'I suspect you h...
sensitivity than...

Jordan said lightly.

Dom looked towards the ceiling. 'Here we go. The woman trying to see more in a man than is really there. Listen, I do my job, I go to bed. End of story.'

'Mr Average.'

'You got it.'

'Do you watch sunsets and wonder about how God created such a beautiful sight?'

'On occasion. Is that such a big deal?'

'It just means that you're not as average as you'd like me to think you are.'

Dom held up his hands in mock surrender. 'Okay, okay, I'm deep as a damned well. Satisfied?'

Jordan laughed delightedly. 'It's all an act, isn't it? This whole poker-face, tough guy thing of yours.'

'Oh no.' Dom moved closer. 'Trust me, it's not an act...'

Dear Reader

Welcome to Silhouette Sensation® in the new millennium. As always we've got plenty of terrific reading for you, so come and forget the daily grind with us—indulge yourself!

Let's start with a very special man, January's **Heartbreaker** from Sharon Sala—*The Miracle Man*— he's the kind of guy most women would choose to father their child—if only they dared!

The Tough Guy and the Toddler by Diane Pershing pretty much speaks for itself, and *Like Father, Like Daughter* from Margaret Watson kicks off a set of linked books from this talented writer. Look for *For the Children* in March.

And last but never least, is favourite author Paula Detmer Riggs with a cracking read about a cop and his ex-wife whose son is abducted and how, once the boy is found, they become *Once More a Family*.

Enjoy!

The Editors

The Tough Guy and the Toddler

DIANE PERSHING

*Silhouette, Silhouette Sensation and Colophon are
registered trademarks of Harlequin Books S.A., used under licence.*

*First published in Great Britain 2000
Silhouette Books, Eton House, 18-24 Paradise Road,
Richmond, Surrey TW9 1SR*

© Diane Pershing 1999

ISBN 0 373 07928 1

18-0001

*Printed and bound in Spain
by Litografia Rosés S.A., Barcelona*

DIANE PERSHING

cannot remember a time when she didn't have her nose buried in a book. As a child she would cheat the bedtime curfew by snuggling under the covers with her teddy bear, a torch and a forbidden (read 'grown up') novel. Her mother warned her that she would ruin her eyes, but so far, they still work. Diane has had many careers — singer, actress, film critic, disc jockey, TV writer, to name a few. Currently she divides her time between writing romance novels and doing voice-overs. She lives in Los Angeles and promises she is only slightly affected. Her two children, Morgan Rose and Ben, have just completed college, and Diane looks forward to writing and acting until she expires, or people stop hiring her, whichever comes first. She loves to hear from readers, so please write to her at P.O. Box 67424, Los Angeles, CA 90067, USA.

To my advisers:
Brian Banks, L.A. County Sheriff's Department,
and Kathy Bennett, L.A.P.D.
Thank you both for your insight and patience.

Chapter 1

"And on the KRAD radio weather front," the voice on the car radio chirped, "it's another sunny day in southern California, temperatures up to eighty-four in the valleys, while the rest of the country is shoveling itself out from under snowstorms. Hey, are we lucky or what?"

As she changed lanes to pass an elderly woman in a slow-moving sedan, Jordan found herself wondering how radio newscasters and disk jockeys managed to keep talking with that upbeat, smiling cadence. To her, they all sounded like happy robots.

As though the newscaster had read her mind, he changed to a more serious tone. "This just in! Police in Inglewood have asked for your help."

A female voice, much less polished, came on the radio. "Be on the lookout for a white male, age twenty-six, driving a dented light blue seventy-nine Chevy Malibu, license plate number two-four-five eight-eight-two. The suspect has kidnapped a small child, who is still in the car, which was last seen in the vicinity of Airport and Seventy-ninth Street. Call nine one one if you spot the car, but do nothing else—the driver of the car is believed to be armed and dangerous.''

The cheerful announcer came back on. ''And now a word from…''

But Jordan was no longer listening. A kidnapped child, she repeated silently, as she sped along the freeway. How horrible. How frightened the child must be. And the mother. The chill of remembered fear rippled through her for both of them. Even without knowing any details, Jordan imagined what the child's mother must be going through—the terror, the worry, the guilt. She would be praying now, hoping against hope that everything would turn out all right. She might also be asking herself what she could have done differently, better, sooner, so that this might not have happened to her baby.

The same questions Jordan had asked herself this past year.

''The poor woman,'' she said aloud, shaking her head, so lost in remembrance that she almost missed the fact that El Segundo Boulevard was the next off ramp. ''Silly woman,'' she muttered, meaning herself this time. Sometimes she got so caught up in sorrowful reflection, she forgot to pay attention to what was in front of her.

She managed to steer her Land Rover to the right lane and made a smooth exit off the freeway, then turned right as she'd been directed and headed west, toward the ocean. She was on her way to the home of a woman who wanted to sell her extensive wardrobe. Some of the clothing might do well at Riches and Rags, the resale boutique where Jordan worked.

As she passed a large complex of run-down looking apartments, a car shot out of an alleyway, pulled in front of her and sped up, dark gray exhaust filling the air. At first she was too busy swerving and braking for the details of the car to register, but when they did, her heart leaped to her throat. It was a light blue Chevy Malibu, the same model she'd just heard about on the radio.

Too much of a coincidence, she told herself. That kind of thing doesn't happen.

But, on the other hand, why not? Someone would spot the car eventually and call it in. Why not her?

What had been the license number? ''Twenty-four some-thing?'' she said aloud. Swallowing a small rush of fear, she stepped on the accelerator, gaining on the vehicle until she was close enough to read the rear plate. Two-four-five eight-eight-two. Was that the number they'd given on the radio? How could she be sure? And was it important that she be sure, or should she report it anyway?

The child, she reminded herself. The most important thing was the child. Jordan peered through the Chevy's rear window, but all she could see was the back of the driver's head, which seemed to be a man's. Where was the child? Was he small enough to be sitting in the passenger seat and not be seen? Was he lying on the seat? In the trunk? Dropped off somewhere already? Injured? Dead?

''No,'' she admonished herself. She could not afford to let her mind drift into obsessive what ifs, not with a child's life on the line. Trembling with the effort at self-control, she picked up her car phone and called 911.

After she reported what she'd seen, Jordan was thanked crisply and told to do nothing more. She was to go about her business, to cease following the car. The authorities, she was assured, would take over.

But as she disconnected the car phone, Jordan knew she couldn't do that, not yet. What if they didn't get there in time? What if they were too late to save the child? She needed to keep the Chevy in view. Just for a little while, she told herself. Until the police showed up. Without doing anything foolish or heroic, she promised herself.

Her hands gripping the steering wheel, Jordan kept her distance and followed the light blue vehicle along El Segundo for several minutes as it headed west all the way to Vista del Mar, the wide street that bordered the ocean. When it turned down a narrow road, she did, too, finding herself on a winding path that had been designed for a single car only.

She heard the whirring blades of helicopters and looked up. Several of them were ahead, flying over the shoreline. Police. Thank God. But others, too. The media were also out in full force—Channel 6 News Now! was written on the side of one.

The circus had already begun, she thought sourly. Good news for the kidnapped child—rescue was on the way. However, not good news for her. She knew that circus all too well. And it could get out of hand all too quickly.

Jordan told herself it was time to leave, to get out of everyone's way. To do that, she needed to turn around. She was headed toward a rise, over which the light blue car had just disappeared, when the sound of sirens made her stomp her foot on the brake before she reached the crest. Several police vehicles came careening behind her on the narrow path. There was no room for her to turn around or, it seemed, for anyone to pass her.

Whirring helicopter blades, honking horns, flashing lights, the incessant whine of the sirens—it was all too much to tolerate. Jordan put up all her windows, slammed the gear into Park and stayed put, having no choice. She clamped her hands over her ears. The noise. Dear lord, it was unbearable.

One police car swerved around her, siren screaming, through the dry brush on one side of her and over the hill. Another followed, doing the same thing on the passenger side. Two more pulled up behind her, and men and women came rushing out, running toward the hill, paying no attention to her.

Whatever was about to happen was out of her eyesight, as her vision was still blocked by the rise. Part of her wanted to leap out of her car and see what was going on. But, no, she told herself. What she needed to do was to stay put, keep out of the way, let the professionals do their job. As her heart beat a furious rat-a-tat-tat, Jordan remained in the same position for what seemed an eternity. Please, she prayed silently, let the child be all right. Let him survive this, so his mother doesn't have to go through the soul-destroying pain of losing him.

After a while, Jordan heard what sounded like instructions being given over a bullhorn, followed by silence—except, of course, for the noise of the whirling helicopter blades. She pressed the button to lower one window a fraction so she could hear better but remained safe in the cocoon of her car, safe for the moment from the noise and potential violence on the other side of the hill.

When she heard a male voice yelling, "Come out with your hands in the air!" Jordan tensed and waited for gunshots. But when seconds rolled by without any, she began to hope.

Then came the piercing sound of a child wailing in fear.

Jordan's clenched hands tightened. Oh, God, was the child okay? Had the man hurt him? Safety be damned. She had to leave the car, had to know!

She had turned off the ignition, unhooked her seat belt and was about to open her car door when a loud tapping on her windshield startled her. She looked up to see a man glaring at her with a stern expression on his face. He wore dark wrap-around sunglasses and was dressed in a rumpled tweed sports jacket, white shirt and loosened tie. His hand gestured for her to roll down her window.

Who was he? she wondered, a fresh wave of panic washing over her. Where had he come from? She had no idea, but she wasn't taking any chances. Pressing the door lock switch, she shook her head. She saw his mouth tighten, then he reached into his pocket and pulled out a wallet, flipped it open and showed her a badge. Los Angeles County Sheriff's Department, it said. He repeated his instruction to roll down her window.

She pressed the button and lowered it a couple of inches. The man—the plainclothes policeman, she supposed he was—came over to the driver's side and said gruffly, "Excuse me, ma'am—"

"How is he?" Jordan interrupted.

The officer seemed startled. "How's who?"

"The little boy. Is he okay? Did the kidnapper harm him?"

The man stared at her, or so it seemed—it was hard to tell what went on behind those sunglasses—for a moment, then said tersely, "She's fine."

"She?" Jordan repeated. How strange, she'd been so sure the child had been a little boy. Which made sense, of course, she thought sadly, a lot of sense.

"Didn't you hear the sirens?"

Jordan glanced up, startled. The officer had been talking, and she'd been drifting again. "I'm sorry," she said. "Yes, of course I heard them."

"Then why didn't you get out of the way? You interfered with a police pursuit." She noted the hint of a New York accent, in the dropped Rs, in the way he spoke too rapidly, punching his words like fists.

"I know that," she said, trying to explain. "I'm the one who—"

"You put yourself," he interrupted her, "and the kid in danger by hanging around. What if there'd been gunfire?" His tone remained neutral, almost impersonal, but she could sense the cold anger behind it.

She was being attacked and didn't care for it in the least. "But there wasn't gunfire, was there? Besides, I couldn't get out. I mean, it all happened so fast, I was—"

"Fine, whatever," he interrupted with an impatient wave of his hand. "I could cite you for this, you know." She might not be able to see his eyes behind his dark wraparound sunglasses, but there was no missing his barely banked temper. "Why don't you get this tank of yours out of the way now, all right?"

Tank? Her top-of-the-line Land Rover? Tank? That did it!

She threw open her car door, causing the officer to step back quickly to avoid being hit. She scrambled out, slammed the door and faced him, her hands propped on her hips. He had three or four inches on her, but she looked him straight in the eye. "Listen. I don't know your name or what your rank is, but your attitude needs some work."

The details of his face were clearer. The hair was thick and dark and curly, badly in need of a trim. The sunglasses rested on a nose that was crooked and looked as if it had been broken more than once. He had olive skin, the shadow of a dark beard and a wide mouth. A scar cut across the right side of his full upper lip, now lifted in a sneer. He was older than she was but probably not yet forty.

His hands were fisted at his sides. "My attitude, as you call it, is a hell of a lot better than you deserve. Now, if you don't mind, I got work to do. Your car is blocking us and needs to get out of the way right now." More than anything, he reminded her of a boxer. Or a gangster. A thug. Not the well-groomed, clean-cut policemen she saw around her neighborhood.

"You're blocking *me*, in case you hadn't noticed," she fired back her answer. "What do you suggest I do? Sprout wings?"

At that moment, a younger, dark-skinned man, also in a sports jacket but not appearing in the least bit unkempt, came hurrying to them. Resting a hand on the angry one's shoulder, he said, "Hey, Dom, my man, take it easy, okay?" He shifted his attention to Jordan and smiled. "Nice work, ma'am. Thanks for calling nine one one, Ms—"

"Carlisle," Jordan said, pleased to be talking to someone other than this ape for a moment. "*Mrs.* Carlisle. And you're welcome."

The one called Dom took in a breath. Obviously he'd just realized the part she'd played in the child's rescue and—she hoped—deeply regretted his bad manners.

She directed her attention to the younger one. "All I care about is that the little girl is safe."

"She is."

"May I see?"

She didn't wait for permission. Brushing past the one named Dom, she climbed the few steps to the top of the rise and surveyed the scene below.

The sparkling waters of the Pacific spread out from a rocky, weed-strewn beach. The Chevy was parked at an angle, both its passenger and driver's doors wide open. Nearby, a sobbing little girl had her arms around the neck of a uniformed female officer. A skinny man, his hair caught in a ponytail, his hands cuffed behind his back, was being led to a waiting police car.

The child was safe, Jordan thought, offering thanks and letting down the tight knot of inner tension she'd been sustaining. Sometimes it worked out.

Dom felt *real* stupid, and he hated feeling stupid. Jaw tight, he glared at Mrs. Carlisle's back, his gaze unconsciously raking over the slim, tall shape of her. She was about five-eight, he figured. Skinny, too, model skinny. Which meant she probably either starved herself or threw it up, the way they all did.

She had sleek, short, stylishly cut auburn hair and wore a cream-colored blouse tucked into matching pants. Silk and expensive, for sure. Earlier, when she'd sat in the car, he'd observed the thin face, the hollowed cheekbones, the designer sunglasses. Her hands on the steering wheel had been perfectly manicured, a huge rock and matching wedding ring on the third finger of her left hand, a hand that had never known a day's work. A new Rover, a state-of-the-art car phone, a cream-colored leather bag on the seat. Money. Rich bitch type, he thought, haughty and condescending.

Man, he knew the kind. Working out of West Hollywood, he was right next to Beverly Hills, and he'd had it about up to here with spoiled women whose chief complaint was that the gardener's truck was parked two inches too close to her driveway or that a homeless person had dared to actually walk down her street. In Beverly Hills he had to rein in his temper and assume the poker face he'd used today with Mrs. Carlisle. But his feeling of disgust didn't change, whatever shape his facial muscles took.

The woman turned, glanced at him dismissively, then turned to Steve Fenoy, his partner. "Please tell your surly friend to take his bad temper out on someone else," she said in a low-pitched, husky voice. "I ought to report him."

"Go on," Dom retorted. "It won't be the first time."

"Don't tempt me."

"Dom," Steve said under his breath. "Cool it."

Dom kept glaring at Mrs. Carlisle, and she glared right back. She stood tall, her small, high breasts outlined by the silk of her blouse, her hands on her narrow hips. Some of the gold strands in her hair glinted in the late afternoon sun.

"Dom, my man," Steve warned again, and this time Dom heard him and knew his partner was right. He'd been more than rude. Hell, he'd dumped on the woman.

His excuse was he and Steve had been cruising nearby, at the tail end of an overtime shift, and Dom had been way past tired, getting onto downright exhausted, when they'd heard the APB. So they'd responded. Between the chase, the tension about the kid and the fear that a civilian would get caught in a crossfire, he'd unloaded on the handiest thing around him—Mrs. Carlisle—before he knew he should be awarding her Good Samaritan of the Month.

Now he'd have to apologize. Damn.

He'd always hated saying he was sorry. When he was a kid and the priest or his mother would make him apologize, he usually had to punch a wall or something afterward to relieve the sense of frustration.

Okay, he told himself, he wasn't a kid anymore. He'd apologize for barking at her. But still, why *had* she hung around after calling in the sighting? She been told not to, damn it; that was SOP on 911 calls. Was she some sort of thrill seeker? Publicity hound? Most of the helicopters were from the local news teams. Even now, vans filled with reporters and cameramen were on their way, about to come screeching to a halt behind the police vehicles, which were still behind the hunter green Rover. Maybe Mrs. Carlisle got off being in the spotlight.

If she wanted the spotlight, she was about to get it.

But he still had to apologize. Get it over with quickly, he told himself. As the saying went, Just do it.

He walked up the small incline, all the while muttering a curse under his breath. When he faced her and saw her tightened mouth, he knew his volume hadn't been low enough.

He held his hands up, palms out, in a placating gesture. "Okay, listen, Mrs. Carlisle," he said gruffly. "I, uh, shouldn't have been rude like that. It was all the tension from the car chase, and I let off steam."

The woman removed her sunglasses and stared at him assessingly. A fringe of dark lashes surrounded eyes of an unusual color, a translucent light green. They struck him, somehow, as being sad eyes, old eyes. There were shadows beneath the lids that all the expensive cosmetics in the world couldn't hide. She had flawless skin and a great mouth, with a bow in the center of the full upper lip. Dom felt his stomach knot up as the realization kicked in—Mrs. Carlisle might have been a pain in the ass, but man, was she something. Not just groomed and pampered and carefully made up to look her best, but naturally, heart-stoppingly beautiful.

"Anyhow," he went on, his voice suddenly hoarse, "I'm sorry."

"Well… I was tense, too," she said.

"Yeah, it gets like that."

He shuffled his feet, not sure what to say next, but was saved from having to decide by the sound of shouts coming from below. The news media had arrived in full force. Van doors slammed. Orders were barked, cameras and microphones positioned.

Dom cursed under his breath again. "Here they come. The vultures."

Mrs. Carlisle's eyes followed his gaze, then they widened in horror. "Reporters? Oh, no!" As she shook her head, he sensed panic emanating from her in waves.

"What's the matter?"

Instead of answering him, she ran down the hill toward her vehicle. He followed, heard her say, "I have to get out of here." She turned and gazed at him, her hands clasped together tightly against her chest. "I don't want anyone to know I'm here. Please. I need to get out of here, but I'm blocked in."

Dom studied her for a moment, but there was no reason to doubt her. There was real anxiety there, like the fear of a cornered animal. Why? he wondered, but there was no time to dwell on his question. He made a quick decision. Hell, he owed it to her.

"Steve," he said briskly, ushering the lady to the passenger side, "tell the guys to keep Mrs. Carlisle's name out of it as long as possible. Do what you can. I'm taking the lady home." He opened the door and said, "Get in. I'm driving."

"But—" She seemed confused.

"You want to get out of here? I'll make it happen. Got it?" With no further hesitation, she got in. He slammed her door and hurried to the driver's side. "I'll call in later for a ride," he told Steve as he slid into the seat.

"But how will you—" the woman asked.

"Seat belts," he said, buckling his. "Leave it to me."

He gunned the exquisite machine, expertly maneuvered it between two police vehicles, then headed up and over the hill toward the ocean. "If you don't want to be seen," he told his passenger, "duck your head." Dom yanked the wheel to the right, roared past the parked Chevy, then proceeded to career along the beach parallel to the water, taking the high-priced machine over rocks and ruts and weeds, letting the four-wheel drive do what it did best.

Several helicopters circled overhead. They followed the Rover's trail for a few minutes, then seemed to lose interest and returned to the more exciting scene of the child's rescue. Dom swung the Rover into what appeared to be a grove of trees, which masked a small, winding, private beach road. They bumped along this path for a while, finally emerging onto the highway a mile away from where they began their dash to escape.

Neither he nor Mrs. Carlisle spoke the whole time, but when they were headed north on the smoothly paved tarmac, she put her hand over her heart and gasped, "Oh! I've never been on a ride like that before."

"That's what this baby was built for."

Jordan gave herself a moment to catch her breath. Relieved to have escaped the press—in her experience, they were vultures who fed on the carrion of people's pain—she felt as though she'd just been driven through an obstacle course in a tacky amusement park, which didn't seem that farfetched an image.

What a time she'd had! While on her way to see a potential client, she had gotten involved in a car chase with an armed kidnapper, been verbally assaulted by a policeman, nearly been ambushed by the media and held on for a wild car ride. The past hour or so had been like something out of a fevered dream. If it wasn't so serious, she might feel like laughing.

Instead, she glanced at her driver. He seemed more relaxed now that they were away from the action. Although she had the feeling the word *relax* wasn't quite appropriate. The man had a tightly coiled presence about him, as though he were ready to pounce at the slightest provocation.

"How did you know about that road?" she asked him, deciding to keep their conversation to a neutral ground.

"I used to drive a patrol car around here. Where to?"

"Hmm?"

"Where am I taking you?"

"Oh, Beverly Hills."

"Figures," he said under his breath.

There it was, another little barb. The man was impossibly sullen and rude, she thought, even if he had just saved her from a horror show. The fingers of her right hand reached for her rings, and she played nervously with them. She slanted him a narrow look. "So, you're not only tactless, you're judgmental."

He shrugged but said nothing. She should leave it alone, she told herself. After all, why should she care what this man thought about her?

But, for some reason, she did.

"Tell me," she asked archly, "your attitude—is it all women? Just women who live in Beverly Hills? Or is it just me?"

"I've never met you before," he replied.

Another nonanswer. Was he trying to bait her or brush her off? Forget it, she told herself. Don't waste your energy.

For a while, she stared out the window at shopping malls and gas stations, at huge trucks and sports cars racing past them on the freeway. They hit some rush-hour traffic near the airport, but it thinned out as they headed toward Santa Monica. Eventually, however, Jordan found her attention wandering again to her driver. She studied him—the stubborn set of the jaw, the broken nose, which could have been disfiguring but on him was somehow…interesting. Sexy, even. She still hadn't seen his eyes, but in profile, he reminded her of someone, an old movie star.

Oh, yes, she thought. John Garfield. *Body and Soul.* Street fighter turned boxing pro. She'd always liked him in that one. Oh, and *The Postman Always Rings Twice,* from the forties. With Lana Turner. The two of them had had a lot of chemistry in that one. Quite a turn-on, as she recalled.

What? Jordan was taken aback by the direction of her thoughts. A sexy broken nose? Chemistry? Quite a turn-on?

Words and phrases that weren't part of her vocabulary, not any more. Nothing and no one had turned her on for so long, Jordan thought wryly, she'd often wondered if she'd ever experience that particular sensation again, or if she'd remember what to do if it happened. That part of her, the sensual-woman part, had shut down. Forever, it seemed. She was a widow, yes, but she'd felt like Reynolds Carlisle's widow long before he'd made her one in reality.

She glanced once again at the man driving the car, then purposefully focused her gaze front. She might compare this Dom person to John Garfield, but there was no way she would ever find this rude, opinionated policeman attractive. Thug types weren't for her. No, what she was probably feeling was gratitude. He might be surly, but he'd put himself out for her.

"Will the little girl be all right?" she asked him.

"Depends on who she's going home to." He shrugged non-committally. "A crack-addicted mother, maybe, or a hooker. A teenager who had a kid at fourteen so she'd have someone who loved her. Who knows?"

"Oh, no." Jordan felt as though cold water had just been thrown in her face. "Are those the only scenarios you can come up with?"

"Sorry, lady, but that's what I see every day on the job."

"Please don't call me lady," she snapped.

"Fine."

"Are you as hard and uncaring as you seem?" It was out before she could stop it, and she regretted it immediately. She didn't want to give him the satisfaction of knowing how much he annoyed her.

But her question seemed to stop him momentarily. Keeping one hand on the wheel, he scraped the other over his face and stubble, then rubbed under his dark eyeglasses as though he was tired.

"No, I'm not uncaring." His tone was less aggressive. "There's just so much I can do, so much any one cop can do. We don't deal a lot with fine, upstanding folks, Mrs. Carlisle, like you probably are. We deal with victims or scum—they're the ones who get in trouble. Most of 'em are doomed, some of 'em have a chance, and I hope to hell they get it and take it and run with it. But I have to shut down. If I don't, I'll go under. That answer your question?''

It was more of a speech than she'd expected and, she suspected, more of a speech than he'd intended to give. She nodded. ''I see.''

They drove along in silence, past the office towers of Century City and toward the Santa Monica mountains, the wide ridge that separated the valley from the rest of Los Angeles. The silence was much easier now, Jordan noted and was grateful. As they exited the freeway at Sunset Boulevard, she said, ''Thank you for taking me home, Sheriff, or whatever they call you.''

''Sergeant.''

''Sorry. Sergeant what?''

''D'Annunzio. Detective Sergeant Dominic D'Annunzio.''

Dominic D'Annunzio. The two words and the way he said them filled her head. Visions of stocky Italian men with thick eyebrows and thicker accents, large women stirring huge pots of steaming pasta…

Hold it, Jordan told herself. If Dominic D'Annunzio had pigeonholed her as the Beverly Hills type, she'd just pigeonholed him right back, hadn't she?

''Left here,'' she directed, ''and look for the fourth house on the right.''

Fourth house, indeed, Dom thought as he turned into the driveway. More like a small castle. Tall trees rose on either side of the private road, which continued for about fifty yards to end at imposing wrought-iron gates. Beyond them lay a vista of green, gracefully sloping lawn fronting a tree-shaded, three-story stone building, complete with turrets and broad balconies. Ah, he thought mockingly, the good life.

After turning the motor off, he handed the keys to Mrs. Carlisle. She took them, removed her sunglasses, met his gaze and said, ''Thanks.''

His breath hitched in his throat. Those eyes, he couldn't help thinking again, they were incredible. Like pale green marbles. But the dark shadows underneath—why were they there?

He had more questions. The whole drive he'd wanted to ask her why she'd run from the press when most people coveted their fifteen minutes of fame. He'd wanted to ask her what the fear was about.

But he was a civil servant, and she was a married lady from Beverly Hills, and he didn't need to know any more about her than he already did. "Mind if I use your car phone to get a ride?" he asked.

Her hand flew to her mouth. "Oh. I should have offered to drop you off."

"Nah. I'll get a patrol car to swing by. No problem."

He made his call and was in luck. There was a car from his West Hollywood precinct at Beverly Hills City Hall at the moment. They would be right by to get him.

Dom got out of the car. But the woman continued to sit in the passenger seat as though she had no desire to move. She must be beat, he thought. She'd been through a hell of a lot, for a civilian. Come to think of it, he was pretty damned tired, too. He stifled a yawn at the thought. He wasn't as young as he used to be, and these all-nighters could be killers. A bottle of beer and a bed sounded real good right about now.

"Look," he said, propping one hand on the Rover's roof and leaning in, "you go on in. My ride'll be here in a moment."

She nodded distractedly but stayed where she was, staring at the mansion. There was something haunted in her expression.

"What is it?" he asked.

"I hate it there," she said quietly.

Her reply surprised him, and his natural cop's curiosity made him want to know more. He slid into the driver's seat, keeping the door ajar, and looked at her. "Why?"

She didn't answer for a few moments. Then she angled her head and gazed at him, the expression in her eyes so filled with suffering, he wondered how she managed to remain upright. "Have you ever lost someone you loved more than life itself?"

That one threw him, but good. So did all the images that suddenly assaulted him—Theresa, lying on the floor in a pool of blood. The funeral, the rain hitting the coffin like tiny daggers, the sound tearing away at what was left of his heart.

"Yeah," he muttered before shutting off the pictures. "My wife."

Mrs. Carlisle nodded, then let out a deep sigh. "Then you understand. My little boy, I lost him last year." There were no tears in her eyes, but the tragic loss was stamped on every inch of her face. Her fingers played nervously with her rings. "That's why I hate the press—back then, they wouldn't leave me alone. I wasn't allowed to mourn in peace. Coming back here reminds me of what I no longer have and will never have again."

Their gazes remained locked, but Dom had no words. What could he say? What could anyone say to a loss like that? All the money and possessions in the world couldn't replace her little boy. And it was wrong, against the natural order, to lose a child. Parents, even spouses, you lost them—that was the way life worked. Someone got left behind, sure, but you got on with your life. But a child? Some people never recovered from that one.

"That's tough," he said.

He wanted to touch her hand, to tell her that he knew—God, how he knew—just what she was feeling. But two quick honks interrupted the moment. Dom turned to see a patrol car behind them in the driveway. His ride was here. Good, he thought. The less time spent in the presence of so much pain, the better—for him anyway.

But a part of him didn't want to leave Mrs. Carlisle. Hell, he didn't even know her first name, but he still found himself reluctant to say goodbye. Stupid notion, he thought, but reached into his wallet for one of his cards.

"Here," he said, handing it to her. "In case you want to report my surly attitude."

His remark seemed to startle her out of her reverie. "I don't think—"

One side of his mouth quirked up. "Nah, I didn't mean that. Look, take it," he said, wondering at his persistence. "In case you, you know, ever need anything…"

Dom let the sentence trail off, but he kept his gaze on hers. Why was he saying this? Hell, she had a husband, didn't she? And obviously enough money to smooth most of the rough edges in her life. Why would she ever need anything from him?

Finally, she nodded and took the card. "Thank you. That means a lot," she said in that husky voice of hers. A bedroom voice, he thought, then shook away the impression as totally out of line.

"Yeah." He got out of the car, waved at the patrol car, then turned again to Mrs. Carlisle. "Hey, good luck," he said.

Her mouth curved in the first hint of anything resembling a smile he'd seen from her. "Not my strong suit," she said, then took in a fortifying breath and got out of the Rover. She came around to the driver's side and slid into the seat without another glance at him. When she pushed a button on the dash, the wrought-iron gates swung open. He watched as she drove through the gates, watched them swing slowly shut afterward. Mrs. Carlisle never looked behind her or waved goodbye.

As Dom lifted his own arm in a half gesture of farewell, it came to him that he'd never see her again. He frowned. The realization made him feel empty somewhere deep in the vicinity of his gut.

Still, he kept his gaze focused on the Rover's taillights until the tall, stately gates shut with a firm—and final—clang.

Chapter 2

A week had passed and Jordan was almost back to normal. Or as normal as she ever got, she thought with a smile, as she closed the front door behind her. In this past week since the child's rescue and the subsequent discovery of her as the 911 caller, the attendant press attention had taken its toll. She was tired. Good tired, for a change. She had spent all day at the shop, which had been just what she'd needed—hard work, distraction, the concentration on other people and other lives instead of on her own. Tonight, she looked forward to a leisurely hot bath, maybe even a good night's sleep.

Brushing one hand through her hair, she reached with the other for the pile of mail on the small antique pine table by the front door. As she did, Cynthia appeared from around the corner, perfectly dressed as usual in a soft silk dress, heels, her white hair styled immaculately.

"So, you're home," her mother-in-law said.

Jordan smiled. "Did you have a nice day?"

"I had a doctor's appointment, remember?"

"And is everything all right?"

Cynthia didn't answer her question. She was still attending

to her own agenda. "I had to get Connie Lehman to drive me," she said, accusation dripping from every word.

"Why didn't you ask Sofia?" Jordan answered, referring to the live-in housekeeper and trying to keep her voice pleasant.

Cynthia waved her hand dismissively. "She has enough to do around here."

What her mother-in-law did not say out loud was, *You should have been here, instead of at that awful shop. You should be here with me all the time, as a dutiful daughter-in-law should be, especially one I support financially and provide with a place to live.*

Jordan ignored the familiar stab of guilt that Cynthia always managed to arouse in her and sifted through a couple of catalogs, a bill from Neiman-Marcus. "I'm sorry, Cynthia," she said, keeping her tone level. "Maybe next time we can make the appointment for one of my days off."

"I don't understand why you have to work at all."

"No, I know you don't."

Cynthia would never understand. But Jordan had realized three months ago that if she didn't have something else to do with her time than listen to Cynthia's complaints, attend luncheons and shopping expeditions and charity functions, she would descend into the pit of despair that had been beckoning her since Michael's death. Her mother-in-law's life was not hers and never would be.

So she'd gotten herself a job at Riches and Rags and now she had a purpose. Jordan loved well-made clothing and interesting accessories, got a kick out of matching styles with customers. This job represented a first tenuous step toward some sort of future, a looking ahead instead of looking back. Cynthia might not understand, but Jordan would not give it up.

"Monsignor Larsen is our guest for dinner tonight," the older woman said. "He'll be here in half an hour."

She'd forgotten. There went her hot bath and quiet time to herself. "I'll be ready."

As Cynthia, with her customary sniff of disapproval, walked away, her high heels clicking on the marble floor, Jordan's attention was caught by an envelope addressed to her in large block letters. There was no return address.

Curious, she opened the envelope. A piece of paper was folded over a snapshot. Jordan glanced briefly at it as she unfolded the paper. It was a blurry Polaroid of a child on a swing.

Does this child look familiar? The letter was printed in the same block letters. *Could it be your son? Is there a reward offered for information? Please say nothing to anyone else—this is between you and me. If you bring in the police, forget the whole thing. You'll never see Michael again. You'll be hearing from me.* It was signed, *A Friend.*

Jordan studied the picture more carefully, and as she did, she felt her heart speed up. The child was towheaded, about two or three, with a shy smile. Oh, God, she thought as her hand flew to her rapidly beating heart. It did. It looked like Michael.

But that wasn't possible. Michael was dead.

Pain twisted throughout her body, a pain that was so familiar it felt as though she'd been carrying it all her life instead of only a year. She gripped the edges of the photograph and stared. The image was not clear, but something inside her cried out. Michael? Could it be?

Clutching the letter and its contents to her chest, she crossed the marble entrance hall and made her way up the broad staircase to her bedroom suite. Once inside, she leaned against the closed door, gave herself a moment to calm down, then again studied the picture. How was it possible? she asked herself, all the while knowing the answer. It wasn't.

This was some sort of sick joke. For months after Michael's death, she'd received all kinds of letters and phone calls from crazy people telling her his passing had been God's judgment for her past sins. Some offered to hold seances. Charities had asked for donations in his name. Reporters had hounded her every move, recorded her every breath. Michael's death had ceased to be her private loss—it became fodder for anyone with an agenda.

And this letter, she told herself, was from yet one more crazy person. It was nothing. The picture meant nothing. She threw it on her dressing table on her way to her bath. Discarding the pantsuit she'd worn that day, she showered, letting the hot water soothe her tense muscles as she tried to order her thoughts into some coherent state.

But her rebellious mind kept returning to that blurry picture, to that smile that was so like Michael's. Of course it wasn't her son, she told herself, it couldn't be. Jordan's picture had been in the papers again this past week, that was all, and had acted as a catalyst for some cruel, twisted person.

After drying off, she sat at her dressing table, tunneling her fingers through her wet hair. Against her will, her gaze returned to the picture, setting off the ache and the memories. Michael had been a beautiful child, with her pale green eyes and his father's white-blond hair. But that smile—it had been his alone.

She remembered the day she'd been nursing him and he'd opened his eyes, looked up at her, let go of her nipple and smiled shyly at her. His perfect little mouth turned up slightly more on the right corner, a little hesitant, offering a gift.

"He smiled!" she'd cried out. "Reynolds, look, he's smiling."

Her husband, who had been fussing with his cuff links, had walked over from his huge walk-in closet. "Let me see," he'd demanded.

But Michael had gone back to nursing. Reynolds had stared at the child for a few more minutes, then had said, "It was probably your imagination," and had gone back to his closet.

Her husband's cold, dismissive remarks had been something she'd almost gotten used to in all their years of marriage. But that day, she knew it hadn't been her imagination. Her son had smiled at her, with loving trust in his eyes.

She squeezed her eyes shut as another stab of grief assaulted her. Never to nurse him again, to feel his small mouth tugging at her breast in order to receive the sweet liquid gift of life. She should throw the picture away, but somehow she was unable to force herself to do so. She opened her eyes and gazed at it again, wishing it were more in focus. Michael would be two and a half now, the same age as this child appeared to be. Reluctantly, she set the photo down. Why was she doing this?

It was masochistic to dwell on this, she told herself, as she applied mascara to her lashes.

In the mirror was the reflection of her large sitting room with its thick carpets, the plump gray love seat and chairs. Through the doorway, she could see the separate bedroom with its pedestal bed. It was an enormous bedroom suite, as spacious as the entire first floor of the small ranch house in Wyoming in which she and her older brother had been raised.

But the sumptuous surroundings barely registered. If everything in the Carlisle home was the best money could buy, she had long ago stopped being impressed. External riches covered up a hollow existence.

And she was part of that existence, knew it and hated it. She didn't want to be here, was uncomfortable living off the Carlisle family money. She was not the type to be dependent on the goodwill of others, but the terms of her late husband's trust had left her with nothing. She was too old to model again and had despised that life, anyway.

In the past year, she'd been trying to regain her strength, both emotional and physical. For the present, she was biding her time until she could make the break. She hoped it would be soon.

Unable to help herself, Jordan picked up the picture and looked at it. Michael? Alive? Was it possible?

Please say nothing to anyone else, the letter said. The *anyone* was underlined.

But how could she not? She felt as if she would burst. Someone. She needed to talk to someone about it, get some perspective. How she would have liked to pick up the phone and get a reality check. Family? Her brother and she weren't close. Her parents were dead. Friends? One of her two close friends was working in a Brazilian rain forest and was unreachable. The other lived nearby but was an inveterate gossip.

As her mind scurried about for someone to share this with, the in-house phone buzzed. She picked it up. "Monsignor Larsen is here," Cynthia told her.

"I'll be right down."

Cynthia? Could Jordan share this with her? No. Her mother-in-law had her good moments, but their relationship was tenuous, at best. All through Jordan and Reynolds's marriage, Cynthia had seemed to feel that Jordan was responsible for her son's unhappiness and let it be known, never directly, but in subtle ways. Sometimes, Jordan thought, Cynthia even held her responsible for Reynolds's death in that fiery crash, the same one that had killed Michael.

No, she couldn't tell Cynthia. Then who? She drummed her fingers on the dressing table. She knew she had to talk to someone or she would implode. As her gaze wandered over the top of her dressing table, as though searching for a clue, it fell on the business card she'd tossed next to the phone. Dominic D'Annunzio. The policeman she'd met a week ago during that awful day with the kidnapped child and the hovering news helicopters.

Why had she placed the card there? she wondered. Why hadn't she filed it in her desk or thrown it away?

If you bring in the police, the letter said, *forget the whole thing.*

No, she told herself, not Detective D'Annunzio.

But… What had he said there at the end? To take his card and to call him if she needed anything? She desperately needed someone to talk to about this, even if it was just to be told to forget it.

Anything, he had said.

Without giving herself a chance to change her mind, she picked up the phone.

An entire morning in court, testifying on a robbery-rape case, was not Dom's idea of a good time. He'd made the collar, had done it by the book, the case was airtight. But that didn't stop the perp's lawyer from trying to chew him up on the stand, making veiled accusations about police brutality, the planting of evidence, the whole nine yards. Dom had sat there and taken it with a straight face, answered the questions without losing his cool or his temper.

But the anger sat there inside him, churning. He was a good cop, a damned good detective, and he knew it. The lawyer was showboating for the jury, trying to tap into an anti-cop bias, and that kind of thing pissed him off.

By the time Dom returned to West Hollywood at two o'clock, his mood wasn't real upbeat. It didn't get any better when he was greeted by the sight of all the paperwork on his desk, files and forms and reports he'd been meaning to get to for weeks. Mumbling a curse, he picked up his messages, shuffled through them. Steve, wheeling his desk chair over from the adjacent cubicle desk area, said, "Hey, Dom, my man, you had a call yesterday from that lady."

"What lady?"

"You know, the looker, the nine one one caller from last week." He handed him a yellow message sheet, then wheeled his chair to his neat, orderly desk. Jordan Carlisle, the message sheet read, followed by a number.

At the sight of her name, Dom's irritation vanished like smoke and was replaced by a gush of something warm in his gut. Smiling, he leaned back in his chair and stared at her name. Jordan Carlisle. A classy name for a classy dame.

If one week ago, Dom had no idea who she was, now he knew all about her. So did most of L.A. For those few days after the car chase, Jordan Carlisle, Beverly Hills socialite and former model had been identified as the 911 caller who had led the police to the little girl's rescue. Her picture and her life story had been splashed all over TV screens, although the lady herself, through the family lawyer, had declined interviews. Then some new scandal erupted, and Jordan Carlisle's name disappeared.

Dom, meanwhile, curious about the woman whose life and his had intersected briefly, had done a little background research of his own. He read about her discovery at age fifteen by a camera crew in a small town in Wyoming, about the ensuing three years as a teen model, her fairy-tale marriage twelve years ago to Reynolds Carlisle, a young man with old money. And all about the parties and charity functions, the birth of a son.

Then, last year, both the child and the husband had died in a car accident.

It had struck Dom as odd that, when they'd talked, Mrs. Carlisle had spoken about the kid's death but hadn't mentioned that in the same crash she'd also lost her husband. He wondered if that was significant—the leaving out of that little fact—or if it had been a momentary lapse.

Whatever the answer, he now knew that she was a widow, not a married lady, which altered the equation a little. Not that he cared one way or another, he assured himself, or that it was any of his business. They were worlds apart and fantasizing about her wasn't worth his time.

Even so, each day for the past several days, he'd taken out the file he'd assembled on her and studied the pictures of her. And, each day, he'd had a hard time connecting the glossy, self-confident celebrity in the photos with the unhappy woman he'd met. She'd stayed in his head most of the week. The eyes, mostly, had haunted him. Large and sad, filled with a pain he knew all about, even though he'd shut out most of the memories associated with that pain.

Sitting at his jumbled desk, he picked up her file again, held it in his hand without opening it. So, she'd called him, had she? Call her back, she'd requested, so yeah, he would do that. No problem. Dropping the manila folder on his desk, he reached for the phone.

But, for some reason, his hand stopped in midair. It was weird—it was like some sort of premonition. If he called her back, he'd be setting something in motion, something out of his control. Dom liked to be in control.

Premonition? Where the hell did that come from?

"Bull," he muttered to himself. All he was doing was returning a call. He picked up the phone and punched in the numbers.

"Carlisle residence." The voice on the other end of the line had a slight Eastern European accent. The maid, he assumed.

"Mrs. Carlisle, please."

"Mrs. Cynthia or Mrs. Jordan?"

"Mrs. Jordan."

"Whom shall I say is calling?"

"Detective D'Annunzio."

"One moment, please."

He shuffled through some paperwork while he was on hold, listened to the background noise in the squad room—phones and beepers ringing, conversation, laughter. About a third of the sixteen detectives in the unit were in at the moment, each in a work cubicle or hanging out at the coffee machine. He liked it here; it felt like home.

"Detective?" Her voice startled him, and he sat up straight in his chair.

"Mrs. Carlisle?"

"Yes." She emitted a relieved rush of air. "Oh, thank you for calling me back," she went on in that same husky, low-pitched bedroom voice that had blown him away a week ago. The shock wave of pleasure that ran through him took him by surprise, but he cut it off ruthlessly.

"Sure. What can I do for you?"

Again, she seemed to hesitate before she spoke. "Well, you'll probably think me crazy—" She left it hanging, waiting for him to jump in.

But he didn't. Sixteen years on the force had schooled Dom to let silence do the work.

"I wonder if—" She sighed. "Listen, you said to call if I needed anything."

"Yeah."

"The thing is, I need to talk to someone who—"

Again, she left the sentence hanging. Again, he waited her out. "I'm sorry," she said finally, "I'm not doing this very well, am I?"

"How about you come right out and say what's on your mind?"

"Yes, of course. All right. I need advice from an expert, someone in…your field. But not official advice."

"Meaning?"

"What I tell you must be in confidence and not part of any official report or anything like that."

A warning bell went off in his head. "So what you're saying is, you need a cop but don't want any cops involved." Before she could answer, he added, "What is it, blackmail?"

There was a long pause before she responded. "I'm not going to say anything until I have your word."

She was making conditions, was she? "Listen, Mrs. Carlisle," he said bluntly as the back of his neck stiffened. "I *am* a cop. It's what I do, it's who I am."

"Fine." Her voice turned chilly. "I'm sorry I bothered you. I thought if— Oh, never mind."

She was about to hang up, and the realization made him blurt out "Wait a minute," before he had a chance to think. He scratched his head, considered. He'd told her if she needed him for anything, she should call, hadn't he? Why had he said that? Idiot, he called himself. Fool.

"Look," he said, annoyed with himself but trying not to let it show. "Tell me what this is about, okay? I can't make any promises, but I can tell you I'll be as discreet as possible."

"I—" She paused, then said, "Yes, all right. But not over the phone."

"I'm off at eight tonight. How about I swing by your place about eight-thirty?"

He heard her long sigh of gratitude. "Thank you."

That evening, as was their custom, Cynthia and Jordan watched TV together in Cynthia's sitting room. The older woman's heart condition prevented her from climbing stairs, so her bedroom suite had been moved to the ground floor near the entrance to the house. Most nights, before Cynthia retired to her silk and brocade bedroom, Jordan had taken to watching the news with her—local, national, international. Even though Cynthia kept uttering tsk, tsk at all the violence, the truth was the older woman soaked up the details of that day's horrors with a relish that bordered on the macabre.

Tonight, Jordan could have been watching a Disney cartoon for all the attention she was paying. She was on the alert, waiting for the doorbell to ring.

When it did, she got up quickly. "I'll get it," she told her mother-in-law as she hurried from the room. She hadn't told Cynthia about her visitor because she hadn't wanted to go into an explanation about the letter.

When she opened the door, Dom stood there, one hand propped on his hip, one arm leaning on the door jamb. The sight of him aroused the same reaction as a week ago—once again, he reminded her of an attractive, grown-up street tough. He was dressed in a well-worn brown and tan tweed jacket, unbuttoned, and pants that were a different shade of brown and did not quite match. An inexpensive brown tie was loosely knotted under a wrinkled white shirt collar. There was no stomach paunch over the waistband of his pants, and she had the sense of well-honed muscles beneath his clothing.

He was chewing gum and his expression seemed guarded. On his cheeks and stubborn jaw was the suggestion of a dark beard shadow. And—there was no denying it—she found the sum of all his parts extremely sexy.

Careful to keep herself composed, Jordan said, "Detective, thank you for coming."

He nodded. "Mrs. Carlisle."

As he entered the large hallway, she could smell a faint odor of healthy male sweat mixed with wintergreen-flavored gum. The juxtaposition made her smile for a brief moment, then she became aware of the way her nerve endings were humming in his presence, was conscious of the rapid fluttering of her pulse.

Could she blame these physical reactions on the fact that she'd barely slept the night before? That all day long she'd been on the edge, wondering how the detective would react to what she was going to tell him?

No. Jordan tried not to lie to herself. Her response to Dom was not about the letter, or not totally. In one part of her, there existed a sense of emotional and physical excitement, almost exhilaration at being in the presence of this surly, cynical policeman once again. For some reason—she was mystified as to why—this man, of all the men she'd met recently, seemed to jump-start her long-dormant juices.

Cynthia, in her billowing blue dressing gown, had followed Jordan to the door and stood staring at him. After Jordan made the introductions, she explained, "The detective has been kind enough to come here. There are some details he and I need to discuss…left over from that incident last week."

Jordan could have predicted Cynthia's haughty sniff. In the week since the child's rescue, Jordan had been treated to several lectures about not getting involved in other people's problems, about not putting herself in danger and not courting the attention of the lower life form known as the press.

"Follow me, Detective," Jordan said.

She heard Cynthia sniff again but ignored it as she led Dom into a small family parlor off the main entrance. As she closed the double doors behind them, Jordan acknowledged that Cynthia would not approve of the closed doors, but her business with this man was both personal and private. She turned to face him.

He stood very close, his dark brown eyes studying her dispassionately while his jaw muscles clenched and unclenched as he chewed his gum. She wondered if he was aware of the powerful impact he had on her. He was the definition of total, overwhelming masculinity, nothing soft or tentative, all hardness and male brawn.

She made her mouth curve into a polite smile. "May I get you something to drink? Coffee?"

"I'm all coffeed out, thanks."

"I'm going to have a drink, if that's okay."

He shrugged. "Hey, whatever."

As she crossed to the bar, she said, "Won't you take a seat?"

In the mirror over the bar, she saw him gaze around the room, taking in its details—the two small off-white couches, the antique chairs, the gleaming silver pieces on the glass shelves that lined one wall, the soft lighting, the Aubusson rug. He sat on one of the chairs, a Duncan Phyfe. He was not a huge man, but he seemed way too large for the delicate piece of furniture. She mixed herself a Scotch and soda—she needed something to settle her nerves.

The lady was highly agitated, Dom observed. When she'd introduced him to her mother-in-law she'd kept twisting her rings, like she'd done in the car last week. Those two rings—a large diamond, a wedding ring with smaller diamonds—represented major big bucks, enough to feed a family of five for a couple of years. Not surprisingly, there was evidence of major big bucks all around him. The house, the furnishings, the people in it, were all upper Beverly Hills at its most upper Beverly Hills.

The woman looked like she belonged here, her long legs encased in beige-colored pants. She wore a matching sweater and pearls at her throat and on her ears—expensive and real, he was sure. His gaze was drawn to her image in the mirror, to the way the sweater hugged her small, high breasts, not in an obvious way, but it was enough to send a jolt of awareness through him.

It was back, that same feeling of arousal she'd provoked the last time he'd seen her.

Dom didn't want to be attracted to her. What he wanted was a cigarette, but he'd given them up four months ago. So he sat back, chewed his gum, tried to relax in his chair, but it wasn't easy. Who the hell had invented these little, spindly pieces of furniture? he wondered. Had they been made for small females only? Or midgets?

He watched as she used silver tongs to put two ice cubes into a crystal glass, then poured in a nice dollop of booze over them.

"How is the little girl?" she asked.

"Who?"

She glanced over her shoulder. "That little girl who was kidnapped? Is she all right?"

"Oh. Yeah, she's fine."

"Did she— I mean, did you find out any more about her family?"

There was hesitancy, almost dread, behind her question, and Dom was mystified at first. Then he remembered. Mrs. Carlisle had been horrified by his downbeat description of most of the people and families he dealt with. Mrs. Carlisle, he reminded himself, was a civilian.

"Yeah, and you can relax. She has a mother and father and a big brother, a nice, middle-class family." Her stiff posture eased slightly, and he went on. "The kidnapper was the mother's younger brother—he's schizophrenic and had skipped his meds. He's back in the hospital now, and so you have your basic happy ending.''

"Thank God. And thank you for telling me."

She took a quick slug of her drink before carrying it to the couch near his chair, where she set it on a coaster atop the highly polished coffee table. Perching on the edge of the couch, so their knees were only inches apart, the woman fidgeted with her rings again but said nothing.

She was keyed up, having a hard time with whatever was bugging her, so he helped her out. "So, what did you want to talk to me about?"

She seemed startled by his abrupt question, then favored him with a self-mocking smile. "Of course. I'm sorry. Here." She picked up an envelope that was lying on the table, removed a photo from it and handed it to him. "Please look at that."

Dom glanced at a picture of a kid on a swing, then at her. "Yeah?"

"I— Do you think it's possible?"

"Is what possible?"

"The little boy looks like my son...." She gazed at him imploringly through large, anxious eyes. Dom was struck again by their eerie pale green color, the long lashes. And by those faint shadows underneath the eyes, shadows that revealed strain, despite the grooming, despite the attempt to seem in control.

"So?" he prompted, not sure where this was leading.

"I'm wondering if it's possible he could still be alive. This came with it."

She gave him the letter. He read it once, then a second time, then muttered an oath under his breath. He'd seen this kind of thing before, too many times, but it always evoked in him the urge to beat the crap out of whoever wrote it.

Setting the letter and the picture on the coffee table, Dom leaned in with elbows on knees, met her gaze and gave it to her straight. "Most likely it's a scam, Mrs. Carlisle," he said bluntly. "Don't get yourself all worked up. After a tragedy there are all kinds of ghouls who trade on other people's miseries. Your picture was in the papers last week. Some lowlife saw it, decided to have a little fun at your expense, maybe collect a little money.''

''Yes, yes, I keep telling myself that, but this feels different.''

''It always feels different—they count on that.'' He shifted again. How in hell was a body supposed to be comfortable in this toy chair? Sitting back, he lifted his hands and dropped them to his lap. ''Look, I'm not familiar with the case—''

''Of course you're not,'' she said quickly. ''I shouldn't have—''

''No, it's okay,'' he said. ''I didn't mean that. There was a car accident, right? Was your son ID'd? Was there any doubt?''

Biting her bottom lip, she closed her eyes and shook her head. ''No, I guess not. I mean, the bodies were…burned beyond recognition, but there was no doubt, no.'' Raising her lids, she stared into space, her eyes reflecting a painful memory. ''I waved goodbye to my husband and my son, and two hours later, they were both dead.''

Dom said nothing. What was there to say? Then he managed to speak. ''Gee, I'm sorry.'' Lame, but it was all he could come up with.

She picked up the photo again and gazed at it. ''It's just that it looks so much like him.''

He shrugged. ''Yeah, well. It's not a very clear picture, is it?''

''I know, but the smile. It's Michael's smile.'' As she clutched the picture to her, her eyes filled. ''I wanted so much to believe.''

Watching this display of suffering, Dom felt inadequate. Stupid. Awkward. In his line of work, he was used to crying women, and the way he usually dealt with them was to distance himself, turn off. But it was hard to ignore Mrs. Carlisle's tears, hard to remain detached from her pain. The woman needed comforting, which was not his strong suit. Theresa had been in charge of compassion. He didn't have a lot in him.

Theresa. At the thought of his late wife, he felt an uneasy knot of discomfort harden in his gut. Stay away from this woman and her tears, a voice told him. He was reacting to her way too strongly. Something about Jordan Carlisle wiggled past his cop's defenses and called to him, tugged at him the way Theresa used to tug at him.

Which was crazy. You couldn't get two more different women than Theresa D'Annunzio and Jordan Carlisle. Okay, then why was he thinking about them in the same moment? This whole situation felt confusing, and Dom didn't like feeling confused. Didn't like it at all.

Mrs. Carlisle cried silently. The tears flowed, gliding smoothly over her cheeks. Her lower lip quivered, her hands clutched the picture like it was a religious icon. What could he—should he—do? Pat her hand? Hug her? No, he wasn't a hugger—some guys on the force could pull that off, not him. Offer her a handkerchief? His was used, and there didn't seem to be a handy box of tissues lying around.

What had Theresa told him? That men didn't need to rush in to fix things all the time, didn't always have to have solutions. Let people tell their story, Theresa had said. Maybe that was all they needed—someone to listen. Well, hell, he had ears.

"Look," he said, "maybe you'd like to, you know, talk about this a little." He shrugged with discomfort. "If you want to," he added.

She used a knuckle to swipe at the moisture on the lower lids. "But I barely know you."

"Yeah, well—" He shrugged again. Might as well go for it. "I'm here, and I'm willing. Tell me about Michael."

Chapter 3

What was she doing? Jordan asked herself. Weeping, falling apart in front of a virtual stranger, a policeman, to boot. How had she arrived at this state? She felt uncharacteristically exposed and vulnerable. She hadn't cried in months, but that didn't seem to matter.

Through the misty film of her tears, she tried to shift her focus to Dominic D'Annunzio, to his face with its furrowed, unsmiling brow. He sat in his chair, his elbows on the chair's arms. He seemed watchful, waiting. A bit tense, but not judgmental or disapproving, thank God, the way most strangers—most men—were in the presence of a woman's tears.

Tell him about Michael, he'd said. And she knew she wanted to, desperately *needed* to talk to someone. The letter had begun the flow of memories, the stripping away of her defenses, and this man, with his simple, ''Tell me about Michael,'' had completed the job.

Composing herself seemed to be a good place to begin, so she rose from the couch and walked away from him, rubbing her arms as she did. She took a moment or two with her back to him, studying a small, ornately framed water color of lilies in a pond, while she swallowed her tears. Finally, she turned to face him and asked, "Do you have kids?"

He shook his head. "Uh-uh."

"It's hard to explain, especially to someone who hasn't experienced it."

"Try me anyway." Still no smile, but at least a small nod of encouragement.

She came closer, sat on the couch, leaned over the coffee table, took another sip of her drink, then set it down. "You see, Detective," she began, then stopped. "Is there something else I could call you other than detective?"

He raised one thick eyebrow in surprise, then shrugged. "Dominic, Dom, whatever."

"All right. Then, please, call me Jordan."

Her request seemed to make him squirm. "Yeah, sure."

"Well, Dominic—" She smiled. "No, Dom, I think." She focused on her hands, which were in her lap; automatically her fingers played with the five-carat perfect diamond. "The simple truth is when Michael was born, I understood why I was alive. Up to then, it was as though my life had no purpose." Looking up, she met his unsmiling scrutiny. "Oh, sure, it had *looked* good. There had been fame and money and parties and all that—" She dismissed it all with a wave of her hand. "But inside—" she made a fist and pressed it right beneath her breasts "—in here, nothing but emptiness. Then Michael was born—" her fist relaxed, fell to her lap "—and everything changed. Suddenly I didn't feel useless, directionless anymore. Now I had a purpose, to be Michael's mother, to love him, to teach him about life, to prepare him for the world."

Biting her bottom lip, Jordan fought a fresh onslaught of tears. *No,* she told herself. She didn't want to cry, wanted instead to talk it all out, to tell Dominic D'Annunzio about the miracle.

"I was a good mother," Jordan went on. "It came to me out of nowhere just what to say and do, when to comfort him, when to let him fuss, you know. I fought my husband, my mother-in-law." She laughed briefly. "I was fierce. They didn't know what to do with me."

"What did you fight about?"

"Oh, things like they wanted me to have a nanny, to leave his care to someone else. I put my foot down. *I* would care for him. Then my husband didn't want me to nurse him—he was afraid I'd never get my figure back. No, I told them. I'm here, I don't work like a lot of women have to. I want to do this, I told them. I *will* do this. Like I said, fierce."

"A mama lioness with her cub." Dom said this with a hint of admiration on his face and one side of his mouth turned up slightly.

She smiled. "Believe it." She went on, leaning her head against the couch cushion. "He was beautiful," she said dreamily. "Oh, I know all children are beautiful to their mothers, but truly. Not just the cute face—that's easy, children are adorable and plump, and their skin is soft. No, inside. Michael was—" Pausing, she sought the right word. "He had a sweetness to him," she said finally, "that wasn't like other children. Look, I can show you."

Eager to do just that, Jordan vaulted up, crossed the room to a book-lined alcove that was next to the bar. She removed two thick cream-colored volumes from the shelves and brought them to the coffee table. "I have pictures," she said, setting them down, then resumed her seat on the couch once again.

She opened the cover of the album and turned the pages slowly, reliving those first few months of Michael's life. There was the wrinkled newborn, the first bath with the towel wrapped all around him. Baby Michael in his grandmother's arms, his father's arms, his mother's arms.

When she found the one she'd been looking for, she stopped, smoothed a hand over the page. It was a picture of Michael on his knees near a bed of flowers, clutching the stem of one in his fat little hand, caught in the act of glancing at whoever was taking the picture, an expression of pure joy on his face. Jordan felt her heart cracking under the strain of the memory of that day. One precious moment in time, captured forever.

It had been early last year, and she and Reynolds had just had another fight. This one was about her unwillingness to go to yet another party with the same spoiled, wealthy people he'd been friends with since childhood—each of them, men and women, on their second or third marriage. She knew how it would go. There would be too much drinking and catty remarks and golf stories. One or two of his friends would come on to her, and she would wriggle out of it as gracefully as possible. Reynolds would disappear for a half hour, and when he returned, his clothes would be a little less immaculate than when he'd left, and there would be a trace of lipstick somewhere on his shirt.

No, Jordan had told her husband that day, she would not go to his stupid party. Since Michael's birth she'd been speaking up for herself more and more, and Reynolds's scowl had been fierce. She'd grabbed her camera, picked up Michael and driven him to a nearby park. There she'd set him down near the flower beds and watched him, fascinated as he examined the blooms, clapped his hands at a buzzing fly. His child's interest, his joy at these simple things, had allowed her insides to return to some semblance of calm. As her son had fingered the petals of a daffodil, Jordan had picked up the camera and called his name. When he looked up, she'd snapped the picture.

She pointed to the photograph. "See?" she told Dom. "That's who he was. That's the real Michael."

Dom leaned in, straining his neck in an attempt to see what she was pointing at, but the angle of his chair made it difficult. Glancing at him, Jordan seemed to notice his discomfort because she said "I'm sorry," moving over on the couch and patting the cushion next to her. Her invitation was innocent enough, but he found himself hesitating. For some reason, he felt safer keeping a physical distance from her.

Safer? he asked himself silently. What was being safe all about? He was here to help her out—she'd asked, and he'd accepted. He shifted from the chair onto the couch, so that he sat next to her on the overstuffed cushion. Still, he was careful to keep several inches between them as she showed him a couple more snapshots of a blond-haired, chubby-cheeked little boy.

"There he is with his yellow ball. And on his first birthday." Angling her head, she offered an apologetic smile. "Am I being awful? There's nothing worse than having to look at other people's pictures, especially of their children.''

Her eyes, he thought, drawn into their depths against his will. They were the strangest color of green. Translucent. And that mouth, the way she smiled, the teeth white and even, the lips full and oh, so tempting.

"Hey, I asked," he said gruffly. "It's okay."

"Sure?"

"Yeah."

Man, was it hard to concentrate. Dom kept being distracted by the woman sitting next to him and the impact she made on his senses. This close, he could smell her fragrance, a mixture of expensive perfume and clean, lemon-scented hair. Sexual awareness throbbed in every part of him. He wanted to caress her hair, stroke her skin, to feel the touch of her fingers on every part of him.

Schooling his face to keep from revealing any of his thoughts, Dom forced himself to concentrate on the pictures, offering appropriate grunts of acknowledgment and appreciation. Picking up the recent snapshot she'd received, he tried to compare the faces. There was some similarity, sure, but not enough to make a big deal over. And okay, the kid was cute, but he was a kid. Dom knew how that went—he had a bunch of nieces and nephews, and according to all his siblings, the sun rose and set on each one of them.

He and Theresa had had bad luck in the baby-making department so, long ago, he'd stopped planning to be a father, ceased fantasizing about a little miniature version of him sitting on his knee or catching a softball. He'd put that part of him away, and that's what Jordan Carlisle would have to do. Put it away.

Her little boy, she needed to remind herself, was no longer living and breathing. The sad but real truth was that Michael Carlisle, this child whose face was spread over all the pages of this album, was now a statistic.

But not the woman, Dom added silently, she was not a statistic. Again, he inhaled the fresh smell of her as his gaze moved to the album. Her hands on the pages were beautifully formed, with long, slender fingers and clear polish on her nails. Lamplight glinted on the large diamond.

Jordan Carlisle. A real upper-crust name; it went with the jewelry, the house, the woman. Jordan Carlisle. Perfect. No one in his world was named Jordan. They were Maries and Sallys and Annes, not Jordans. So, okay, he and Jordan didn't hang out at the same places—that didn't alter the fact that, like it or not, there was something between them, some…connection. An invisible wire, electrified, ready to go off any moment.

On his part, anyway. Glancing quickly at her profile, he wondered if she was aware of that connection, but then decided that, nah, she was too wrapped up in happy-painful memories to be paying much attention to him.

The album reflected her recent past, its snapshots revealing a whole other Jordan Carlisle than the one he knew. Here was a loving mother with child, romping in the sand at the beach, riding a bike with the kid in a small seat behind her, her legs long and bare in shorts and tennis shoes. Jordan, waving and laughing. Relaxed. The way she could be, he saw, but not the way he knew her. He hadn't seen that side of her yet. The pictures showed Jordan before her world fell apart.

He knew all about that. He'd been a different man before the obsession for a baby had started eating at Theresa. Not softer—he'd never been soft a day in his life—but less closed off than he was now. Loving another human being made people nicer, kinder, he figured. Hopeful.

"Here," Jordan said, snapping him out of his reverie. He'd been thinking about Theresa again. Why now? It had been three years, and her memory had faded.

As Jordan indicated one more photograph, Dom observed the slight tremor in her hand and how she bit her bottom lip to keep from crying again. This was hard on her, it was obvious, and the effort to hold on to her composure was costing her.

The picture showed the kid in front of the house, one thumb in his mouth, his feet turned in slightly, hugging a brown stuffed animal with his free hand.

"He was about fifteen months old when I got him that dog," she said shakily. "He loved it so."

Abruptly, she rose from the sofa and walked to the floor-to-ceiling windows at one end of the room, continuing to speak as she did. "We couldn't have a real dog because Cynthia is highly allergic, so I found that one, a pretend puppy, and from the moment he got it, he never let it out of his sight. It was like some kind of talisman, a kind of, you know, a friend to have when you got scared. Michael was a little shy until he got comfortable."

Angling her head to face him, she smiled softly at Dom. "Kind of like me. But then when he knew someone, he was all right. He was quick to walk, slow to talk, but he was doing both fine when—"

Her breath hitched, and she bit her lip again, in an obvious effort at control. Averting her gaze, she moved the curtain aside and seemed to stare out at the night.

Dom stood, started to walk toward her, but stopped. The instinct to reach out and take her hand was strong, but he didn't follow it up with action. Clenching his fists, he held back, kept his distance. That push-pull thing was here again, although he wasn't quite sure why—only that physical contact with Jordan Carlisle didn't seem like a smart thing.

"He was doing fine when what?" he prompted.

"When he died," she said, still staring out the window at nothing but black night.

What could he say? What was left to say? They both lapsed into silence. She was still shaky, he saw, so he walked in her direction, saying, "Look, we don't have to talk about this anymore."

She shook her head but didn't look at him. "No, I want to. Give me a minute."

Another few moments of silence went by. Then the phone rang and was quickly picked up somewhere in the house. Jordan turned as Dom glanced at his watch. Almost nine-thirty. He was on duty again in less than eleven hours.

"I'm sorry," she said quickly. "Do you have to leave?"

"Not for a little while."

"Sure?"

"Yeah." He scratched his head. Were they done? Had she told him all she could? Did he want this time with her to be over?

No, he did not.

"Do you feel up to telling me about the accident?" Dom asked. "More details, I mean. If you want to."

She examined her rings, and he wondered if she knew what a giveaway that nervous gesture was. She was pretty easy to read anyway—everything she felt showed on her face. Her heart-stoppingly beautiful face.

"Detective—" she began, but he cut her off.

"Dom."

"Oh, yes, Dom." Placing her hand on his arm, she said softly, "I want to thank you for taking time to come here, and all. I really appreciate it."

His skin burned where she touched him, even through his jacket, and the gratitude on her face made him feel squirmy. "Hey, forget it."

She moved away, made a beeline for the bar. "I'm going to get another drink. Sure I can't interest you?"

"Yeah, okay, I'll take a Scotch."

Man, he needed one, he thought. The woman made him uncomfortable. Obviously, she, too, needed some fortification. Was she a lush? he wondered with the cop part of his brain. She exhibited none of the signs, but it was possible. Tragedy often turned a lot of one-a-day recreational drinkers into candidates for AA.

He watched her as she walked toward the mirrored built-in bar, her slim hips swaying slightly. Dom removed the gum from his mouth, discarded it in a crumpled wrapper he found in his pocket, then deposited it in a heavy crystal ashtray on a side table.

As he did, he asked himself what he was doing here. And why was he staying? She'd given him an out—it was late, he was tired—but he hadn't taken it. Which was nuts—he'd put in twelve hours already, hadn't taken a day off in over two weeks. He was wiped out, running on nervous energy. The letter was a scam, he'd done his bit. So why was he here?

Instead of answering his own question, he found himself walking toward the bar. "Can I help?" he said.

"No, thank you."

Even so, he stood behind her while she mixed the drinks, gazing at the back of her neck. Her hair had some brown and blond mixed in with the auburn and was cut so that it tapered into a slight V. At the point of the V, a soft, blond line of down continued downward, past the clasp of her pearls—which shimmered in the soft lighting—disappearing beneath the neckline of her sweater.

Her neck was long and graceful, her skin nearly as pale as the pearls. He longed to run the pad of his finger over that line of down, wondered how her skin would taste.

Why was he staying? asked that same nag of an inner voice. Why was he having a drink, prolonging the encounter? And fantasizing about the taste of her?

There was no way the two of them belonged together. Dom preferred his women more down to earth, more Wal-Mart, less Neiman-Marcus. And she obviously went for guys in thousand-dollar suits and home gyms, which had nothing to do with the way his hormones clanged loudly in her presence.

But, even more worrying than this physical reaction was his need to get to know her, to learn all there was to learn about her, more and more and more, as much as she would reveal. Which was not like him, but there it was.

So, to answer his question, he was still here because, somehow, he couldn't see himself cutting off her reminiscences, hopping up, waving goodbye and taking off. Couldn't see it, didn't want to.

What he needed to do, however, was to go back to being a cop. Return to being Mrs. Carlisle and Detective Sergeant D'Annunzio. Yeah, that's what he needed to do.

Soon, he assured himself, staring again at the jeweled clasp of her pearl necklace and at the tiny mole beside it. Real soon.

Jordan sensed Dom's presence behind her—solid and strong, but also warm. It was as though he gave off heat, like a furnace.

It had the strange effect of rattling her and comforting her at the same time. In fact, in the past few moments, the atmosphere in the room had changed. Up to then, her grief and the pictures of Michael had made her tune out everything but her own emotions. Now the air was heavy with this new element.

She glanced into the mirror behind the bar, and as she did, Dom's eyes met hers. It was hard to decipher the look in his eyes, but it was intense. She was aware of how dark he was, especially in the backdrop of the room's white and beige tones. Dark hair, dark eyes, olive skin, the beard shadow. He was a half a head taller than she was, but he seemed even larger than that. Overwhelming and powerful. Hulking.

She turned to give him his drink, and face to face, their eyes locked. She saw it then.

Hunger.

Raw, primitive desire.

A brief flash of it before he pulled the shutters closed. It was not her imagination. She was too used to men and the way they looked at her, wondering if she would be a trophy, to miss the signs.

With abrupt movements, Dom took the drink from her, then turned away. After downing half of it, he walked around the room, staring at pictures, vases, knickknacks, keeping his back to her. Avoiding her.

So, Jordan thought with wonder, Dominic D'Annunzio wanted her. She stood still and let the realization wash over her. It felt…nice. No, wrong word. Not nice. Exciting. And a little scary, too. This felt like unknown territory. Even with all her experience of men, she wasn't familiar with this type of man and his particular set of rules.

Jordan hadn't had much success with lovers, hadn't enjoyed much pleasure in bed. But that didn't seem to have soured her on the possibilities, did it? From the start, she'd found Dom disturbingly sexy and now she knew it was mutual. She'd seen it in Dom's eyes—a naked yearning for her. He'd let her glimpse it for just a millisecond, and then it was gone.

She followed his movements as, obviously unsettled, Dom prowled the room. She wondered briefly what it would feel like to have all that restless energy inside her and felt a warm shiver go through her at the thought. He stopped in front of a framed wedding picture, Jordan and Reynolds on the day of their marriage, and stared at it, but said nothing.

Drink in hand, Jordan walked over to the picture and stood next to Dom, aware of him with that extra sense, now that she knew how he felt. Both of them studied the formally dressed bride and groom.

"I was so happy that day," she said. And she had been, impossibly young and filled with the dream of a solid, secure future.

Her speedy journey from dirt-poor and naive to the jet-set world of high fashion had been more than she could handle emotionally. In the beginning, of course, at the age of fifteen, she'd loved the attention, the fuss, the money. But after a couple of years, when everyone wanted a piece of her and she'd stopped feeling like a person and more like a commodity, after her family had begun to "invest" her money for her and every man she met wanted to bed her, underage or not, she'd been on the verge of collapse. That's when Reynolds had come along, riding up on his white horse.

A white top-of-the-line Mercedes, in actuality. He'd been raised in privilege and had been singularly unimpressed with her fame, which was a nice change.

He'd been determined to have her. He'd wooed her with thoughtful gifts, corrected her grammar, taught her about wine and how to select the best quality jewelry. When he'd weeded out his competitors, he'd informed her she'd better marry him because he was what she needed. Barely eighteen years old and already exhausted by life, she had agreed.

In her wedding picture, her face was wreathed in a happy smile. Her happiness that day had been real, but it had not been in love happy. It had been relieved happy. Finally, there was someone to lean on, someone whose arms would be large enough to take her in, to protect her from a world that puzzled and terrified her.

Jordan glanced at Dom's profile as he continued to study the portrait. "Nice picture," he said finally.

"It was a nice day."

"Did it stay that way?"

He angled his head to face her, piercing her with those coffee-brown eyes of his. See-all, seen-all eyes. His expression was grim. Again, she was struck by how thoroughly out of place he seemed in this delicate room with its neutral shades and aura of quiet good taste. He brought not only darkness with him, but also street smarts, rough edges, eyes that had seen all the worst mankind could offer.

He repeated the question a shade more insistently. "Did it stay that way?"

She answered with a shrug. "Does anything?" she asked.

He stared at her a little while longer, his face impassive, then shrugged also. "Sometimes it does." He said it offhandedly, but she sensed there was more to it.

Then she remembered. Yes, of course. His wife had died, he'd told her. Here she was, so wrapped up in her own tragedy she'd forgotten that until this moment. His marriage must have been successful, one of the good ones.

"So," Jordan said softly, placing her hand lightly on his arm, "you must really miss your wife."

Something flashed across his face, some emotion she could not read and that he made sure she couldn't by drawing the shutters again. "Yeah." He turned away from her, and her hand fell to her side. "But I'm here to talk about you."

Again, he'd closed down abruptly, which, for some reason, hurt more deeply than it should have. She stared at his back as he nursed his drink and checked out some more family pictures on the wall. She rubbed her arms. There it was, that chill in the room again.

All right, Detective, she wanted to say. I get the message. Do not probe, he was telling her. Do not talk about my wife.

And, after all, she asked herself, why should he? She'd made her business his, but he hadn't invited her to do the same.

She walked over to the couch, recovering her poise as she did. "To answer your question," she said dispassionately, "my marriage was not a very happy one. Sometimes I'm guilty that I don't mourn Reynolds more, but I'm afraid the truth is, the

loss of my son overwhelms anything else I may be feeling.''
She downed the rest of her Scotch in one gulp. She was not
much of a drinker, but she wanted the warm feeling back.

Her glance fell on the open letter sitting on the coffee table.
She reached down and plucked it up. ''So,'' she said as the
smooth liquid worked its magic, soothing, buffeting. ''Where
were we?''

He stood facing her, the two floor-to-ceiling windows that
opened to the terrace behind him. He had his drink in one hand.
The other was in his pants pocket, jiggling his keys. ''Tell me
about the day of the accident.''

''Oh, yes.'' Perching on the arm of the couch, she said,
''Reynolds came up to me and announced that he was taking
Michael for a drive—alone. I remember being surprised. He
never did that, you know, father and son kind of thing. And I
remember Michael didn't really want to go, not without me. He
was in that real mommy phase—I was the beginning and
end of his existence.'' She chuckled a little, but Dom's expression remained impersonal, watchful, which made her feel
foolish.

Looking down, she picked at a piece of lint on her pants.
''Anyhow, that day, Reynolds was adamant, he was taking his
son for a drive, out for ice cream, maybe, or to the zoo. So I
waved goodbye to them. Michael was in his car seat in the
back, and he turned around to look at me the whole time the
car moved down the driveway.''

Her voice cracked on that last word, but she was determined
not to cry again. Enough tears, she told herself firmly, way too
many. She would tell the story and be done with it.

''It was after lunch, one or so. I got word by late afternoon
that the car had been found over an embankment off Mulhol-
land Highway in the hills above Malibu. It had gone over, some
nearby brush caught fire, and by the time the fire fighters and
police got there, everything—the car, the bodies—was pretty
well burned.''

''Then how did they know whose car it was? How were they
able to contact you so fast?''

''Apparently, part of the license plate hadn't burned.

And…oh!'' The sob rose out of nowhere. Damn it! She'd been doing so well. Her hand flew to her mouth to muffle the sound.

After a moment, she made herself continue. "The puppy, the stuffed puppy had been thrown clear. It was found on the hillside nearby. It had a real dog collar with a tag on it. 'My name is Pup-Pup,' it said, followed by my phone number. That's how they found me so quickly." She bit her lip, hard. She would *not* break down.

Leaving his post by the window, Dom walked toward her and stopped, the coffee table between them. He still had his drink in one hand, but the thumb of the other was looped over his belt, which had a pager and a badge clipped to it. He had a gun, she assumed, and wondered idly where he wore it.

For a time, he seemed to be checking her out, almost clinically, for any further signs of emotional distress. Then he asked, "What caused the accident? Had he been drinking? Had he blown a tire?''

Meeting his gaze, Jordan shrugged. "They never found out. There were skid marks on the highway, as though he'd tried to put on the brakes. No alcohol. And it was impossible to tell anything about tires or anything else. The car was just about totaled.''

"Were they sure it was an accident? Could it have been suicide?''

It was too much of an effort to continue to make eye contact, so Jordan looked down as she played with her rings. "There was some talk about that, for a little while, anyway. I was pretty sure it wasn't suicide.''

"That's natural.''

She shook her head. "No. You don't understand. Reynolds wasn't like that. He was too—'' She sought the words. "He was a vain man, narcissistic. If he were going to kill himself— and I don't think the thought would enter his mind—he would do it more cleanly. Pills, maybe, or gas.'' She looked up, met his gaze. "So he wouldn't appear…flawed in death.''

"Look, Mrs. Carlisle—''

"Jordan.''

"Oh, yeah." He drew his brows together, as though puzzled. "Is that your real name or one of those made-up ones?"

The change of subject surprised her, but it also lightened the atmosphere in the room, so she welcomed it with a small smile. "It's real. For the River Jordan. My brother is named Galilee. Bodies of water in the Holy Land. You see, where we grew up, well, it was pretty parched in that section of Wyoming."

He nodded, finished his drink, set the glass next to hers on the coffee table. As he checked his watch again, she knew he was preparing to leave.

"Would you like me to pull the file," he asked, "see if there's anything there? Not that it'll do much good, if there was a positive identification of the bodies."

"There was. Reynolds's dental records, the puppy, the child's bones were the right age. No, there was no doubt in anyone's mind, not even mine, that Reynolds and Michael both died in that car crash."

Her breath caught in her throat again, unexpectedly, and she felt another sob threatening. She tried to contain it by holding her fisted hands to her solar plexus. "I'm sorry. You think you're through crying, and then it all comes up again."

"Yeah."

"You know all about mourning, don't you? Because of your wife."

His mouth tensed again and he seemed to hesitate, then nodded once. She knew that he wanted out of here, away from her and her stupid tears.

She snatched the picture from the coffee table and looked at it. "I'm a fool aren't I?" she said angrily. "I allowed myself to hope again. I wanted it to be real." She glanced at Dom. "Michael," she said brokenly, "was the one good thing I ever did in my life. And my life ended a year ago."

She lost it then, totally and thoroughly. Her hands crumpled the photo as she raised them to her eyes. Long, choking sobs of unfettered grief racked her body. "Go," she tried to tell Dom. "I don't want you to see me like this."

She didn't observe but felt the moment when he took two quick steps toward her. There was a brief hesitation, but only for a second. Then she felt his hands covering her clenched ones, easing them away from her eyes and pulling her to a standing position. He brought her arms around his waist and pulled her close to him, wrapping her body in a broad, muscular embrace.

She sagged against him, and, oh lord, it felt natural and right, as though Dom was an everyday, available source of comfort. As she hugged him tightly, she cried onto his shirt, soaking the front with salty tears.

While her cheek rubbed against the wool of his jacket, he stroked her hair awkwardly, murmured soothing words in his gruff voice. It was such a huge relief to be able to do this. And after a while, when the sobs diminished, she was aware of the smell of him—wool and male sweat and that faint hint of wintergreen. What had happened to his gum? she wondered suddenly, not at all sure where that thought had come from.

His strong heartbeat throbbed against her cheek, a little rapidly, she noticed, the same as his breathing. In a single moment, his hand stilled on her neck and the atmosphere changed, from warmth and comfort to something more sensual—and a lot less comforting. It was disconcerting to be so aware of Dom with every pore of her skin. Still holding tightly to him, Jordan drew her head away from his chest and gazed at him, a question forming on her lips.

But then she saw his eyes. It was there again, that fierce hunger. And just like that, her own hunger rose to the surface.

She just had time to close her eyes before she heard his muttered ''Damn,'' and his mouth descended to hers.

Chapter 4

Dom knew what he was doing. Hell, he always knew what he was doing. Not only did this come from having to watch his back growing up on the streets of Brooklyn, it came from that sixth sense cops developed after years on the job, so that you were never caught unawares, so that there was always a part of you on the lookout—observing, assessing potential danger.

So, yeah, he knew what he was doing—he was giving in to an overpowering, totally irresistible impulse to make contact, flesh to flesh, with Jordan Carlisle. To sample that inviting mouth of hers, to taste her as he'd been wanting to do all evening.

What took him by surprise was her response. It was immediate and breath-robbingly intense. The moment his mouth met hers, it was like they'd slammed into each other. It was as though a blowtorch of passion had fused them together. She made a guttural sound in the back of her throat, then her lips parted in invitation, and he shoved his tongue through. She tasted of Scotch and tears, and she met his tongue with her own. As he drank deeply from her mouth's moisture, he brought his hands around to frame her face, angling it for a better, even deeper connection.

There was nothing tender going on here—none of that first, tentative, exploratory merging of mouths, no holding back to give each other time to adjust. No, what this was, Dom knew, was instant heat, combustible enough to set off a sizable flame. His hands moved again to the back of her head. His fingers plowed through her silky soft hair to dig into her scalp. Reaching under his jacket, she splayed her hands across his back, pressing her body to his chest. He groaned as the points of her nipples dug into his shirt front, setting up a trembling along his thighs, making heat pool between his legs and giving him an instant, unmistakable erection.

If his ferocity took him by surprise, hers made him feel downright primitive. Animal responding to animal, both in heat. His instinct was to open his mouth even wider, to take her, all of her, inside him and devour her. Pushing his arousal against her stomach, he deepened the kiss. His teeth scored her lower lip. His heart pounded loudly in his ears.

Too loudly.

It was not his heart. Someone was knocking on the door.

Dom and Jordan broke apart immediately, stared briefly at each other. Her face registered the same shock he was feeling, then she shook her head as though she had just awakened. Quickly, she averted her gaze.

"Jordan?" a voice called, followed by another knock on the door.

Hastily brushing her fingers through her hair, she responded, "Come in, Cynthia," then leaned over the coffee table to gather the photo albums into her arms.

Dom tensed as the door opened. Mrs. Carlisle, Senior, entered the room to see her daughter-in-law clutching the family albums to her chest. Even with her pale skin uncharacteristically flushed, Jordan had managed to school her face into a look of pleasant inquiry. "Yes?" she said evenly.

"I...thought I heard someone crying."

Dom angled his body away from the two women. His arousal had been swift. His and Jordan's mouths had met and, pow, his male equipment had been ready to give service. The abrupt ending to their kiss had taken its toll—his nerve endings trembled with small aftershocks.

"Yes, I was crying," he heard Jordan say. "I...well, it was nothing to worry about. I'm fine now."

What he needed, Dom figured, was a couple of moments to get back to normal. Downtime, the guys on the force said. While he waited for his shallow, rapid breathing to get regular again, he ambled over to a bookshelf and pretended to study some of the volumes. Were there still traces of Jordan's pale peach lipstick on his mouth? he wondered, and ran his tongue over his lips to see if he could taste any. No, he decided, even as the thought of Jordan's luscious mouth reversed some of his cooling-off effort.

Sliding his hands into his back pockets, he continued to turn away from Cynthia Carlisle. The back of his neck felt flushed with an emotion that took him a moment to ID. Then he got it.

Guilt.

Son of a bitch, but that knock on the door had made him feel guilty. It was like he'd been caught necking in the back row during choir practice. The thought made him smile briefly.

"I didn't mean to interrupt anything important," he heard the mother-in-law say.

"You didn't," Jordan replied easily. "I was just showing Dom—" She caught herself. "—Detective D'Annunzio some pictures, and I'm afraid I reacted a little strongly."

"Oh."

He heard the older woman sniff loudly. Typical, he thought with irritation, that sniff of disapproval, not just of him, but of all cops, probably, creatures who had their uses but who should be let in by the back door and told to wipe their feet. On the other hand, he made himself consider with a little more generosity, the lady had lost her son and grandson last year, so maybe he could give her a little slack.

Whatever. It wasn't important. It was time to bail.

He adjusted his tie, smoothed his jacket and turned to face the two women. "I was just leaving, Mrs. Carlisle," he said. "Your daughter-in-law has been most helpful." Keeping his face impassive, he nodded to Jordan. "Thanks for your time."

Their gazes met for an instant. He could have sworn he saw a brief flash of amusement in hers before she said, in a lady-of-the-manor fashion, "Let me just put these albums back and I'll walk you out." With that perfect poise of hers, she crossed to the small, book-lined alcove and returned the thick volumes to their shelves.

The dragon lady shifted her gaze to him. Again she sniffed. Maybe, Dom thought, she had sinus problems. Jordan turned to her mother-in-law and raised an eyebrow. "Was there something you needed, Cynthia?" she asked coolly, and he had to admire the way she did it. If their little physical encounter had aroused any guilt in her, she was a champ at covering it up.

"Not really," the elder Mrs. Carlisle said, continuing to glare at him, then shifting her gaze to Jordan and to him again. Her brow wrinkled with puzzlement. It was as if she could sense some undercurrent in the room but couldn't put her finger on just what it was.

Yeah, well, in her wildest dreams, Dom thought sardonically, she couldn't have imagined that steamy kiss he'd shared with her daughter-in-law. In her wildest dreams.

"I'm getting ready for bed," Cynthia said, "and just wanted to say good-night."

"I'll be back in a moment," Jordan said, sweeping past her, "and I'll say good-night then. I'm just going to see our guest out."

"No need," Dom said, following her to the door of the room.

"The fresh air sounds good."

As they left Cynthia Carlisle staring after them, Dom felt like chuckling. He got it now—the older woman reminded him of none other than Sister Mary Magdalena, the head nun at his boys' Catholic school, the one who always managed to nab him and his friends at their small, youthful misdeeds. A grown man of thirty-six no longer had to account for his actions to anyone, but that old childhood training went deep.

"Where did you park?" Jordan asked as he opened the front door for her.

"Out on the street."

They walked down the long driveway in silence. The night was quiet, as it usually was in this area of prime real estate, the north of Sunset section of Beverly Hills that was nestled against the mountains. The harsh whirling of helicopters or kids gunning their motors or blasting rap music out of their car speakers—there was none of that here. Loud, jarring, peace-shattering noise was for the rest of the city, which seemed far, far away but was, in actuality, only a few miles to the south and east.

Dom glanced at the woman by his side, wondering what she was thinking. Her long legs easily matched his stride. Her profile, as she looked straight ahead, revealed nothing.

Dom was used to making snap judgments and quick decisions, usually knew what the next two or three moves in any situation should be. But not with her. She threw him off. Strange. The whole thing was strange. Just moments before, the two of them had been on the verge of—what? A quickie roll in the hay? Doubtful. Not there, at that time, in that house.

And probably never, he figured. Their kiss had been one of those spontaneous acts that happened once and that was it. A sudden, out-of-time moment and then adios. He muttered a low curse under his breath. He didn't want it to be just one time, damn it. He wanted to taste more of her, all of her.

"What?" Jordan said, stopping. "Did you say something?"

"No."

"Oh."

They walked on, Jordan's heels making a slight clicking sound on the flagstone path. Muted ground-level lights illuminated their way. Damp patches on the stone indicated recent watering. That special smell of freshly mown and watered grass rose to his nostrils. It was a sweet smell, one that signaled early spring, that sense of new life forming and unfolding. Funny, not since Theresa's death had he been as aware of the change of seasons as he was at this moment.

Theresa. A small twinge of uneasiness hit him at the thought of his late wife. He didn't want to be with Jordan and thinking about Theresa—didn't like the confusion it created in his head—but that seemed to be the case whether he liked it or not.

As he breathed in the smell once again, he found himself yawning and covered his mouth.

"You're tired, aren't you?" Jordan said.

"Yeah, I'm pretty wasted." What he was was overworked, stretched way too thin. It was by choice—he preferred longer hours to lonely time at home—but still… He really needed to hit the sack.

Alone, he guessed.

They stopped at the gate. Through the wrought-iron fence, he could see his car, which was parked under a street lamp. American, six years old, ninety thousand hard miles on it. There was a long gash across the passenger door where some gangbanger in his neighborhood had scraped a key, a dent in the right rear fender. And dusty—who had time to wash a car?

Suddenly he saw it through Jordan's eyes. His Dodge sure didn't belong here among the lush, perfect grounds with their elegant trees and beds of flowers and bushes that had been trimmed and tamed to within an inch of their lives. Hell, not even the gravel on this part of the driveway would dare to get too messy.

Dom was a messy kind of guy. Not dirty, just messy. And he was comfortable with—even proud of—his blue collar roots. He was a beer and spaghetti—never pasta—man. He'd never been one of those jokers who lusted after big bucks and fancy cars and servants. Not ever.

But tonight, standing here with this woman, the truth was he felt like a slob, a tired, worn-out slob. The sooner he got away from here, the better.

Jordan pushed the button, and the gate slid open silently.

Dom walked to his car and she followed him. When he got to the driver's side, he rested one hand on the door frame and turned to gaze at her. She seemed composed, and he wondered if he was imagining the flicker of nerves he sensed beneath her skin.

"Well—" he said, then shrugged.

She offered her hand. "Thank you so much for coming."

He took her hand in his. Soft, smooth skin. His fingers and the pads of his palm were callused, and much larger than hers. He continued to gaze at her, still not sure what the next move was but wanting to see something in her eyes that he had no name for.

In the light from the overhead street lamp, shadows hollowed her cheekbones. Her complexion looked ghostly, but her face was so perfectly formed, it was easy to see why the camera loved it. Smooth face, smooth skin, smooth hands. She belonged here. She was part of all the smooth perfection of her surroundings.

Realizing he was still holding her hand, he dropped it quickly. "Should I apologize?" he found himself asking—the words came out before he even knew they were being formed.

"For what?"

"Kissing you."

A brief flash of humor crossed the alabaster face. "I believe I kissed you back."

"Yeah, you sure did," he said with a small smile, then frowned. "But you were pretty upset, not in a real good place, and, well, maybe—"

"Maybe you took advantage of me?" she interjected sardonically.

When he shrugged, she set her hand on his arm, lightly, the way she had a couple of times that evening. "Thank you for asking, but I needed what you gave me, Dom," she said quietly, that husky voice of hers rich with emotion. Removing her hand, she placed it over her heart. "I can't tell you how much you helped me tonight. It's been such a long time since I've been able to pour out my heart to someone."

"So the kiss was my reward?" He winced the minute he said it, wanted to take the words and shove them back down his throat.

She looked startled. "Excuse me?"

Terrific. He sounded like some petulant kid who had been spurned by the prom queen. "Look, forget it. I'm wiped out. I don't know what the hell I'm saying."

She seemed on the verge of answering him, but didn't. And really, he thought, there was nothing more to say. It had been one of those what-the-hell moments, was all. She'd needed comfort, he'd needed to get his hormones stoked. It had been one stupid kiss, nothing else. In the scheme of things—as his dad had used to say when one of the kids came running home with a black eye or a tale of betrayal by a friend—in the scheme of things, it didn't signify a whole hell of a lot.

So, yeah, big deal, he could handle it.

He inserted the key into the car door. Then, remembering why she'd summoned him in the first place, he turned to her again. "Look, about the letter—"

"I'm going to tear it up," she said quickly. "It would be nothing but foolish to expect to see my son again." With a small, vulnerable smile, she added, "And I have a horror of appearing foolish."

He nodded. "Yeah, I know what you mean. Okay, then. Good night."

He opened his car door, but was stopped again by the light touch of her hand on his arm. "Dom?"

Again he turned. "Yeah?"

"We probably won't meet again...." She left it dangling. He could pick it up and run with it or leave it where it was. There was something in her expression that he couldn't read, and just then, he didn't want to.

Close the door, his inner voice commanded. Get out of here. Run.

He nodded. "Yeah, we probably won't, so—" He shrugged, not sure just what to say. "Have a good life," was what he came up with.

His remark made her flinch slightly, then she recovered. "You too," she said softly.

He got into his car, gunned the motor and took off.

Cynthia was waiting for her by the door when Jordan returned to the house. "Why were you crying in front of that man? Why were you showing him the family albums?"

"It just happened, Cynthia." Absentmindedly, Jordan checked her appearance in the antique mirror by the mail table. "We got to talking, and I told him all about Michael—and Reynolds," she added quickly. "And then I showed him pictures."

"But why? Why bring all that up again?"

Her mother-in-law was honestly stumped. Jordan could see it by the pained look in her gray-blue eyes as she asked the question. She wished she had Cynthia's capacity for shutting down feelings, for putting all of life's hurts into a little box and burying it somewhere in her soul and then just getting on with her day-to-day existence.

But she was not made that way. She didn't let go easily.

"It just came up, that's all. I'm sorry if I upset you. Look, why don't you go on to bed. It's late."

Her mother-in-law continued to gaze at her, obviously wondering about her. She'd seen that question in Cynthia's eyes before. *Who is this person I have been stuck with? Why aren't Reynolds and my grandson here instead of her?*

For that brief moment, Jordan felt sorry for the older woman who hadn't deserved to be left alone any more than Jordan had. Impulsively, she kissed Cynthia on the cheek. "See you in the morning," she said. "It's my day off—would you like to go shopping?"

"Oh." A look of surprise crossed her face. "Well, yes, that would be nice. I'm supposed to meet Mabel Arness for lunch— will you join us?"

Usually Jordan said no to invitations like this one. Lunch with any of Cynthia's friends meant listening to idle chatter and mudslinging. Tonight, she accepted. "I'd love to. Sleep tight."

She ran up the stairs to her room. After she closed the door behind her, she threw herself on her bed with relief. Clutching a lace-edged pillow to her breast, she stared at the high cream-colored, plaster ceilings with their curlicued molding. Lord, lord, lord, she thought as she finally allowed all her delayed reactions to flood through her.

There was a mass of them—all complicated—and she felt almost giddy from the onslaught.

Hope had been raised by the letter, but was soon dashed by reality. Tears of grief she'd been holding in for so long had been released in the presence of a stranger. With that same stranger's kiss and her own passionate arousal, her womanly reflexes had come to life for the first time in a long time. Such a very long time.

Wanting to sink into the ground when Cynthia knocked, but covering it up. That familiar childhood shyness as she walked Dom to the car, not sure what to say to him. Her surprise at the brief hint of vulnerability he'd allowed to slip out.

The yearning to feel his mouth on hers again. The shock of his rejection. "Have a good life," he'd said, as though nothing special had happened to him, the way it had happened for her.

Yes, a torrent of sensations, both physical and emotional, had been released tonight. So many emotions. Too many. She felt drained, depleted of energy.

Weary, she rose from her bed and padded over the thick carpet toward her bathroom. It was time to wash up and get into bed. Time to put an end to all this introspection and fantasizing. No more emotional roller coasters for her. Time to get on with her life.

"Terrific, Nancy," Jordan said into the phone. "See you at four." She hung up and called to Lisa, who was straightening up the sweater shelves. "Got her."

Lisa glanced at her, one blond eyebrow raised. "Got who?"

"The complete pile of rejects from Nancy Tremaine's

closet.'' Jordan grinned. She knew what the word ''rejects'' meant to Nancy—barely used, top designers, year-old and in perfect shape. The jackpot. ''You'll salivate when you see what she considers out of style.''

Lisa grinned. ''Nancy Tremaine. Mrs. Gilbert Tremaine, Junior. Wow. Glad you're here, Jordan. Love your contacts. Nothing like the personal touch.''

Lisa's praise warmed her, and again she was so glad fate had brought the two women together.

Several months before, after Jordan had attended a foreign film in West Los Angeles—one of her secret passions—she'd wandered into Riches and Rags, which was just down the block on Santa Monica Boulevard. It was a for-profit store, but even so, she'd been expecting something only slightly better than a charity thrift shop and had been pleasantly surprised to find such beautiful clothing, so lovingly displayed.

After walking around the store for a while, she'd gotten to chatting with Lisa Davidson, the shop's owner, a woman of her own age. On impulse, Jordan had offered to work there part-time and to use her connections to purchase the discarded wardrobes of some of her Beverly Hills circle. At the time, she thought it would be a hobby of sorts, something she could do to get her mind off herself. However, in the three months since she'd been there, she and Lisa had begun discussions on Jordan becoming a partner.

Clothing had been a passion of Jordan's even in Wyoming. She'd always played dress up, using discarded rags and bits of fabric to create costumes for her brother and her. Riches and Rags, with its colorful apparel racks, walls hung with scarves and hats and belts, its two large windows looking out onto busy Santa Monica Boulevard, gave her a sense of belonging and ease she never experienced under Cynthia's roof.

The bell jangled, and two designer-jeans-clad young women walked in. Jordan checked to see if they needed any help, told the elderly lady pawing through the Last Chance blouse pile she was available for assistance, then went to the front counter. The invoices were filed, the mailing list updated and, for the present, at least, no one needed her attention. There was, for this single brief moment, nothing for her to do.

Which meant her mind shifted to Dominic D'Annunzio again, as it had, off and on, in the five days since he'd been to the house. There had been no new notes about Michael, but she hadn't torn up the letter and picture as she'd promised to do. Instead, she carried them with her in her purse, reluctant somehow to put out the small flame of hope they'd aroused. She was foolish, she knew it. Dom would counsel her to put all that firmly behind her.

However, putting Dom behind her, as she'd intended to do—as he'd made it clear he wanted her to do—seemed to be more of a challenge.

His face kept invading her head at odd moments. The memory of that kiss could still make her knees melt. What was it about this street-savvy cop that attracted her? His strength, she supposed. Not just physical strength, although his hands had gripped her forcefully. Her hands had been impressed by the rock-hard firmness of his chest and the ripple of muscles down his back. He could crush her with one squeeze, she supposed.

No, the strength she was talking about came from the aura of power she sensed from him. Power and dependability. Without knowing him well at all, she knew he was a powerful, dependable, capable, *strong* man. And strength of character was one thing she completely lacked. Michael had been all that was good about her....

No! Jordan admonished herself, looking around the busy shop and wondering if she'd said it out loud. No, she repeated silently. She was not to think that way anymore. Since childhood, she'd been tearing herself down, and it had to stop. The grief therapist she'd gone to last year had passed along pretty good advice—when the old tapes of self-doubt and self-loathing began to play in her head, she was to counter them by finding something of worth about herself and concentrating on that.

Something of worth, Jordan said silently, as she picked up a feather duster and swiped it along the counter. Yes, she had some admirable qualities, she knew that. She was always on time, took responsibility seriously. She didn't steal or cheat at cards. Pretty boring stuff, she thought with a smile, but starting small was okay. What else? She was a loyal friend. When she loved, she loved fiercely.

Loved fiercely. She stopped the movement of the feather duster in midair. Barely realizing what she was doing, her free hand flew to her mouth. Dom's kiss had been fierce. Possessive. Knowing. Her fingertips traced the path his lips had taken. How could she ever forget the way his tongue and hands and mouth had kindled a fire in her she didn't know existed?

"Daydreaming on the job, are we?"

Lisa came bustling to the counter, ready to ring up a customer. Startled out of her reverie, Jordan jumped, which made Lisa grin mischievously. She was just under five feet and slender, with a nice, unremarkable face and a mane of riotous golden curls. The curse of the frizz, Lisa called it, but, to Jordan, her employer-friend's hair perfectly reflected her glowing inner vitality.

"I'm sorry," Jordan said shamefacedly, moving to one side to give Lisa room. "I'm afraid I was drifting a little."

"Nothing wrong with that." She ran the customer's credit card through the scanner. "I do it all the time." Lisa's brown eyes danced as she went on. "Hey, you've earned all the dream time you want. Between Helen Wasserman and Nancy Tremaine, our stock is primo. We need to come up with some big-time way of thanking both of them. Not just the usual note this time. Flowers, maybe, huh?"

Jordan nodded, but her mind had vaulted off into a different direction than thanking clothing donors. She'd never really thanked Dom for all the time he'd given her, had she? She'd said the words, of course, but still, shouldn't she do more? She prided herself on her manners. Saying a proper thank-you was the civilized way to behave.

On the other hand—and she had to ask herself the question—was this some feeble excuse she'd just come up with to make contact with Dom again? Hmm. She considered this. Maybe. Quite possibly.

As the shop bell jangled and new customers entered, Jordan decided she would have to think about this a little more.

"Hey, Santos," Dom yelled at the new kid as he passed Dom's cubicle, "where'd you get the tie? It's like a solar eclipse—look right at it and you go blind."

"Come on, Dom," the latest, and youngest, member of the detective squad said. "My girl gave it to me. She says with my coloring I can wear bright stuff."

Chuckling, Dom tipped his desk chair back and clasped his hands behind his head. "Yeah, well, bright is one thing. You could shoot that tie into the sky on July fourth, and the whole world would see it."

Several more smart-ass remarks about his tie trailed Santos as he made his way up the aisle of cubicles. To his credit, the kid took the kidding good-naturedly.

From his adjacent desk, Steve glanced at Dom. "At least he's got a new tie. You're still wearing those church bazaar rejects."

"Hey, don't knock it," Dom said, fingering his brown tie with small green polka dots. "This baby only cost me three bucks."

"You got robbed." Steve pushed back his chair and got up. "I'm getting some java—you want any?"

"Nah."

Work, Dom said to himself, studying his desk. He needed to get to work. He sifted through the mess of files on his desk with some vague thought of alphabetizing them when his hand came to rest on the one he'd hand-labeled Carlisle. His own personal Jordan Carlisle file.

He opened it. There, on top, was that publicity photo from Jordan's modeling days. Glamorous. Her shiny mouth curved in a small smile that hinted at sex without spelling it out. As he stared at the photo, he could practically taste her, even felt his tongue rolling around his mouth, craving just one more sip. Now that he'd sampled her, he wanted more.

As though on automatic, his gaze shifted to the upper right-hand side of his desk, to the framed picture of Theresa he kept there. She, too, was smiling at him, but her smile was open and friendly, no secrets.

Theresa Maeve Flynn, she'd been before they married. Never a beauty, but lovable, with a major-league Irish temper. A little on the plump side, always dieting and complaining about her hips, even when he told her he loved the extra flesh. She'd stuck with him through his training, married him, made the move with him to the west coast, where he'd wanted to live since coming here on a family vacation to Disneyland.

They'd both left their families behind. A loyal cop's wife, she'd never complained about being so far away from those she loved, although their phone bills to the east coast were pretty high. His job consumed him, but they'd both assumed there would be kids to fill Theresa's days. Then a series of miscarriages had weakened her. She'd died from the final one.

And he hadn't been there—he'd been out on a drug bust the night she died. A stab of self-loathing hit him, the way it did most times when he thought about that night and the months preceding it. He was a good cop, but not a good man. He raked his fingers through his hair. There it was again, that synonym for self-loathing. Guilt.

Something about Jordan and his attraction to her brought up the guilt he felt about Theresa. It wasn't one of those ''I feel unfaithful to my late wife when I'm with you'' kind of things. Hell, he wished it were that simple—if it was, he could deal with it. Nah, it was more complicated than that, and he wasn't at his best figuring out complex emotions.

All he knew was being with Jordan, kissing Jordan had felt terrific everywhere except in his head. He'd been with several women since Theresa's death, but kissing Jordan Carlisle had been different. There had been some element to it other than pure lust. And that made it complicated.

Damn it, he liked his life simple.

He picked up Jordan's picture and stared at it. "Have a good life," he'd told her the last time he saw her. Good advice. Yeah, that about summed it up. He put the photo back in the file folder and, with a silent goodbye, was on the verge of tossing the whole thing into the wastebasket when his hand stilled.

No, he thought. Not yet. Yeah, she brought up complicated emotions, ambivalence, guilt, the whole nine yards, but so what? He could handle it. And besides, he was just not ready to let Jordan Carlisle go.

At five o'clock, when Jordan was in the small back office collecting her purse and getting ready to go home, the phone rang. She picked it up. "Riches and Rags. How may I help you?"

"D'Annunzio, here," Dom barked into the receiver.

The brusqueness in his voice took her aback for a moment, but then her insides filled with warmth at the fact that he'd called her. "Carlisle here," she responded with a smile, lowering herself onto the desk chair.

After a pause, he said, "So, how are you?" just as gruffly as he'd greeted her. For a moment she wondered why, but the answer came to her right away. He was nervous, she realized. The big, street-tough cop had decided to call her and was not feeling smooth and in-charge about his decision.

She couldn't help the smile that curved the sides of her mouth. "I'm all right, thanks, and you?"

"Okay." His attitude seemed less abrupt when he added, "Have there been any more notes?"

"No, nothing. You were right. Someone was playing a joke."

"Pretty sorry joke," he muttered. "You okay about it?"

She fingered the picture of the little boy that was still in her purse. No, not really, she wanted to say, but refrained from doing so. "Yes, I'm okay."

A moment of silence went by before he said, "Well...I, uh,

just wanted to check up on you, you know, to see if you're all right.''

Oh, Jordan thought, with a sense of disappointment. That was why he'd called, a sort of follow-up to his visit. Maybe it wasn't nerves that had made him sound gruff. Maybe he was in the middle of a difficult case and he'd taken a moment out to check up on her. Maybe the call wasn't personal.

She played with the phone wire. ''Well, thank you for calling. In fact, I'm glad you did. I wanted to say thank-you, you know, for everything.''

''Forget it.''

''No, really, I mean it. Thank you.''

''Yeah, well, fine. You're welcome. Look—''

''Yes?''

''I was wondering, maybe…''

She waited, a small spark of excitement building again. ''Yes?''

''Would you like to grab a cup of coffee or something, sometime?'' The gruff voice was back.

Yes! Jordan thought. Her initial impression had been right— Dom was nervous about calling her. Which meant it *was* personal. The realization filled her with an almost giddy sense of happiness.

''I'd love to,'' she gushed. ''In fact—'' A new notion popped into her head, a crazy notion, but, playing nervously with the phone wire, she went with it without giving herself a chance to think. ''Dom, will you let me buy you dinner?''

''Excuse me?''

''I want to take you out to dinner, to thank you.''

He didn't answer right away. Then he muttered, ''You don't owe me anything.''

''Yes I do.'' Now that she'd said it, it felt exactly right. Her confidence grew as she went on. ''First you rescued me from the media, then you came to my house after work and gave me advice, you listened to me going on and on about my son, you let me weep all over you, so, yes, of course I owe you something.''

Dom's hand gripped the receiver a little harder as he swiveled in his chair to face the back wall. In Jordan's little list of his good deeds, she'd left out the last part. The kiss. Wiped it away like it didn't exist. "Look," he said brusquely, "I was just doing my job, okay?"

"No," she countered, "you did more than your job, and I insist on thanking you properly."

Thanking you properly. Images of silken sheets, pillows tossed to the floor, her pale alabaster body rising and falling with her heavy breathing as she lay, sated, in his arms. The picture made him shift his position. "Hey, Jordan, let's not make a big deal out of this. If it'll make you happy, you can buy me a drink."

"No," she said insistently. "Dinner. How's tomorrow night?"

"Well..."

Hell, Dom thought with a frown, he'd had some vague idea about a cup of coffee, sometime in the future, and now she was taking the ball, running with it, and pinning it down to the next day, which made him really squirmy. He called himself an idiot for wavering like this, something he never did. There was this war in his head between reluctance and a sense of excitement. He wished he hadn't called her. He was damned glad he'd called her. He hated ambivalence, didn't believe in it.

"Are you—" Jordan began, then laughed. "I don't know the terms. Are you on duty or something?"

"Actually, tomorrow's my day off."

"Good," she said briskly. "If you don't have any plans, please let me buy you dinner." When he didn't reply, she said with a smile, "You do eat, don't you?"

He found himself responding with his own smile. "Oh, yeah. Too much, sometimes."

"It doesn't show," she said, and he heard the admiration in her voice.

That was followed by a glaring silence, as though Jordan realized she'd ventured into territory that she might not want to visit. "So," she went on brightly, "what do you like? Indian, Japanese, Thai? Steak, fish?"

"Hey, you put it in front of me, I eat it."

"I'll bet you do," she said throatily.

Again, an embarrassed silence. Between the two of them, he thought wryly, this whole phone call was sounding like two green teenagers with no experience, tiptoeing on a conversational minefield.

Dom swiveled his chair and sat up straight, determined to take some kind of action. "Okay, I accept. Tomorrow night's fine."

"Wonderful. How about eight o'clock at Bistro Rodeo?"

Dom frowned. She was going fancy, but then what did he expect from a Carlisle? A corn dog? He would have to wear a jacket. His one decent one was in the cleaners. He'd have to swing by and pick it up. On his days off, he preferred not to wear a jacket, but what the hell. "Okay, sure. Do you want me to pick you up?"

"No, I'll meet you there. Bye."

She hung up, so he did, too, but he kept staring at the phone, not sure how to feel. He sensed he was being watched. He looked up into Steve's brown-eyed gaze. His partner had wandered in somewhere during his conversation with Jordan and had a look of speculation on his bronze face.

"Setting up a date, are we? The woman has questionable taste. Who is she?"

Dom shuffled some paperwork, shrugged indifferently. "Jordan Carlisle."

"That the Beverly Hills lady?"

"Yeah," he grunted.

"You got something going on there, my man?"

Dom looked straight at his partner and nodded. "Sure," he said, arranging his features into a sardonic, bored mask. "The dame's giving me fashion tips."

Chapter 5

Jordan was early, ten minutes early, in fact. At home, she'd been restless and fidgety, had changed her outfit three times. Finally, disgusted with herself, she'd settled on a dress, donned it and headed to Bistro Rodeo. So, here she was, sitting at the restaurant's bar, sipping a martini and waiting for Dom.

Her gaze roamed the room, over the graceful potted palms in the corners, the modern art on the walls, the crisp white tablecloths, gleaming silver and crystal. She'd been here many times with Reynolds and had thought it was a good choice. Now she wondered if Dom would like it, or even if she did anymore.

"Jordan?"

Her head whipped around at the sound of her name, then the smile on her face faltered. "Hal," she said politely, as the large, ruddy-faced man approached her.

"Hey, great to see you." Hal Cooper leaned in, arms wide. With a neat maneuver of her body on the bar stool, she managed to avoid his embrace and accepted a wet kiss on the cheek.

"How've you been, Jordan?" he said, beaming at her. "We've all missed you."

Really? She hadn't missed him. Hal Cooper had been one of Reynolds's oldest and best friends, dating back to the exclusive private high school they'd both attended. Of the whole bunch she'd been forced to socialize with during her marriage, Hal had been the one with the busiest hands.

"How is Sherry?" Jordan asked, naming his wife.

"Oh, you know Sherry—" He winked conspiratorially. "Still dieting, still shopping."

"Well, send her my love."

"Sure." He stood back a step and raked her up and down with his gaze. "You look terrific. I always told Reynolds he got the biggest prize of all of us."

Her answering smile was not warm. "Thank you."

Again, he sidled up to her and leaned a hip against the side of her chair. He was close, way too close. His breath smelled of the fat cigar he'd probably just put out. It made her stomach churn. "So, you here with anyone?" His tone was sly. "Because if not, maybe I could—"

As it was impossible to shift any farther without falling off the stool, she hopped off and kept a couple of feet between them. "Thanks, but I'm waiting for someone," she said, her gaze roaming the room. Relief poured through her as she spotted Dom. "And here he is now."

Her rescuer, she added silently—the man who seemed to always show up at the right time. He was at the maître d's desk, where he was being directed to the bar.

She kept her gaze on Dom as he walked through the crowded entryway in her direction. While his eyes darted here and there, observing the crowd, taking it all in, his face wore that same brooding, on-guard look that seemed to be its habitual expression. He held himself like a boxer waiting for his opponent to make a move—perpetually ready to defend himself.

When he spotted her, she could have sworn there was a faint change in that harsh face of his, a lightening up, pleasure, even. But it was so subtle, it could have been her imagination.

With the part of her mind that always assessed people's wardrobes, Jordan applauded the nicely cut charcoal gray jacket and black pants, cream-colored shirt and subdued tie he had chosen. He was clean shaven—it was the first time she'd seen him so—and his thick, curly black hair was neatly combed. As her mother used to say, the man cleaned up real good. So, Jordan thought, aware of a giddy sensation just below her breast, he, too, had made an effort this evening. For her.

As he grew closer, she felt a telltale flush of excitement heating her cheeks. She even had to repress an urge to giggle. Who'd have thought she would ever feel this innocent again?

"Hello," Dom said, placing himself right in front of her and gazing at her from under hooded eyelids. She took in the olive skin, the thick black eyebrows, the sensual Roman mouth of his ancestors with that intriguing scar in the right corner. She must remember to ask him about that scar.

"Hello," she said breathlessly.

Dom's gaze shifted to her left, and he raised an inquiring eyebrow. Jordan turned to see what had grabbed his attention.

Hal. She'd forgotten he was there. Her glance moved from Hal to Dom. The two of them were sizing each other up and, in that brief instant, it was obvious that neither liked what he saw. If they'd been bulls—and maybe they were—they would have been pawing the ground and flaring their nostrils. The tension was palpable.

Jordan put her arm through Dom's elbow and said brightly, "Hal, meet Dom. Dom, Hal."

Quickly, she grabbed her clutch purse from the bar and smiled at Dom. "Shall we?" As she steered him away, she called over her shoulder, "Love to Sherry," then turned her full attention to Dom. The impact of his extremely masculine presence was pretty powerful and she had to swallow before she gave his arm a squeeze and said, "Glad you could make it."

He nodded. "Yeah," he said, peering one last time at Hal. She could tell by the way the thick muscles of his biceps clenched that he was still in defensive mode. The don't-mess-

with-me expression on his face reminded her of Al Pacino or
Robert De Niro in bad-guy roles—the type whose fate it was
to sleep with the fishes.

"Who is that guy?" he asked her.

"No one important."

They were shown to their table, a small one in the corner,
as she'd requested. As they sat, a uniformed busboy set down
a basket of bread and tubs of sweet butter. The waiter—clean,
courteous and slightly effeminate—handed them menus, then
said, "May I start you both off with a cocktail?"

"A vodka martini," Jordan said, "very dry, two olives."

"Same," Dom said, his gaze darting restlessly around the
room before it returned to settle on her.

"Funny," she said, "you don't seem the martini type."

"I'm not." He shrugged. "When in Rome…" He seemed
to study her for a moment before he said, "So."

"So," she repeated.

He assessed her some more. For the life of her, she couldn't
read his expression. "How's your day been so far?"

"My day?" she said stupidly, as though there was someone
else at the table whose day he could have been referring to.
"Fine," she said automatically, then thought about it and, with
a small smile, said, "You know what? It really has been. Fine,
I mean."

"Good."

"And you?"

"Good."

"Busy?" she asked.

"Always. The bad guys just keep on coming."

Small talk, Jordan thought. There it was again, that tension
in the air between them. She sensed an edginess in Dom. Of
course, she wasn't exactly the picture of a relaxed, confident
woman, was she?

As she usually did when feeling off-kilter, Jordan slid into
her hostess mode. She touched his hand briefly, then removed
it. "I'm glad you could come tonight. I really am so grateful
to you."

A crease of annoyed embarrassment crossed his brow. "Hey, I didn't do that much."

"Maybe not, but…" Wanting to make him understand, she searched for the words. "Have you ever had the experience of needing to talk about something and trying to talk about it to all the right people and then suddenly you find yourself unburdening yourself to—"

"The wrong people?" With one eyebrow raised sardonically, he finished her sentence for her.

"No." At first she felt flustered, then annoyed. She'd been trying to make a connection, and he was being deliberately obtuse. Baiting her in some way. "I wasn't going to say that. I was going to say unburdening yourself to someone you don't know very well at all."

"Ah." He seemed to give it some thought, then said, "No, I've never had that experience."

"Oh."

If Dom had been trying to deflate her, that remark did the trick. As she opened her mouth to respond, the waiter appeared with their drinks. When he'd left, Jordan glanced at her martini, then at Dom. "If I offer a toast, will you bite my head off?"

For a moment, she swore he had no reaction to her question. Then, with a slight loosening of the muscles around his mouth, he asked, "Am I being a jerk?"

"You could say that. But…I have a feeling you're angry. Is it at me? Something I said or did?"

"Nah." Expelling a breath, he closed his eyes, opened them again, then shook his head. "No. You've done nothing, Jordan."

"That's good to know…Dom."

Jordan. Dom.

The way Jordan emphasized his name made Dom aware that this was the first time either of them had used the other's first name. He felt a slight shift in the atmosphere and allowed himself a rueful smile. She smiled back and, just like that, the ice was broken.

Good thing, too—he'd been about to jump out of his skin.

All that day, the knowledge that he would be seeing Jordan Carlisle that evening had kept him strung tighter than a piano wire, and he'd brought that mood with him to the restaurant. The minute he saw her, he realized all over again how much he wanted her. But he didn't want to want her, not this much. He took a deep breath and made himself relax.

"How about if I offer the toast?" he said, to make up for his surliness. "I'm afraid if you do it, you'll start slobbering all over me with gratitude again."

That got a laugh out of her. "I don't slobber." She held up her drink. "You're on. Let's hear it."

Terrific. He'd opened his big mouth. Now, what the hell was he going to say? Here's looking at your gorgeous eyes? A toast to that sexy mouth of yours, which I haven't been able to forget since I tasted it? Or, more impersonally, to your health, to my health, to the world's health?

He settled for, "Here's to a good dinner and good company." Neutral. Not real exciting, he thought, but hey, you went with what you had.

"I'll second that." They clinked glasses then sipped.

The martini was good. He popped one of the olives in his mouth, took another slug, then set down the glass. The liquor warmed him, settled him down enough that he allowed himself to look at Jordan. Really look at her, and what he saw was real fine.

At their two previous meetings, she'd worn slacks, but tonight she wore a dress, some sort of soft, flowy thing with a scooped neck and no sleeves. Feminine. She had long, pretty arms, but the dress's color was what struck him. An ice-cream color, kind of a pinky peach, and it brought a glow to her cheeks. "Nice dress," he offered.

"You like it?" Her eyes lit with pleasure. "It's from the shop."

"Shop?"

"Oh, that's right, you don't know where I work."

"You work?"

"Part time, for now. But I hope it will be full time soon."

He'd had no idea that she had a career of any sort. She'd retired from modeling, that he knew, and figured she spent her days being a rich widow. "Tell me about it."

And she did, all about it—how she'd happened on Riches and Rags, how much she admired Lisa for starting her own business, how good she felt about recycling other people's cast-offs to women who really appreciated them. As she spoke, her eyes shone with happiness and enthusiasm, and he felt a kind of melting in his gut that was more than booze doing its job.

This was the Jordan he'd seen in the family album, the Jordan without the emotional baggage of her tragedy. It was good to see her looking happy, but somehow, he wished he wasn't witnessing this side of her. He didn't want to think of her as being a complex person of varying moods—a real, flesh and blood, extremely attractive woman.

Somewhere in there, he went to work on the bread basket and they ordered dinner and a bottle of wine. Jordan didn't finish her martini and didn't touch the bread. Not a lush, he decided, or much of an eater, either.

"—and so," she said, "if I can swing it, I'm going to buy into the business. I've never done anything like this before. It will be a challenge, but I'm really looking forward to it."

"Sounds good."

Jordan leaned an elbow on the table and rested her chin in her hand. "Okay," she announced with a mocking smile, "enough about me. Your turn."

"For what?"

"Tell me about you."

Oh, no. He hated talking about himself. "What do you want to know?" he asked guardedly.

"Do you miss your wife very much?" Her hand flew to her mouth. She seemed startled that she'd said that, as though she hadn't planned it. "Oh, dear. I thought I wanted you to tell me about your work, but that question about your wife just slipped out." After a short, apologetic laugh, she went on, "Ah, well, you know what they say about slips. So, I admit it. I'm curious."

Tonight, of all nights, he didn't want to discuss Theresa and the complicated emotions that thinking about her brought up in him. It wasn't a door he wanted to open, not with Jordan. As he felt his jaw tensing, her expression changed to a frown.

"You have that look on your face," she said.

"What look?"

"That off-limits look." She touched his arm lightly, then removed it. "Dom, I didn't mean to pry. I guess it's just that most of what we've talked about has been me, my problems, my pain. You know so much about me, and I know practically nothing about you."

He scowled. "Yeah, well, I'm not one of those nineties guys, the kind who spill their guts all over the place. Back at the station, we had to take these sensitivity training classes, you know, where you say 'I feel your pain' and all that. I wasn't much good at it."

Dom's obvious discomfort mixed with disgust made Jordan want to laugh. She tried not to, but a bubble of mirth came out anyway.

"What?" he asked suspiciously.

"You look like you're about to get force-fed some castor oil."

He seemed to consider it for a moment, then one corner of his mouth turned up. "Yeah, Theresa used to say I was not exactly a touchy-feely kind of guy, but—" He stopped in mid-sentence and frowned.

"But?" she prompted.

He shrugged. "I guess she liked me anyway…most of the time." For a brief moment, the look in his eyes was pained and bleak, but then it was gone. "Anyway, enough about that."

Jordan stared at him, moved by the shifting emotions she'd seen on his face. Dom had been in love with his late wife, it was obvious, probably deeply in love. As that realization hit her, Jordan was surprised at the spurt of jealousy that rose in the back of her throat like bile. Not a nice emotion, she admitted with shame. Not even a reasonable one. Human, she supposed, but unattractive.

Lighten up, she told herself. Steer away from Theresa. "I suspect you have a lot more sensitivity than you let on," she said lightly, returning to their previous topic.

He looked toward the ceiling. "Here we go. The woman trying to see more of the female side in the man than is really there. Listen, I do my job, I drink my beer, I go to bed. End of story."

"Joe Average."

"You got it." He tore off another hunk of bread and slathered butter on it. Obviously, he expected that to be the end of this discussion, but she wasn't through, not yet.

"Do you read books, go to the movies?"

He lifted a shoulder. "Sure."

"Do you watch sunsets and wonder about how God created such a beautiful sight?"

"On occasion. I mean, sure, I see things I like, I pay attention. Is that such a big deal?"

"It just means you're not immune to the world and the people in it—" she smiled "—and not as shallow as you'd like me to think you are."

He held up his hands in mock-surrender. "Okay, okay, I'm deep as a damned well. Satisfied?"

At that moment, as the old bread basket was removed and a new one set down, Jordan laughed delightedly. "It's all an act, isn't it? This whole poker-face, tough-guy thing of yours."

"Me? A tough guy?" He considered it, then nodded. "Yeah, sure. I guess I am. But, trust me, it's not an act."

"I'm sorry. I didn't mean—"

"No, I'm not offended. It's just that where I grew up, in my part of Brooklyn, you didn't have a choice. Early on, you learned to take care of yourself or you wouldn't make it."

"But you went into law enforcement."

"Yeah, well, back then you had three choices—you could be a priest, a member of the Mob or a cop. The priest was out, but as for the other two, it was a toss-up, trust me. Theresa was the one who decided for me. If I'd chosen to join the wise guys, I would have lost her."

Theresa again. Jordan wondered if he knew how his voice, his whole attitude gentled when he spoke her name. This time, Jordan felt no jealousy, just a strange emptiness. She wanted someone's voice to soften when he spoke her name, wanted someone to love her that deeply. No one ever had, and that old insecure inner voice of hers was fond of telling her she didn't deserve it.

She was grateful when their dinner was served—fish for Jordan, lamb chops and new potatoes for Dom. It gave her a moment to shake off the effects of too much wistful reflection.

"Anything else I can get you?" the waiter asked. "More bread? Fresh ground pepper?"

"Uh-uh," Dom said.

Jordan smiled at the young man. "We're fine."

Dom dug right in, but Jordan found herself watching him instead of eating. The play of muscles around his jaw as he chewed, the pleasure on his face as he swallowed. He reached for his water glass, drained it. A nearby busboy filled it immediately. Dom nodded curtly at the young man, then frowned at her. "Aren't you going to eat?"

"Oh, yes." For the first time, she picked up her fork, then found her attention caught again by the way Dom attacked his dinner with gusto. As he glanced up again, he caught her staring at him. "What?"

"I take it you like your meal," she said with a smile.

"Yeah, it's delicious. Really good. You like yours?"

She took a bite. "Yes, the fish is very tasty."

His elbow brushed his napkin, making it drop to the floor. It was immediately picked up by a busboy, and a clean one was handed to him. "Waste of laundry soap," he muttered, then looked at her. "You keep watching me. Do I have butter on my tie or something?"

Caught. Might as well come right out with it. Setting down her fork, she rested her elbow next to her plate and balanced her chin in her hand. "You have the most fascinating face."

He set down his fork and jerked a thumb to his chest with an are-you-putting-me-on? look. "My face? Fascinating?"

"Yes. It hardly changes expression at all, just a small muscle movement here and there."

He wiped his mouth with his napkin. He really did have a beautiful mouth, she observed, with full, sensual lips. She wished she could forget how those lips had felt on hers— maybe then she'd get her appetite back.

"Yeah, well, that's what I was talking about," Dom told her. "Never let them know they're getting to you. Keep your cool. Never show fear." Again, one corner of his mouth turned up. "Street rules. Learn 'em or you're history."

"Never show fear," she repeated. "So, are you afraid? Here? Tonight, with me?" She held her breath at her audaciousness; as before, it had just popped out. She'd tried for a teasing tone, but didn't think she was very successful.

There was a small moment of silence while he took in her question, considered it, then shrugged again. "Maybe. Yeah," he admitted, and she could have sworn he was embarrassed.

His gaze fell on her full plate. "Hey, you're not eating."

As a change of subject, Jordan observed, it lacked a certain grace, but it made the point. Getting inside Dom was more difficult than digging up a petrified tree stump. Why was it so important, she wondered, to be allowed past his facade? What did she want from the man? More than he was willing to give her, that was obvious.

"I've had a few bites," she said.

Dom shook his head in wonder. "My mother would be on you like the rent collector if you didn't clean your plate."

"Tell me about her."

"My mother?" This time his smile was real and unguarded. "Mom's the best. Always hugging, always feeding people. Like those Italian women in the commercials, except she's not fat, she's tiny. She eats, don't get me wrong, but she has more energy than all of us put together, so she burns it off. There were eight of us kids, so she never sat down. She'd take one look at you and say, 'What's the matter—you don't like my cooking?'"

Jordan sighed. "I know. I'm too thin."

He raised an eyebrow. "You could use a little meat on your bones. You know, just enough—"

Dom had been about to say, "Just enough for a man to grab hold of," but checked it, settling instead for, "Just enough so you're healthy. Hey—" he held up a hand, palm out "—it's none of my business."

"It's all right. I asked you. And it's true, I have lost weight this year. Okay." She picked up her fork, cut into her fish. "I'll eat."

A frown formed between his brows as he watched her pick daintily at her food. He felt funny, not ha-ha funny but strange. The woman had a way of making him feel off-kilter. He kept trying to keep his distance and she kept picking away at his wall. The result was he felt out of step, thrown by his reactions to her questions.

Yes, he was afraid of being with her. She'd nailed him with that one. Afraid of what, exactly? He knew what he wanted from her. A bed. Hot sex. Oblivion. Hell, that was the easy part.

So maybe he was afraid of what she wanted from him. Yeah, maybe so.

He drained his glass of wine and was about to reach for the bottle when, as though summoned by a magician, the waiter appeared and beat him to it. After the smiling young man had lifted the bottle and poured his wine, he asked, "Everything okay sir?"

"Terrific."

Jordan must have caught the hint of sarcasm in his tone, because when the waiter had left, she asked, "What's the matter?"

"I just don't like people…hovering over me all the time. It makes me uncomfortable. When I eat, I like to be left alone."

"They do hover here." She worried her bottom lip, as though fretting over an unsuccessful tea party.

"Hey, it's okay," he said quickly. "The food's delicious." His gaze swept the room, taking in the well-groomed diners, the low lighting, murmuring waiters, discreet music. Top of the heap. Class A. If you liked that kind of thing.

"Yeah," he went on, "it's a great restaurant."

"I hear a 'but' in there."

He shrugged. "It just isn't my usual kind of hangout, that's all."

"What is your usual kind of hangout?"

"More of a joint. Beer, pool, you know." He chuckled. "Believe me, you'd hate it."

He didn't know what reaction he expected, but it wasn't the gleam of mischief that shone in Jordan's eyes. She met his gaze straight on. "Oh, yeah?" she challenged. "Try me."

He stared at her, then felt his mouth curve in admiration. "You're on."

She was like a totally different person, Dom thought, as he sipped an ice-cold brew and watched Jordan sink the six ball in the corner pocket. Gone was the sleek woman with the elegant manner. Get her away from that upscale environment, and suddenly she was a regular human being, or as regular as someone with her looks could be.

They were at his favorite hangout, Morgan R's, and the Marina del Rey dockside restaurant and bar was packed. There were sporting events on two large TVs on either side of the bar, rock music blared from the loudspeaker, and the crowd was the usual assortment of cops, locals and tourists. Also a lot of single guys on the make. Since Dom had brought Jordan here, several of them had given her the eye, but she'd handled them. If they didn't take the hint, one look from Dom had done the job.

For the past hour, Jordan had been shooting pool, first with him, then with her current opponent, a retired cop named Nick Holmes. Nick, who was one of his best buddies, wasn't beating her too badly. She had to concentrate hard on her shots—she was rusty, she'd told him earlier when she'd come over to the table for a sip of cold beer. But, she'd added with a lift of an eyebrow and a cocky smile, the night was young.

He sat back in the booth, nursed his beer and watched her through hooded eyelids, appreciating her every move and—damn it all—found himself comparing her to Theresa.

His late wife had never liked coming to Morgan R's—she preferred to entertain others with home-cooked meals. It was no problem for him to go, she would tell him, to let down with the guys after a long day—just so long as he always came home to her.

I'm with Jordan tonight, Dom told himself. Hell, he was thrilled to be with Jordan tonight. So, he needed to get off memory lane and back to the present.

As though she'd heard him and decided to help him along, Jordan came to the table, laughing. A fine sheen of sweat gleamed on her face, and there was a glow in her eyes. Holding a pool cue in one hand, she rested the other on a cocked hip and grinned. "Ready to shoot some more pool, mister?"

He rose, took the cue from her hand and gave it to Nick. "How about we take a little walk instead?" Dom asked her.

The cool night air hit them the moment they stepped outside. Without even thinking, Dom removed his jacket and put it around Jordan's shoulders. Then, almost as automatically, he kept his arm around her. He wanted contact with her, had been wanting to touch her all night.

"Thanks," she said, and just as naturally, put her arm around his waist and leaned into him as they walked. The only restaurant on this section of the dock was Morgan R's, so once they got a few feet away, the noise and music subsided. There was a hazy half-moon in the sky, and the sounds of creaking wood and waves lapping against the wood pilings filled the night.

Dom liked holding Jordan this way, liked how she seemed to fit into the curve of his arm. Her hair smelled good. They would walk a little, he figured, and talk a little more and see what developed.

"So, you're a pool shark," he said.

With a small laugh, Jordan replied, "Not even close. But back home in Wyoming, the pool hall was the only entertainment in the area. Incidentally, I also ride horses, mend fences and can milk a cow. Can you do any of those?''

''Nah. But I can pick a lock and duck under a subway turnstile and have been known to break records running down fire escapes.''

''City mouse and country mouse, that's us.''

Chuckling, he steered them to the railing that overlooked the harbor, and for a moment they watched the moored boats bobbing gently in the water.

How lovely this was, Jordan thought. Peaceful. Since they'd left Beverly Hills, she'd relaxed considerably. Not only did being with Dom out here on the marina feel good, but so did the hum of sexual tension in the air. Dom's arm around her felt protective. His body was solid and sturdy with its thick muscles and obvious strength.

''Jordan?'' he said.

''Hmm?''

When she angled her head to look at him, he brought his free hand up to stroke her face. Yes, she thought, closing her eyes. This is right. The sensation of his callused fingertips on her heated skin was subtly erotic and she responded with a quiet moan of pleasure. He turned their bodies so they faced each other, then planted soft kisses on her eyelids, her forehead, over her nose and cheeks and chin. Such soft kisses, she thought, from such a hard man.

Finally, he touched his mouth to hers, sliding his tongue between her lips and probing the moist flesh within. He took his time exploring her, and as he did, a slow, steady, pulsing heat oozed through her bloodstream, hardening her nipples, creating an ache between her legs.

It was a sweet ache, but powerful. This was the kind of bodily reaction she'd heard discussed among other women, but she had rarely experienced. Indeed, Jordan hadn't known much real sexual urgency and had wondered if she were incapable of it.

She didn't have to wonder now. Lord, she wanted this man and she wanted him badly.

Splaying her hands across his broad back, she used her tongue to let him know that whatever he wanted to give her, she would gladly accept.

Suddenly, Dom pulled his mouth away, bringing an abrupt end to their kiss. His withdrawal was a shock to her system, but before she had time to recover, he'd gripped her face between his hands and stared at her, something tangled and dark written across his features.

"What?" she managed to say, her disappointed body still craving his touch. "What's the matter?"

Mute, he stared at her a little longer, then dropped his hands and turned away from her, once again peering out at the boats and the ocean beyond. "What?" Jordan asked again, clutching at his arm. "Tell me, Dom."

He shook his head. "You'll take it the wrong way."

"Try me."

He rubbed his hand over his face wearily, then leaning an elbow on the railing, he angled his face to meet her anxious gaze. "When I'm with you, Jordan," he said slowly, "I think a lot about Theresa. Not," he added quickly, as he saw her look of dismay, "how I wish she were here instead of you, or how much I miss her, or any of that stuff, I swear."

He'd been right, Jordan thought, she was taking it the wrong way. How could she not? Swept up in an embrace with a man she was not only attracted to physically but starting to care about on a much deeper level, then to have the cold water of reality thrown in her face. When Dom was with her, he thought about his late wife.

"Jordan? Did you hear what I said? It's not what it sounds like."

She took a moment to gather her composure. She should ask him to drive her to her car, she supposed. She felt stupid, embarrassed, as though she'd done something wrong, as though his thinking about Theresa was because she, Jordan was lacking in some way.

He held her by the shoulders. "You're not listening."

"Yes, yes. I am." She had to focus on what he was saying—it was important. "You're thinking about your wife."

"See, it's like Theresa's some kind of, I don't know, voice in my head."

"And what does the voice say?"

"Not to make promises I can't keep."

That one seemed to come out of left field. "Excuse me?"

"I'm afraid you'll ask more of me than I can give. Not sex, I'm not talking about sex. Is this making any sense at all?" He looked utterly miserable, and she felt totally confused.

"Dom, I...I don't know what to say."

He dropped his hands from her shoulders, gripped the top of the railing with both hands and stared at the water. His profile was that of an ancient Roman, the corners of his mouth turned down. "Hey, I don't blame you."

There was silence between them for a while before Jordan, also looking out to sea, said quietly, "You loved her very much."

"Yeah. Lot of good it did her."

Startled by the depth of bitterness in Dom's voice, she glanced at him. "What do you mean?"

He shrugged. "She died."

There was something going on here, some undercurrent she hadn't picked up on before, and she latched on to that small thread of knowledge greedily. "How did she die?"

"She bled to death on the bathroom floor."

"My God," Jordan gasped as her hand flew to her heart.

"She'd been pregnant, one of those tubular things. The tube burst and she was alone and couldn't get any help. I was out on a drug bust at the time. I came home and found her."

Horrified both for Dom and a woman she'd never known, Jordan said nothing for several moments, then managed, "How awful."

They were both quiet for a while, then she ventured another question. "Is that what this is about? Do you blame yourself for her death?"

He frowned, then nodded. "Sometimes." He angled his head

to look at her straight on, his face twisted with conflict. Shadows from the lights on the water danced on his visage, making it seem strange, almost grotesque.

Then he raised both hands as though warding off an evil spirit and announced, "That's it. No more questions, okay?"

She took one of his hands and brought it to her cheek and held it there. "No more questions, I prom—"

Beep-beep-beep! The sound pierced the night, making Dom jerk his hand from her grasp. "Damn," he said under his breath.

He reached for the pager at his waistband and turned it off. As he unhooked it to see the readout, Jordan pulled his jacket tighter around her. She was trembling, not just from the chill. Her body was all swirling sensations, her mind confused.

"I have to call in," Dom muttered.

"I thought this was your day off."

"The day ends at midnight. Come on."

Wordlessly, they hurried to Morgan R's, where Jordan waited while Dom made his phone call. When he hung up, he shook his head. "Sorry, something's come up. I have to leave."

"What is it?"

"The less you know about my work," he answered tersely, "the better you'll sleep. Come on, I'll get you back to your car."

They said good-night to Nick, then Dom drove them toward Beverly Hills. They didn't speak much on the drive. His face had that shuttered, protected expression again. Did he regret telling her about Theresa? Did he regret kissing her? Was he anxious to get away from her? Jordan wished she could read him, wanted to understand him.

"Dom?"

"Yeah?"

"I would like to know about your work. It's part of who you are."

When he didn't respond, she sat back in her seat, disappointed. Then he spoke. "Remember the day we met, when I drove you home and you wanted to know if I was as cynical and hard as I seemed?''

''Yes.''

''Well, the truth is, most of me is. The first two years as a deputy you spend on custody duty—lockup, prisoners, jail. You get real wise in the ways of the criminal mind, and it's not pretty. Since then I've done time on vice and narcotics— real underbelly stuff, nasty people with creepy, sick minds. Now I'm part of the personal and property unit. That means armed robbery, rapes, spousal abuse. That phone call I just got? Looks like a teenage girl was gang-raped, and my partner, Steve, and I have to do the follow-up. I have bad stories from all the years, Jordan, lots of them. I've learned to keep them to myself because after a while, it got so Theresa didn't want to hear them.''

''I'm not Theresa.'' It came out of her so quickly she wasn't sure where it had come from. She didn't say it angrily or petulantly, just stated the fact. Wanted him to hear her loud and clear.

He glanced at her, then nodded. ''No, you're not, are you?''

Another enigmatic reaction, another enigmatic statement. What went on in the deepest heart of this man? Jordan wondered.

When they got to the restaurant, she insisted he drop her off at the valet because she knew he was in a hurry. Before she opened the car door, she kissed him quickly on the cheek. ''I had a lovely time,'' she said. ''You're a lovely man.''

His expression was startled, then he let out a bark of laughter. ''You are too much, Jordan Carlisle, you really are.''

Her mood was pensive as she drove up to the house, parked the car and let herself in the front door, careful to keep quiet. A single light burned in the foyer. As she closed the door, she glanced at the small table.

A special delivery envelope lay on the table, addressed to her, printed in block letters.

Chapter 6

The instructions this time were typed. The sender was still interested in the reward for information about her son. If she wanted to pursue this, on the following night, Saturday, at seven, she was to go to Union Station—alone—to a specific locker and pick up a package that contained proof and further instructions. A locker key was taped to the letter. The last sentence was more strongly worded than the last time. *This is a private transaction. If you bring in the law, it's off.* As before, it was signed, A Friend.

All reflections on the evening with Dom flew out of her head as, thoroughly shaken, Jordan stared at the words written on the page. Again? He wasn't through taunting her yet? The familiar sensations of clammy palms and thudding heartbeats began to overtake her. She tried to summon up anger—how dare someone anonymous play with her emotions this way?

But it was no use, because even as she told herself this was just one more punch line in someone's sick joke, she couldn't help the surge of hope the letter aroused. It mentioned proof, proof of Michael's existence.

She headed up the stairs to her room, telling herself her reaction was foolish. She should throw the letter away, or keep it and, yes, report it to the authorities. This was probably a crime—malicious mischief or something like that.

Certainly she mustn't take it seriously. Some person had decided to play mind games with her by making her think her son wasn't dead. That was bad enough. But for Jordan to act on that, to go to a public place, to an anonymous locker, well, that was not only foolish but possibly insane. This whole thing was like something out of a movie.

Closing the bedroom door behind her, Jordan stared again at the letter. As she did, Dom's voice echoed in her head. *Scam artist. Ghoul.*

But what if—

No, she chided herself. It had been Michael who died in that car crash, of course it had been. She would not give "A Friend" the dignity of even considering it, she told herself. She flung the letter on the floor and sank onto her bed.

But that didn't stop her mind. Why would he or she go to all the bother—the letters, the locker key—why send another letter unless there was something to it?

Her hands clenched into fists on the bedspread. How could she allow herself to hope? And how could she not? If there were one chance in a million that her son was still, by some miracle, alive, how could she not investigate further?

Jordan sighed. Should she go to the train station? Alone? What if there were something dangerous in the locker? Like a bomb?

She laughed weakly. No, no, she was letting her imagination run away with her. The letter writer was someone who wanted her to believe her son was still alive and was going to offer proof. After that would come demands for money. Why kill or harm the fatted calf? So to speak.

Still, she had some trepidation about going alone. What she ought to do was ask someone to go with her.

Dom, she thought immediately, she wanted Dom with her— he would know what to do.

But no, she had to keep this from Dom. *If you bring in the law, it's off.*

Who else could she trust? she asked herself, because, of course, her mind had been made up for her by the sender of the letter. She would take this key and go to the station the next night. With a friend or alone. It didn't matter.

If there was even the slightest chance of seeing her son again, she would jump through whatever hoops were put in her path.

As Saturday was the busiest day of the week, Jordan usually spent it at the shop. So, the next day, she kept herself occupied at Riches and Rags, trying not to count the hours till that evening. When Lisa commented on how industrious she was, Jordan just smiled. At one point, she was on the verge of asking Lisa to go with her, but when the shop owner mentioned that she had a date, Jordan said nothing.

She planned to leave about six-fifteen, to give herself plenty of time to get to Union Station and park. At five forty-five, during a lull in the steady stream of customers, Jordan had an armload of dresses on hangers and was placing each one onto its appropriate rack near the rear of the shop when the front door opened. Looking up, she smiled automatically, then froze in place.

Dom stood there, filling the doorway with his presence. His gaze scanned the room, then came to rest on her. Their eyes locked for a quick moment—he had that intense, brooding look on his face again—before she called out, "Hello."

Out of nowhere, a surge of happiness shot through her. Dom had come to see her. That meant whatever demons he was struggling with—and after last night, she knew there were some serious ones—he wasn't going to disappear from her life—at least, not yet. That was enough to make her smile.

Her next thought wiped the smile right off her face. The timing for his visit couldn't have been worse. Uh-oh, Jordan thought. What do I do now?

Lisa came bustling up to Dom and offered a cheery smile. "May I help you find something, sir?"

He glanced at her briefly, then returned his gaze to Jordan. "No, I see what I came to find."

Lisa followed the direction of his gaze, caught the way Jordan stood, unmoving, and nodded. "All right," she said, then walked casually over to her.

Lisa took a couple of the dresses, moved a few hangers around and hung them on the rack, while she said under her breath, "You okay? This guy some kind of problem?"

"No," Jordan replied, keeping her voice low so the shop's piped-in jazz would cover the sound. "I know him, it's all right. Dom," she called out. "Give me a moment to finish this, okay?"

"No problem," he said. "Take your time."

Lisa whispered, "He's a little scary-looking, isn't he?"

"Only at first." Her mind racing furiously, Jordan lifted another dress from her pile, shook it out and hooked it on the rack.

Lisa winked at Jordan. "So, you've been keeping secrets from me, huh?"

Jordan glanced quickly at Dom. He'd closed the door behind him and moved to stand in front of the wide shop windows. His dark form was outlined by the fading afternoon light. His arms were crossed over his broad chest, and he wore his work clothes—unbuttoned jacket, shirt, loosely knotted tie. A powerful picture.

"No, no secrets," she told Lisa. "He's the policeman I told you about—the one that drove me home after that car chase."

"Oh, right. Rude, Italian and macho, I think you said." She snuck a quick peek at Dom. "But there's more going on now, right?"

"Well—"

"Have you gone out with him?"

"You're a witch. Yes. Last night."

"Aha. And, not being a fool, the man is back for more."

Lisa turned, gave Dom another bright smile, then said under

her breath, "I wonder why scary looking is such a turn-on?
This one looks like he could gobble you up and you'd love
every moment of it. Done the deed yet?"

A startled laugh erupted from Jordan's mouth, but she bit
down hard on her bottom lip to discourage any more. "Stop,
Lisa," she whispered furiously, placing another dress on the
rack. "We haven't—" She swallowed, feeling incredibly ju-
venile. "Well, not yet."

"Really? How can you keep your hands off him?"

"Shush."

Here she was giggling like a schoolgirl, but it wasn't only
because Lisa was a naturally funny person. Dom's presence
seemed to make her all jumpy and nervous, too. Yes, he was
scary looking, and yes—if her body's reaction was anything to
go on—he was sexy as all get-out. If she allowed it, the memory of that slow, sizzling kiss the night before could reduce her
to jelly right here in the middle of the shop.

However, at this moment, she was on her way to a railroad
station locker, a fact she had to keep secret from the man who
had just walked in the door. So Jordan's current list of priorities
didn't include discussing her sex life with Lisa like two teenagers in the girls' bathroom.

Dom let his gaze dart around the shop, not quite sure why
he was here. He'd been in the neighborhood doing a follow-
up interview with a witness to last night's crime and remembered Jordan telling him about Riches and Rags. He'd told
himself he would drop by, see if she was there, say hello. No
big deal.

But now that he was here, now that he was looking at her,
he knew his what-the-hell casual excuse to be here was pure
bull pucky. He was here because he needed to see her again.
Too much had gone down between them the previous night to
try to sweep it under the rug. And besides, he wanted her.

His body was revved and on alert even with only three hours
sleep the night before. He wanted Jordan Carlisle, and today,
wanting her seemed much less complicated than it had last
night. Maybe telling her the truth, talking it through, had

helped. Maybe, like Jordan had said, unburdening yourself to someone else provided necessary release.

Whatever. He wanted her and he'd come here to get her. His body had taken over, had told his mind to take a hike.

However, she'd only smiled briefly at the sight of him. She hadn't glowed with welcome, the way he'd pictured. Instead, she seemed nervous, jumpy. Was she uncomfortable about what had happened between the two of them? Had he been too honest, telling her about Theresa? Or was there something else going on?

Abandoning his post at the doorway, he walked toward her. She was still working through the armful of dresses, hanging them up one by one, taking her time. The other woman was helping her and chuckling at something.

He came to a halt. A long rack of blouses separated them. "This a bad time?" he asked Jordan.

She glanced at him, then away immediately. Keeping her gaze focused on the clothing in her arms, she said, as though uncertain, "Well—"

Again, not exactly rolling out the old carpet. Was she giving him the brush-off? He felt his jaw tighten at the thought. What he ought to do was say adios, sorry to have bothered you, turn on his heel and get out of there.

But before he could, the cute one with the frizzy hair scurried around the rack and breezed up to him.

"Hi, I'm Lisa Davidson, this is my shop." When she offered her small hand, he took it in his and shook it. Her grip was surprisingly strong for such a petite person.

"Dom D'Annunzio," he said.

"Jordan," Lisa called, addressing her but still smiling at him, "Dom here seems a little impatient to speak with you. Why don't the two of you go get a cup of coffee next door? I can manage."

He glanced at Jordan to check her reaction. She seemed flustered by Lisa's offer. "But I was going to straighten up the sweaters before I left."

"I'll do it. Go on." She turned to look at Dom, grinned and

batted her eyelashes at him in a parody of flirtatiousness. "Any more like you at home?"

He couldn't help returning her smile. He liked up-front women. "Three brothers and four sisters, but they all live back east."

"Guess I'd better work on my frequent flyer miles." She walked purposefully to the dress rack, making shooing gestures at Jordan with her hands. "Go on. Get out of here. Talk to the man." She grabbed the rest of the dresses from her in a no-nonsense manner.

Jordan still seemed unsettled, but said, "Well, okay. I'll just get my purse," she told him and headed for the back of the store.

Not exactly enthusiastic, Dom thought, but he'd take what he could get.

While he waited he walked around the shop, checking it out. Lots of silk and lace, assorted colors and prints on the clothing and a faint powdery smell in the air. There were flowers in vases all around, and pictures of old-fashioned women in old-fashioned gowns adorned the walls. Jewelry and silver brushes glittered in glass shelves.

With a frown, he realized he rarely entered this world anymore. His was such a masculine existence—guy talk, guns, metal desks, dust-encrusted cars with worn-out windshield wipers. He rotated his shoulders. He felt a little out of place here among so much daintiness.

"You like my shop?" Lisa asked him above the sound of hangers being pushed around on metal.

"Yeah, it's—" He struggled for the right word. "Real female."

Her laugh was appreciative. "Good. That's what it's supposed to be. So, Jordan tells me you're a cop."

"Yeah," he said, but was saved from further conversation by the sight of Jordan closing a door in the rear of the store and hurrying toward him.

"See you on Monday, Lisa," Jordan said. "Have a great time tonight."

"Hey, you, too."

Dom opened the shop door for her, and she slipped past him, turned right and led him a few stores over to a small café. Inside were several white Formica tables with attached benches and a counter that displayed pastries and bagels. "I only have a few minutes," she said, glancing at her watch. "Sorry. I didn't know you'd be stopping by."

"I was in the neighborhood." He tamped down his irritation at being treated a little like some door-to-door salesman. He had no right to be reacting like this, he told himself. After all, he had popped in on her uninvited, and obviously she had plans.

A date? He felt his jaw muscles tensing at the concept.

Hey, Dom told himself. *Hold up here.* What was this? Jealousy? Possessiveness? Not his style. And anyway, it wasn't as if he had any claim on Jordan's time. It wasn't like they'd been dating for months or anything like that. Whatever was between them was in the future. And, from the way she was acting at the moment, there didn't seem to be much of a future for them, anyway.

Sit on it, D'Annunzio, he told himself. Settle down.

But, man, it was difficult to do just that. The sight of Jordan in a long flowered skirt and green short-sleeved sweater, the smell of her, the memory of the taste of her—all these combined to send his body into hyperactivity, male of the species version.

He had it bad. He hungered for her. In his entire life, had it ever been this strong? This sense of urgency, this compulsion to bury himself in a woman? Never, he thought, never in all the years before, during and after Theresa, and that little fact made him uneasy as hell.

She sat at a small round table by the window, fidgeting with her rings, while he paid for a couple of cups of coffee plus two jelly doughnuts—a belated lunch for him. He set the food down, then slid into his seat.

"Thanks," she said, stirring in some cream.

"I kind of took you by surprise, huh?" he said.

"Yes." With a small shrug of her narrow shoulders, she smiled. "But it's good to see you."

"Is it?"

"Yes, absolutely." She seemed sincere, or he wanted her to be. "Of course."

He felt his inner tension loosen a little around the edges. "Good. Well, look, the reason I'm here—" He paused, took a sip of his coffee, set it down and glanced around the café.

There were eight or so tables in the place, half of them occupied, but at the moment, no one was nearby. So he could do this subtly, could take his time, lead up to it. He could sweet-talk her—hell, he knew how.

But she seemed in a hurry to get someplace, and besides, he had no patience today. None. Action was called for. He would put his cards on the table, see what happened next. He took a deep breath and plunged in.

"Jordan," he began, "I'm not good with words, but here's the thing. With all the stuff that went down between us last night, something might have gotten lost, and I don't want it to get lost. The thing is, I...want you. I have this...craving for you, and I have it bad."

She was obviously startled by his declaration, and a slow pink blush rose over Jordan's cheeks. She managed to set her cup down before meeting his gaze. Until that moment, he hadn't noticed how very pale she was today. Her lips parted slightly while she looked at him with wonder. Her haunted and haunting green eyes had dark circles under them again. Several heartbeats went by before her mouth formed words. "Oh. I see."

He waited, his stomach muscles clenched with anxiety. He hadn't done that very smoothly, had he? It was because he was way too keyed up. This woman did that to him, brought out all the sensations that—until she'd entered his life—he didn't even know he was capable of experiencing anymore. "That's it?" he said. "'Oh, I see'?"

"I guess I'm supposed to say something more."

Damn. She wasn't leaping up and saying let's go. He'd blown it. "Not if you don't feel the same."

"It isn't that—" she began, stopped herself and shook her head. "Dom, it's not a good time—"

"For what?"

"To, you know, get involved."

"Who's talking about getting involved?" he answered. "I'm talking about sex, that's all."

She recoiled as if he'd slapped her, a look of hurt mixed with confusion on her face. That made him want to kick his own butt around the block. He'd said that last bit as retaliation, to punish her for not leaping with joy at the sight of him.

Why? He'd always been blunt, but when had he become cruel? Cards on the table, he'd told himself. Not a hatchet to the head.

Penitent, he put his hand over hers. It was ice cold, and he gripped it, trying to transfer a little of his body warmth to her. How white her skin was, especially next to his swarthy Italian complexion.

"Hey, I'm sorry, Jordan, so sorry. That's my stupid mouth. Attack and think later. I didn't mean it to come out that way. It's just that, well, look, we got this thing between us. I know it and you know it. Come on, say it."

Staring at their joined hands on the tabletop, she nodded slowly. "Yes, of course we do." She offered him a small, forgiving smile. "'We got this thing'," she quoted at him.

Relief poured through him like salve on a festering wound, and he loosened his grip. The door opened, and two teenage girls walked in, giggling loudly. Dom leaned closer to Jordan, keeping his voice low.

"I was concerned that what I told you about Theresa might turn you off of me."

"No," she said quickly, "not at all. I was…honored that you trusted me."

"Good." He expelled a relieved breath. Okay. They'd picked their way through a potential mine field, and the rest should be smooth sailing. "So," he went on with more confidence, "I want the next step, and I hope you do, too. I can't get you out of my head, Jordan. I wish I could, but I can't. I want you out of my head and into my bed—" He stopped, chuckled ruefully. "Forgive the poetry."

Another moment passed while she lifted her gaze to him, stared, then shook her head slowly. "You leave me breathless."

"Is that good?"

Jordan found herself answering Dom's question with a laugh. It was a pretty weak laugh, but she was amazed she could get enough air through her lungs to do even that. Every word out of Dom's mouth so far had taken her completely by surprise. "I don't know what it is. No one's ever come right out and said it before."

"You serious?" His skepticism was obvious. "With your looks, I would think it happens all the time. Didn't you get hit on while you were a model?"

"Yes, but when other men said things like that, it seemed…crude."

"Yeah, well…" His expression was sheepish, or as close to sheepish as she imagined he ever got. "I'm not feeling real suave right now, if you want to know the truth."

There it was again, Jordan thought, her heart turning over in her chest with a thump that must have been audible. One more brief glimpse of vulnerability that made her want to cradle Dom's face between her hands and murmur soothing words to him. Whenever Dom let her in, past the wisecracks and the surly facade, it affected her in a deeply soulful way. "You may not feel very smooth," she said, "but I feel flattered. You do that to me. You make me feel very desirable."

He raised the hand he was holding, turned it palm up, and with his other hand rubbed his callused fingertips over her wrist, the pad of her palm, the spaces between her fingers. The jolt of sensation this caused sent a warm shiver through her whole body.

"Do you like feeling desired?" he asked huskily.

"Yes, of course I do—"

"Then come with me—" he pierced her with the intensity of his gaze "—now."

"Oh, Dom…" As she struggled to find the right words, her glance caught the large clock on the cafe wall. Oh, lord, it was 6:30.

Timing was the secret to a successful life—Jordan had read that somewhere—but at the moment, the timing, hers and Dom's, was about as bad as it could be. Here she was, listening as Dom was saying the words she'd wanted to hear, but she couldn't stay to hear them.

She had to get to that locker. Immediately. And she couldn't let him know that, or why.

She withdrew her hand from his and stood up abruptly. "Look, can we talk about this some other time?"

"Huh?" he said, obviously taken aback. Then he went immediately on guard. Leaning back, he assessed her from under hooded lids. "Hey, Jordan, I'm a big boy. If it's no, all you have to do is say so." One side of his mouth quirked up. "They taught us that in sensitivity class," he added sarcastically.

She'd hurt his feelings. She knew him well enough to see through his flip remarks. But she had to get away from Dom. The way he made her melt inside, if she stayed, she would tell him where she was going, and that would be a stupid thing to do.

"Dom, please believe me. I'm not saying no. It's just that I can't talk about it right now. I have a…previous engagement. I'll call you tomorrow, okay?"

She got her purse and scooted out the door, not allowing herself to look back.

Dom sat frowning in the coffee shop after Jordan's abrupt departure. Previous engagement, she'd said. One of those fuzzy, polite phrases out of the book of etiquette that meant squat. Previous engagement. Did that mean she *did* have a date? It was Saturday night, so why not? Why had he expected her to be waiting for him to show up like some maiden in her castle waiting for the prince? Why had he fantasized that they'd

take one look at each other and he'd whisk her away somewhere—preferably a bed—and they'd pick up where they'd left
off last night? What kind of dream world had he been living
in all day?

Reality time. He and Jordan had shared a couple of hot kisses
last night. So what? By this morning, they'd each of them gone
back to their real lives—his as a cop, hers as the socialite
widow with a part-time job. Sure, she was attracted to him, but
so what? She probably got attracted to a lot of people and
didn't hop into bed with all of them. In coming to her shop,
he'd been operating out of his body's need for her, on his own
timetable and not even thinking about hers.

Angry at himself, he bit off a hunk of doughnut and chewed
it, barely tasting the sweet, buttery texture.

Did she have a date? Was there some guy she was sleeping
with? He hated the rage that came over him at the thought.
Hell, he almost hated Jordan Carlisle for being the cause of
these damned primitive emotions. He'd honestly thought he'd
shut down, that people couldn't have that kind of effect on him
any more. Fool that he was, he'd been convinced that when
Theresa died, he'd buried passion with her.

Surprise, surprise, he thought wryly. Jordan Carlisle made
him see what a self-deluding idiot he could be.

He glanced out the window of the coffee shop. It was night
time now. Traffic moved slowly by on Santa Monica Boulevard. People strolled or hurried along the sidewalk, kids on
skates, babies in strollers. But no Jordan. She was gone. What
he wanted to do was to follow her, to see where she went, what
she did and who she did it with.

Uh-uh. He shook his head. Cool down, he told himself. No,
he would not go there, would not go over the edge and into
what the books called "inappropriate behavior." To follow
Jordan would place him a couple of degrees this side of being
a stalker, no better than some of the low-life weirdos he came
across on the job.

So, no, he would not follow Jordan. He would make other
plans for the evening, because he realized suddenly that he

didn't want to be alone. In truth, from the moment Jordan had walked out of the coffee shop, Dom had felt the loneliness closing over him like a cloudy sky.

He could go back to the station, he supposed, hang out with whoever was on duty.

Nah. Pathetic. He had the evening free—use it.

He went to a pay phone and called his partner. Steve and his wife were always after him to come over for dinner. Maybe he could do it tonight. But there was no answer at Steve's, and when the machine picked up, he didn't leave word.

He punched in Nick's number, and when his friend answered, Dom felt more relief at the sound of his buddy's voice than he wanted to admit.

"Hey, Nick," he said.

"Dom. How's it going?"

"Okay."

"Hey, that Jordan is terrific. How the hell'd you get a woman like that, you bum?"

"You want lessons? Anytime."

Nick's chuckle was appreciative. "No, seriously, I liked her a lot. Have you been seeing her a while?"

"Nah. Not long at all."

"Well, hey, don't let this one get away."

"You know me—it lasts as long as it lasts."

In the silence on the other end of the line, he could almost see Nick nodding. "Love 'em and leave 'em D'Annunzio."

"Like they used to say about you, only different last name. Before Carly, of course. Speaking of which, you two going out tonight?"

"Carly's back in Boston, didn't I tell you? She's getting her apartment closed up and having her stuff shipped out here. Listen, we've set the date. We're getting married next month."

"Huh? You serious?" Why was he surprised—Nick and Carly had been inseparable since they'd met. But now there would be one less buddy to hang out with.

"Totally. And, the thing is, I want you to be my best man. I've been meaning to ask you."

"Well, gee, sure. Yeah, thanks for asking. Really." Nick's request made Dom feel kind of squirmy inside, moved, sort of. What was happening to him? Jordan, that was what. Open up that Pandora's box of emotions and look what you got. In the next minute he'd be weeping into the phone.

Okay, he told himself. Enough of this. "Do I have to wear a tux?"

"Yes. And if I can do it, you can, too."

"Like a bunch of damned penguins," he grumbled. "Well, okay. But that's a month away. Meantime, you want to meet me for a brewskie?"

"Morgan R's. Fifteen minutes."

He was so grateful to Nick for being available that if he didn't know himself better, he'd have sworn he wanted to jump for joy.

At Union Station, passengers hurried by on either side of her as Jordan made her way toward the row of lockers. When she found the right one, she fingered the key in her pocket, hesitating. A feeling of dissociation came over her, as though she'd left her body and was watching it from a distance. It was like a scene in a movie. Slender woman in skirt deciding whether or not to unlock a door, as though her life depended on it.

Foolishness, she told herself. Get it over with and go home.

Stiffening her spine, Jordan glanced both ways, then inserted the key in the lock. She opened the door to see a single, thin manila envelope inside. Nothing else. No bomb—of course not. Laughing nervously, she felt relief flooding her bloodstream as she took the envelope. She wanted to rip it open right away. Instead, she held it in her hand while she found a corner near the freight elevator that was relatively quiet. Once there, she leaned against the wall and opened the buff-colored envelope.

The first thing she pulled out was an eight-by-ten color photo of a towheaded young boy. Her experienced eye registered that this was not a professional portrait. It had probably been blown up from a home snapshot, but it was much clearer than the one last week. It was the same little boy, and—oh, God—yes, it was Michael.

She began to shake then, all over, with emotion. Yes, it had been a year since she'd seen him, and yes, a young child changed a lot in a year—yes, yes, yes, she knew all the arguments.

But unless Nature had played some sort of horrible genetic joke on her by creating two identical children with different mothers, there was no doubt in her mind. This was her child, her Michael.

He was alive!

The shaking was so intense, her knees could no longer support her. She sank onto a small bench. Feeling faint, she lowered her head to her lap and tried to breathe deeply. But her mind wouldn't settle down. How could it? It was difficult to take it in, to make it real.

All the pain, the mourning, the funeral, the depression. And all the while, miracle of miracles, the child she thought she had buried was not dead.

Then who had she buried? The thought intruded. Who was the child in that grave?

No, she couldn't focus on that, not now. There were too many other exhilarating emotions swirling inside her. Tears of relief and joy filled her eyes. Closing them, she rocked back and forth, hugging herself.

"Are you all right?"

Jordan raised her head to see an elderly gray-haired lady with a worried expression on her face. The woman's hands clutched the handles of an aluminum walker.

Jordan smiled. "Yes, thank you. I'm fine. It's just some good news, that's all."

The creased brow relaxed. "Oh, well, that's nice." She steered her walker to the ladies' rest room.

Yes! Jordan thought. Good news. The best news in the world. Her son was alive. Now she wanted him back, whatever it took.

A letter was paper-clipped to the picture. Eagerly, she unfolded it and read it.

"If this is your son," it said, "I believe a reward is in order. Bring five thousand in earnest money to Carlo's, 310 Azusa Street in downtown Los Angeles, Monday night at eight o'clock, rear booth. Please come alone. If you bring in the law, I'll be unable to supply you with any further information." The letter ended with. "I am watching you. A friend."

That last sentence made Jordan look up. Watching her? Whipping her head around, she studied all the passersby, looking for someone lurking behind a post or in a corner. From what she could tell, no one stood watching her, no one seemed to be looking her way, no one made eye contact. But surely, one of the people there was the man who wrote the note.

A ripple of fear replaced her exhilaration. Who was this person she was dealing with? He called himself a friend, but she knew that his motives were purely mercenary.

What was she letting herself in for? What kind of danger was she facing? Unsteady, she rose from the bench, clutched the envelope to her chest and walked briskly toward the exit doors. When she got outside, she ran for the parking lot as though she were being pursued by bloodhounds.

Chapter 7

Dom was at the West L.A. courthouse for maybe the tenth time this year. The courtrooms all looked the same, brown paneled walls, rows of gray seats for spectators, shabby linoleum floor. A partition separated the public from the judge, the lawyers and the defendant. Today, the latter was Joe Hogan, a guy with a long record.

Joe claimed that the person captured on the jewelry store's hidden camera wasn't really him, but his long-lost twin brother. The fact that Joe was caught with the stolen jewelry meant his twin brother had set him up.

To her credit, the public defender who was lucky enough to be assigned this one defended him with spirit and enthusiasm. But not success. The case was wrapped up in two hours and Dom was free to go.

What he should do, he knew, was to head crosstown to West Hollywood. But he was in West L.A., near Riches and Rags.

Which brought up thoughts of Jordan. Or more of them. All morning in the courtroom, he'd been thinking about her. When he'd seen her on Saturday evening, she'd said she'd call the next day, which was yesterday—Sunday. She hadn't called. Now here it was Monday, noon. He went to the pay phone, called in to the precinct to check his messages.

Nothing from Jordan.

Okay, he thought, hanging up but keeping his hand on the receiver. Things like this happened, he told himself. In fact, Dom reasoned, he wasn't always real good about following up on phone calls. So what he knew he should do was forget it—leave the ball in her court. That was what he *should* do.

Should. Great word. Usually used during a war between what was the right thing to do versus what a person really *wanted* to do.

What he wanted was to hear from Jordan, to be with her. His gut instinct backed him up on this one. There was heat between them that couldn't be tossed away or ignored. Yeah, she wanted him as much as he wanted her.

So then why hadn't she contacted him?

Could be a lot of things, of course, but coming up with her reasons when he wasn't in her head wasn't a real smart thing to do. What was also not smart was to drop in on her again. He remembered her telling Lisa she'd see her on Monday, so he knew where she was. Riches and Rags. About three blocks from the courthouse. Still, a guy had some pride.

Disgusted with all this analyzing, he picked up the phone and called the shop.

"Riches and Rags," announced an unfamiliar voice.

"Jordan Carlisle, please."

"Who's this?"

"Lisa?" he asked.

"No, I'm Gretl."

"Oh. Well, Gretl, do me a favor and tell Jordan it's Dom."

"Will do."

What felt like several minutes passed. He fidgeted, had a sudden craving for a cigarette. But those days were over, so he popped a stick of gum into his mouth. More time passed. He played with the foil gum wrapper, got irritated. Being kept on hold was not his favorite way to spend his free time.

Finally, the same voice came on the line. "I'm sorry. Jordan can't come to the phone right now."

Oh, yeah? he thought, but he took in a quick breath and made himself sound civil. "Would you mind asking her to call me?" He gave her his pager number, then took himself off to a favorite Mexican restaurant for lunch.

Two hours later, when he hadn't heard from her, Dom went to another pay phone and punched in the shop's number. Either she really was too busy to speak to him, he figured, or this was her way of telling him to get lost. If she didn't want to see him again, he wanted to hear it straight from her mouth. Did she think he was the kind who would get the hint and just fade away? If she was under that impression, she didn't know Dominic D'Annunzio.

This time Jordan answered. "Riches and Rags. How may I help you?"

"You can help me by talking to me."

She expelled a breath, then said quietly, "Dom."

"Got it in one." He waited. In his present sullen frame of mind—which he suspected was more of an overreaction than the situation warranted—if he said anything, it might be the wrong thing.

"It's nice to hear from you," Jordan said.

"Is it?"

"Oh, that's right. I'm sorry, I was supposed to call you yesterday, wasn't I?" She emitted another sigh. "I got a little, um, distracted."

Something in her voice—a disturbing undertone—made him sit up straighter in his chair. His irritability vanished. "What's wrong?"

"Nothing," she said with feigned lightness. "Just some… family problems."

Maybe there really were family problems, and maybe there weren't, but she was lying. He knew it immediately in his gut and by the way his cop antennae were beginning to hum. "Hey, anything I can do? Are you in some kind of trouble?"

Her sharp intake of breath let him know he was in the ballpark. "Dom, I—" She cut herself off in mid-sentence. "No, there's nothing."

"What, Jordan?" he insisted. "Talk to me."

"I'm sorry," she said much too quickly. "I need to help out a customer. Bye."

She hung up so abruptly, the sound made his head jerk back. As he stared at the receiver, a couple of impressions registered at the same time. Yes, Jordan had been avoiding him, but no, it was not because he'd been pushing her into a physical relationship.

It was something else, something she was both panicked about and didn't want to share with him—maybe even needed to keep from him.

The only thing that popped into his head was that she might have received another note about the kid. Might be that, or it could be something totally unrelated.

Whatever it was, he told himself, maybe he should use this as a reason to stay away from her.

Right. Sure. Like he could.

He glanced at his watch. He didn't really have to get back to the station. Besides, all that was facing him was more paperwork. He'd made a dent in the last pile, but it didn't seem to make a difference. The paperwork just kept coming.

He walked the three blocks to Riches and Rags and went in. Several customers milled about, but he spied Jordan immediately. She stood behind the front counter, sorting through a pile of what look like jeweled pins that lay on a piece of velvet. As he strode toward her, she glanced up, saw him and seemed to go very still.

"Dom," she said with an unsteady smile as he approached. "What are you doing here?" He got that she was trying for casual and offhand, but her body language gave her away. There was a jumpiness about her, even some fear in the eyes.

He went around to her side of the counter, grabbed her hand and headed toward the rear door. "Let's discuss that, shall we?"

She protested weakly as he hauled her out of the shop and

into the alleyway. On either side of the door were piled empty cartons. A high concrete ledge faced a modest parking lot in which were three cars, including Jordan's Rover. Setting his hands on her shoulders, Dom eased her onto the ledge so that she was sitting. Propping one foot next to her, he leaned an elbow on his bent knee.

"Okay," he said. "Out with it."

Jordan wrapped her arms around her midriff protectively. "For your information," she said with some spirit, "I don't enjoy being manhandled."

"I'll remember that. And I don't enjoy being lied to. By the way," he added easily, "you're one terrible liar, at least when you lie to me, and I'm an expert."

"I don't lie," she muttered defiantly, but she didn't look at him, and there was no real heat to her words.

He smiled. "Yeah, I think that's true, most of the time. So when you have something to hide from me, you don't do it too well." The smile left his face. "Come on, Jordan. What's going on? Talk to me."

Her answering look was mutinous. "No, I don't have to, and you have no right—"

He waved away her words. "Don't start with that bull, okay? Did you get another letter about Michael? Is that the problem?"

She gasped, then said quickly, "No." Too quickly.

Yeah, his intuition had been right on the money. Another note from the creep who'd sent the first one, and probably another warning about no cops. Which explained Jordan's whole attitude.

He watched as she lowered her arms, releasing her tight hold on herself. With her right hand she reached for the third finger on the left in that familiar gesture of hers of playing with her rings.

However, only one of those particular articles of jewelry was in evidence.

"What happened to your engagement ring?" he asked.

Her hand jerked back, and she rested a clenched palm on her knees. "What? Oh. It's out getting cleaned."

Shaking his head slowly, he chuckled. "Man, if you ever decide to take up lying full-time, you'd better take a class."

She bit her bottom lip, then made a face of self-disgust. But she didn't say anything else. Just sat there, mute, looking miserable.

He removed his foot and lowered himself onto the hard concrete ledge next to her. With a frown, he gazed at her for a couple of moments while he thought.

The missing ring added a new element to the puzzle and now he could connect the dots. She'd sold or pawned her ring to come up with money. Reward for information, that first letter had said. Was that it? Ransom for her supposedly still-living kid?

A tide of anger and disgust swept over him. Some piece of crud was yanking her chain, and Dom hated that. When he found him, he'd settle the score. In the meantime he had to take care of Jordan to protect her from any more pain.

He lifted the hand that was in her lap and took it in his. It was clenched tightly. Rubbing his thumb over the knuckles, he said quietly, "Hey, Jordan. Come on. This is me. You know you can trust me."

He felt her go still. For a brief moment, he even thought she was about to unburden herself. Then she snatched her hand away.

"You want to know what's going on?" she said with renewed spirit. "Fine. Thanks for the invitation to your bed, but I respectfully decline."

That one threw him, but only temporarily. His answering bark of laughter seemed to be equally disconcerting to her. "Forget going to bed," he said. "That can wait. There's something more going on."

"No, there isn't." She rose, brushed off her skirt and faced him. Her chin came up defiantly, and she continued in that cool, finishing-school way she sometimes had. "I thought about your kind offer the other day, to have sex with you, and I have decided that although I am attracted to you, there is just no room for you, for any man, in my life. It's not personal," she added quickly, her gaze less guarded now. "It's just that I have too many other…matters to deal with."

Dom sat staring at her. Jordan Carlisle was a piece of work. Clapping his hands a few times, he whistled in appreciation. Had to give her credit for the old college try. "Nice speech. Especially that 'it's not personal' part—you even made sure to take care of my tender feelings." He grinned. "It's a crock, of course. But nice."

At his final comment, Jordan's face fell, and all the defiance seemed to drain from her. Holding her clenched hands to her breast, she begged him with anxious, pleading eyes. "Dom, please. Go away. Just go away. Maybe…maybe you need to forget you ever met me."

Openmouthed, he stared at her, feeling the first real flicker of disquiet about their relationship since their conversation had begun. Forget he'd met her? Impossible.

What should he do next? Hell, he'd tried reason, tried strong-arming her, he'd tried encouragement, he'd tried sarcasm. No matter what he did, she seemed determined to keep him at arm's length and he didn't like it. Especially when he became aware of a sensation in his throat and gut that felt strangely like hurt. This woman had the power to hurt him. Somehow he'd given her that power, but damn it, he would not let that get in the way.

Maintaining eye contact with her for a few silent moments, Dom tried to stare her down. But it didn't work. They had reached an impasse.

"Jordan," he said one last time. "I'm trying to help you."

Her face twisted with regret. "I know." She seemed on the verge of saying something more, but she closed her mouth and shook her head. "Don't."

It was time for him to admit it: Obviously, if he was going to do anything for Jordan, it would have to be without her permission.

"So, is that your last word on the subject?"

"It is," she replied firmly. "And now I have to get back to work."

She turned away from him, opened the door and disappeared into the shop, leaving him to stare after her, frustration welling inside, accompanied by a strong sense of desolation.

This section of downtown L.A. wasn't one of Jordan's usual haunts. The city was segmented, each community a self-contained entity, so most Angelenos stayed pretty much in their personal areas of work and home. She'd been in this neighborhood a few times, of course, mostly to attend the Music Center's opera and symphony, and for fund-raisers at USC and the Museum of Modern Art.

But at eight o'clock on a Monday night, only a few blocks from the Civic Center, the city seemed foreign, a strange and threatening animal. And eerily quiet. Here were slums and the symbols that went with the word—liquor stores and check-cashing services, rows of shabby tenements, graffiti-filled walls, litter-strewn vacant lots and shadowed alleyways. Not for the first time, Jordan realized how pampered her life was, how living as she did among the upper reaches of the financial strata made it easy to forget the dark underbelly of American life.

Tense and anxious about the upcoming meeting, Jordan swallowed a surge of fear for her safety as she sought a parking place. She found one a block away from her destination. Tucking her purse under her arm and clutching the lapels of her jacket, Jordan walked quickly and purposefully to Carlo's.

Above the bar was a neon-lit highball glass and a sign that read Cocktails. Several of the bulbs were burned out, and the whole thing made her feel, not for the first time, as though she were a character in an old black-and-white movie, as though she were about to run into a mysterious man in a slouch hat, an unfiltered cigarette dangling from the corner of his mouth.

Shaking off the sense of unreality, she pulled open the door and walked in. The moment she did, the smell of liquor invaded her nostrils, upsetting her already queasy stomach. She found herself in a dimly lit, seedy-looking room. Her eyes adjusted enough to make out a long counter and a row of bar stools on her left at which sat five or six hunched-over patrons. The lone bartender had a shaved head and wore a large white apron wrapped around his enormous gut.

To her right was a wall of booths with cracked red leather upholstery. As she'd been instructed to do, she made her way to the rear booth and sat down. She could see the whole bar and the entrance door. She glanced at her watch. Eight o'clock on the nose.

"Hey!" The gruff male voice startled her, and she looked up.

The bartender was staring at her, not friendly. "You want anything, you have to come up here. We don't got waitresses."

"Thank you," she called, aware that her voice was shaking. "I'm expecting someone."

He shrugged and went back to staring at a small television situated among a row of liquor bottles.

Jordan kept her hands folded on the table and waited while her tension climbed to a nearly intolerable level. She told herself she had to keep her wits about her, had to act self-possessed, but the truth was she had no idea what to expect from this meeting. Every few moments she glanced at her watch, then focused again on the door.

She closed her eyes for a moment as a wave of hope mixed with anxiety washed over her. Michael. Her baby, her—

"Mrs. Carlisle?"

Her eyelids snapped open and she found herself staring at a young man with a friendly smile on his face. He had short, thinning blond hair, old acne scars on his cheeks, hazel eyes and pale blond eyelashes.

"Yes?" she said breathlessly.

"Glad you could make it."

"Are you—?"

"'A Friend.' In person."

Jordan wasn't sure what she'd expected—some hardened criminal type, she supposed, not this small-townish, smiling young man. He wore chinos and a plaid, open-necked shirt. His hands were in his pockets, and he leaned casually against the side of the booth. He just missed being handsome, but he had a pleasant face.

"Want a drink?" he asked.

"No, thank you."

He sauntered to the bar and ordered a couple of shots of Scotch. She realized he must have been one of the patrons sitting there when she arrived and had probably been observing her, waiting to see if she'd brought anyone with her. When he returned, he slid into the booth on the other side, set his drinks on the table and promptly downed one. When he finished, his gaze roamed the room casually, then returned to her.

"So," he said. "you saw the picture."

"Yes."

"Is it your kid?" Holding up his hand, he laughed. "Don't answer. If it wasn't close, you wouldn't be here." He took a sip of his second drink. "You have the money?" he asked pleasantly.

He seemed so at ease, she thought, while she was ready to shriek. Money. He wants money. She forced herself to inhale a deep breath, then release it. She knew she had to hold something back, couldn't be too much of a patsy.

"It's—" she swallowed nervously "—nearby."

His smile faded slightly. "What do you mean, nearby?"

She folded her hands on the tabletop to hide how much they were trembling. "I need some answers from you first," she said resolutely. "Is Michael all right? Where is he? How did he come to be there? Who are you? I need answers."

His eyes narrowed, cold as ice all of a sudden. "You wearing a wire?"

"A what?"

"You know, one of those recording devices to catch the bad man with. Did you tell anyone about this? The cops?"

"No," she protested. "I swear it. You said not to."

He reached over and grabbed her small purse from the seat next to her, opened it and peered inside. There was nothing there except her keys, a slim credit card case, a few bills and change and a lipstick. Closing it, he set it on the table, then reached toward her and patted her shoulders. Before she even knew what was happening his hands had patted her upper arms and breasts, then her back, that ever-present smile on his face.

"Stop that," she said, pushing at his hands, trying to squirm away from him.

"Sorry," he said, but there was no remorse in the remark. "Just looking out for myself."

He reached under the table and, even as she kicked at his hands, patted her ankles, up her calves, over her thighs and hips. When he got to her midsection, he stopped. "What's that?" he asked suspiciously.

"A money belt," she said tightly.

His smile returned. "Good. Take it off and give it to me." When she hesitated, he said, "Money first, answers afterward. My reward for a good deed. That's the rules. Five thousand big ones." His eyes turned icy. "Now."

She looked at him, suddenly frightened of him. The way his gaze turned frigid was creepy. This man meant business, and he held all the cards. But she had to hold something back, had to reserve some bargaining power.

She reached under her jacket, unstrapped the money belt she wore around her waist and set it on the table. His eyes darted around the room then, quickly, he grabbed for it. But she pulled it away as he did.

"No," she said with more bravado than she felt. "I need some answers to my questions."

A spasm of anger crossed his face, then he sat back in his seat, sipped again at his drink. "You're not going to get a lot of answers, Mrs. Carlisle. That's not the way the game is played."

"This isn't a game," she said tightly. "Not to me, it isn't."

"Hey, keep your voice down. Relax. It'll all work out."

She fought for control. Fear mixed with outrage, but she made herself calm down by telling herself that at the end of this nightmare her small, precious son was waiting for her. When she had recovered her poise, she said, "Tell me your name, at least."

He eyed the money belt clutched tightly in her hand. ''I suppose if I grab that, you'll scream.''

''And fight and raise more ruckus than you want to deal with.''

''But then I won't tell you where Michael is.''

''And you won't get any money.''

He smiled again, nodded as though appreciating her move, took another sip. Then he shrugged his shoulders. ''Fine. Five questions, one thousand bucks each. Take it or leave it.''

She hesitated, then said, ''All right.''

He flashed her his warm smile. ''You can call me Wally.'' A salesman. Yes, that's what he reminded her of—someone who sold cars or insurance and had a wife and two children, a home with a picket fence. She almost laughed at the incongruity of the image.

''Wally what?'' she inquired.

''Sorry, just Wally. No last names.'' He held out his hand, palm up. ''And that's your first answer. Let's have it.''

Frowning, she considered him. This was ridiculous. Five questions. It was like some twisted fairy tale where the fate of the golden-haired heroine depended on coming up with some dwarf's name. She opened the bag and removed ten one-hundred-dollar bills, folded them and handed them to him.

He snatched them, glanced around, then stuffed the wad into his pants pocket. ''Next question?''

''Where is Michael?''

''Up north. Don't worry, Mrs. Carlisle. He's safe, and as far as I can tell, he's healthy.''

''I don't understand. How—?''

''That's two.'' He held his hand out again, then made a dismissive gesture with it. ''Look, let's cut the crap, okay? Here's the deal.'' He finished his drink, belched and said, ''Pardon,'' then smiled again.

What she wanted to do was wipe that grin off his face with a slap, but she held herself steady. He was calling the shots. For now.

''Give me the rest of the money,'' Wally said, ''or I walk

out of here right now, and you'll never see your son again.''
She opened her mouth to protest, but he stopped her with a
raised hand. ''In return, I'll give you as much information as
I think you need today. That's it, lady.''

As she gazed at him, all sense of power—imagined or otherwise—drained from her. Oh, lord, she thought, this is a nightmare. What choice did she have but to do what he said?
Mutely, she handed over the leather belt. He removed the rest
of the cash, folded it and pocketed it.

''Okay.'' Resting his elbows on the scarred tabletop, he
leaned in to her. ''Here's the story. I have this sister, her name
is Myra,'' Wally began, and launched into a bizarre tale. As
he told it, he seemed to be enjoying himself, alternately crude
and cocky with self-importance.

Apparently, his sister had left home—this unnamed town
''up north''—four years earlier to break into the movies in
Hollywood. ''Always had stars in her eyes,'' he told Jordan,
''the stupid bitch. And she was pretty, but they're all pretty in
this town.''

The family had lost contact with her. Then, a year ago, Myra
returned home in pretty bad shape. ''She'd suffered some sort
of a nervous breakdown,'' he said. ''You know, all twitchy,
filled with cock-and-bull stories about big-shot producers and
unsold pilots.''

When Myra returned, she had a little boy with her who she
claimed was hers, and there was no reason not to believe her.
Myra had always been a little on the nutty side and since her
return had gotten even nuttier. In the past year, she'd been in
and out of reality, barely able to care for the boy, so their
parents had taken full responsibility for him.

Two weeks ago, when Jordan's rescue story had appeared
in the papers complete with background pictures of Jordan Carlisle and her deceased child, Wally had been in Bakersfield
working and had happened to read an L.A. paper. Something
about the kid reminded him so strongly of Myra's little boy,
he got on the phone and started kidding his sister about it.

Myra went ballistic, denying things she hadn't been accused

of. Suspicious, Wally came to L.A., talked to a couple of people his sister had mentioned and found out that Myra had been seeing Reynolds Carlisle before his death.

"Your husband was paying her rent," Wally said with a knowing smile, and suddenly the whole connection between Myra and Reynolds and the kid didn't seem so farfetched to him anymore. What the hell, he'd told himself. That was when he'd sent the first letter and picture.

Her late husband's peccadilloes were old news, but Jordan wanted to know more about Myra, as much as she could find out. "What's your sister's last name?" she asked, "and how did she wind up with Michael? A child died in that car accident. Who was he?"

"No last names," Wally said. "As for the rest—" He shrugged, obviously indifferent. "Beats me. Besides, you're out of money."

"I don't understand."

"If you want any more answers, I'll need some more cash as a reward for all my hard work."

Angry frustration replaced fear. "This is blackmail."

"Now, now," he said soothingly, an innocent, patronizing expression on his face. "That's not a nice word, is it? No, Mrs. Carlisle, you are free to leave right now, and I have no power over you whatsoever. So, no, it's not blackmail. It's a reward for information, which I have given you." He spread his hands. "Pretty simple, huh?"

"But I need to know more."

"And I need more money," he said, his mouth forming a smug smirk. "Surely the reward should match your ability to pay, don't you think? You're loaded, Mrs. Carlisle."

"I'm not," she protested. "It's not my money. I'm not wealthy, not in the least. I had to pawn my diamond ring to get you what you asked for today."

"Really?" He raised one pale, skeptical eyebrow. "Tsk, tsk. What a sad story." Then he shrugged. "However you get it, I sure hope you can come up with some more, or I'm afraid that will end our association."

"Please, I—"

"Spare me the hearts and flowers, okay? Ten thousand will get you more information, such as the name of my hometown, maybe even details like last names and addresses. Hey," he went on, stretching his arms above his head as though he hadn't a care in the world, "I'm being nice here. I could soak you for a hundred thousand, and you know it. Pawn some more rocks. Steal it. Not my problem. All I know is there is this little boy, and he's either yours or Myra's. And I know where he is. Meanwhile, I have to go now."

He finished the last of his drink and slid around the booth to stand.

No, Jordan thought, he couldn't leave, not now. She pushed herself to her feet and clutched at his shirtfront. "But when can I see my son?"

"I'll be in touch." Wally removed her hands and handed her the bill for his two drinks. "You pay this time," he said cheerfully. "I'll get the next one."

As he turned to go, she grabbed his shoulder. "You can't just—"

Shaking her off, he glared at her. Making sure his back was to the bar patrons, he whispered, "Don't be a pain in the ass, Mrs. Carlisle. Got it?" His hazel eyes met hers for another brief moment. They were empty of all feeling, of all humanity.

If she hadn't known it before, at that moment, she understood that she was dealing with a sociopath, someone who totally lacked compassion, conscience, maybe even a soul. Nothing she could say would sway him from his agenda, which was to drain as much money from her as possible. In so doing, he would dangle Michael in front of her like a cat's toy—the moment she reached for it, it would be snatched away.

Oh, God, she thought, as she watched him saunter out of the bar. Myra was unstable, Wally was sick, and her son was in that family's care. A surge of terror sliced through her unlike any terror she had felt before.

She had to do something, she thought. She would follow him. Force him to tell her…

She grabbed her purse and ran after him but was stopped by the sound of the bartender's gruff voice. "Hey, lady!"

"Yes?" she said over her shoulder.

"Who's paying for the drinks?"

That stopped her. She could make a run for it, she supposed, but this large man would come after her, she had no doubt of it.

She walked to the bar, realizing she was in way over her head. What had she been thinking, that she would follow Wally? Was she capable of trailing him through the dark and dirty streets of downtown L.A., keeping her distance? What if he got into a car and drove off? Her car was a block away. The B-movie image returned, the one where the hero or heroine would hail a cab and say, "Follow that car." In reality, there were very few cruising taxicabs in L.A., none in this section of town.

Briefly, she wondered if all this movie imagery meant the strain she was under was making her lose reality. But she dismissed the idea. This wasn't the movies, this was her life, and Jordan Carlisle, supersleuth, was a bust.

At the bar, she set money on top of the bill. "Excuse me?" she said.

The bartender looked up from wiping a glass. "Yeah?"

"That young man I was just with?"

"Who?"

"You know, the one who just walked out? Do you know him?"

"I didn't see nobody walk out, lady." He seemed bored. "I don't know him, I don't know you, I don't know nothing. Anything else?"

No, she thought, defeated and dispirited. Nothing else. She hadn't done this right, somehow, hadn't come up with a clever enough plan. For sure, she had no idea what the next move was. Still her mind continued to race, trying to come up with some answers, some solutions, anything. Tucking her purse under her arm, she walked toward the exit.

Chapter 8

Dom watched from the shadows as Jordan came out of the sleazy-looking bar. She stood for a moment breathing in the night air as though grateful for oxygen. He stepped forward and put a hand on her shoulder.

She let out a short gasp, but he came around to face her, the fingertips of his other hand pressed on her mouth. "Hey, Jordan, it's okay. It's me."

When he dropped his hand, she stared at him with a look of total surprise. "Dom?" she said. "How did you—" The surprise changed to panic as she glanced wildly up and down the street. "Did he see you?" she asked.

"Who? The blond kid?"

"Yes."

"No." Tucking her hand into the crook of his elbow, he walked them toward his car, which was parked nearby in the red zone. "Come on, get in," he said when they got there.

Again, she glanced up and down the street then at him, panic and confusion on her face. "He'll see us together."

"He's gone. Walking southeast. Nick's following him."

"Nick?"

"Get in the car and I'll answer all your questions."

She did as she was told, and he drove the several blocks to the Civic Center. At the fountains in front of the courthouse, he pulled into a Loading Only zone. They were surrounded by the quiet, darkened stone buildings of the city's hub at night. The only illumination was the colored lights of the fountain.

Dom turned off the motor, leaned against his car door and faced her. He was fighting a war inside between worry for Jordan's safety and anger at her for being here. "What in God's name do you think you're doing?" he said, keeping a tight rein on his temper.

"Me?" She seemed taken aback, then responded heatedly. "You're asking me that?"

"Yeah, I'm asking you that."

She glared at him, defiance in her eyes. "Well, I want an explanation of what you're doing here. And I want it now. How did you know where to find me?"

He took in a breath, tried to slow down the tempo of their interchange. "If I tell you, will you answer me?"

"That depends on what you tell me."

He was aware that he was on the verge of blowing up at her, even if it was fury born of fear. When Nick had called to tell him where Jordan was, Dom had broken speed records getting here. However, at this moment, he sensed that it was not wise to make her his verbal punching bag just to relieve anxiety. Besides, he told himself, he was the professional here, which meant he needed to set the tone.

"I was worried about you, okay?" he said with as much calm as he could muster. "This afternoon, after you clammed up on me, I...got concerned, so I asked Nick to keep an eye on you."

Nick had been only too glad to oblige his old friend. A few months back, Dom had helped Nick track down a sicko who had kidnapped Nick's fiancée, Carly. Nick was retired and teaching Police Procedure at a local college. When Dom had asked him, unofficially, to keep tabs on Jordan for him, Nick hadn't hesitated to agree.

"Keep an eye on me?" Jordan said. "You mean, he followed me?"

"Yep."

"You had me followed? Like a common criminal? How dare you?" She punched her index finger into his chest. "Who gave you the right—"

He grabbed the finger, squeezed it. "You did. When you involved me in this, when you called me up and asked me for professional advice, you gave me the right to do it."

To her credit, Jordan seemed to hear him and at least partly agree with him, because she stopped fighting him. He dropped his grip on her finger, hoping he hadn't hurt her. Crossing her arms over her chest, Jordan leaned against the car door, stubborn defiance in her body posture. "I accept your explanation, but I don't like it."

"I didn't much like it when Nick called me with your location. He popped his head in the bar, saw you talking with the blond kid—" He broke off. "What's his name?"

"Wally."

He nodded. "I came hightailing it down here, got here just as Wally was leaving. Nick took off after him, I stayed to talk to you. So, talk to me, Jordan. I'm gonna guess that he's the one who sent you the note last week."

Her mouth was still set in a stubborn line. He wanted to shake her, but he kept his hands to himself while they curled into fists. "Talk to me, I said," he repeated. "I'm not going away until you do."

She stared at him, those large green eyes nearly translucent as they reflected the fountain's colored lights. Then she seemed to come to a decision. She unfolded her arms and clasped her hands on her lap. "You were right. I got a second letter. I'm just so scared about what will happen if he knows about you."

"He won't, not unless it's necessary. Come on, let's hear it, all of it. Please," he added, less aggressively. Jordan was safe, sitting here in his car with him. He could relax a little. "It's been making me crazy."

She studied him a moment longer, then gave up the last vestiges of her resistance. "All right," she said with a sigh. "It seems stupid not to, at this point."

In halting tones, Jordan brought him up to date—the locker at the station and the picture, the meeting, the story about Myra. As he listened with a cynical cop's ear, Dom's personal fear for her safety increased. She wasn't only a civilian, she was an innocent when it came to dealing with the seamier segment of the population.

He had to reason with her, talk her out of going any further. "What do you know about this guy, Jordan? How trustworthy can he be? You've already given him five thousand bucks. He'll string you along forever."

"Don't you think I know that? But—"

He didn't let her finish. "Do you have any idea what kind of danger you might have walked into tonight?" His fear was heating up his anger again, but he tried, really he did, to hold back. "People disappear from this neighborhood every day, without a trace and without anyone asking questions when they do."

"But the picture." She raised her clasped hands to her chest. "It was Michael."

"Come off it, Jordan."

"*You* come off it, Dom!" she exploded. "You don't have children. You have no idea how it is, how it feels. The little boy in that picture is my child. I'd know him whatever age he was. I'm his mother. And I want him back. If it means exposing myself to danger, if it takes every penny I can lay my hands on, then that's what it will take!"

Her intensity was like a blast of volcanic heat, and as it seared him, Dom felt his vehemence draining away. In its place was a quiet, cold feeling of dread. Sitting in the car with him was a woman whose blind instinct to hold and protect her young might lead her to do something really stupid. There would be no talking her out of it. She would not listen to logic or reason.

Theresa had possessed that same fierce maternalism even though she hadn't yet been a mother. And it had destroyed her. He couldn't let it happen again. He could not, once again, stand by helplessly while a woman put herself in danger.

No, he decided. However much she might protest, he would make Jordan's business his business. This time he would be totally, one-hundred-percent involved. He might have been a loser of a husband, maybe even not much of a man, but he was a good cop, damn it. His expertise would go far toward keeping Jordan safe.

Propping an elbow on the steering wheel, he wiped his mouth and assessed Jordan. Her back was stiff, her gaze determined and intense. Now he had to put his fear for her safety away. Now the cop would take over for the man.

"Okay, I hear you," he said. "You're willing to go all the way, whatever it takes, to see if Michael's still alive. But what I need is to find out more about Wally. Will you go along with me on that?"

After a pause, Jordan said, "Yes."

He removed his pad and pen from his inner jacket pocket and made notes. "Wally didn't mention any last names?" She shook her head. "Works in Bakersfield, but his family lives up north, and he didn't name the town. I need to ID him, see if he has a record. You still got the letters?"

"Yes."

"I'll need them, check them for fingerprints. Tonight, in the bar, did he get his prints on anything you can think of? A drink?"

"Two." Jordan seemed calmer now, caught up in the spirit of investigation, which was how he wanted her to feel. "But the bartender has probably picked up the glasses already."

"Did he touch anything else?"

She thought about it. "Me. My clothes, I mean. He patted me down."

"He what?" Dom barked.

"It wasn't sexual," she said with a nervous laugh. "I don't think he was interested in me as a woman, more like a cash cow."

He shook his head. The little weasel would pay for that one. "The son of a bitch," he said, hardly aware he'd said it out loud.

"Yes, and all the while he kept assuring me this wasn't blackmail, that I was free to go anytime I wanted."

"Covering his bases," Dom muttered.

"I suppose so. But I already gave him the money—" She snapped her fingers. "My money belt."

"Your what?"

"I had the money in a money belt, and he touched it all over."

"You still have it?"

Her face fell. "I left it back there, in the booth."

He started up the motor, rammed the gear into drive. "I'm dropping you at your car. Where is it?"

"A block from Carlo's."

"Okay." Dom punched on the lights and pulled away from the curve, adrenaline rushing through his system. "Get in your car, go home. I'll get the money belt, get it dusted for fingerprints, run them through."

"You're sure he won't find out?"

"How can he?"

"Maybe I'm making a mistake. Dom, I'm worried about your involvement."

He laughed sardonically. "Too late. I'm involved."

"Dom!"

The sharp edge to her voice made him glance at her. It was all there on her face—frustration, exhaustion, fear. He pulled over, kept his foot on the brake, turned to stare at her. "You've got to stop this."

"I know. And I know I keep vacillating, going back and forth about letting you in, not letting you in. I know it and I'm sorry. But I'm so scared." Her expression ripped at him. While her eyes pleaded with him, behind the plea was a vulnerability that made something in his chest turn over. What could he say? What could he do to ease her distress?

The question had barely crossed his conscious mind before he rammed the gearshift into park, unhooked his seat belt, reached over, cupped her face in his hands and kissed her.

At first she jerked with surprise, tried to pull away. But he deepened the kiss, stroked the satiny soft flesh of her cheeks with his thumbs. She stilled, then moaned and opened her mouth to grant access to his tongue.

A slow, simmering heat crept into his bloodstream. All he'd wanted to do was to comfort her, but now he wanted to linger there in the soft, moist recesses of her mouth, to explore and taste all her textures.

But not here, on a dark, downtown street. And not now. Reluctantly, he broke off the kiss. "Don't worry, okay?" he said quietly, smoothing his thumb over her lips. "Leave it all to me."

Her eyelids were heavy as she gazed at him, and he watched as sensual intoxication was replaced by a return to anxiety. Jordan closed her eyes again, ducked her head and turned away from him.

"You think all you have to do is kiss me and I'll shut up. I shouldn't have told you anything. I'm a fool."

"No. You'd be a fool if you tried to handle this on your own."

She shook her head. "I'm so confused. I don't know what's the right thing to do. All I know is I want my son back. If anything jeopardizes my chance to see him again—" She shrugged disconsolately, left the sentence unfinished.

Dom put the car into gear, pulled away from the curb and headed into the night.

A bubble bath usually relaxed her, but tonight the hot water and scented oil weren't doing the trick. Tremors of anxiety, impatience, worry continued to quiver through her. Jordan was a mother whose child was out there somewhere, living a life apart from her, and she ached with longing for him, fear for him.

Was he happy? Eating well? Loved? Or the reverse, mistreated and—

No, she told herself for the umpteenth time. If she did a what-if scenario filled with every mother's nightmares, she might go insane. And what good would she be to Michael then?

She rose from the tub and reached for the large, thick towel draped on the warming rack. As she dried herself off, she played back the entire evening, doubting herself yet again, questioning her actions. Could she have behaved differently with Wally? Could she have said something, done something that might have brought her reunion with Michael any closer?

The good news, Mrs. Carlisle. Your son isn't dead. The bad news, Mrs. Carlisle—you can't have him. Not ever, according to Wally, if she brought in the cops. Was it wise to have told Dom everything? Would that backfire? Would Wally find out somehow, cut off contact with her? Was she relying on Dom too much, expecting more of him than it was possible to deliver?

Dom. Jordan found herself rubbing the towel over her breasts and thinking about him at the same time. Her nipples grew hard at the memory of that kiss. It had come out of nowhere, it seemed, and had made her bones melt. Instant arousal had flooded her, that same arousal that seemed to take place whenever he touched her...

The hand clutching the towel stilled. How could she be thinking about Dom now, about physical attraction, when there was so much else that needed her attention? Even so, as she dried her legs, she reflected on her lame attempt that afternoon—had it just been that afternoon, she wondered—when she'd told him to go away, that she was turning down his offer to share his bed.

Utter foolishness, she thought. She wanted him, of course she did. If these were normal times, she'd be rejoicing at her ability to feel this way. These were not normal times, but in the midst of all the fretting about Michael, Dom was constantly on her mind, in the background, like some tune you heard and couldn't get out of your head.

She had to stop thinking about Dom and her own physical needs. All her energy was required to concentrate on getting Michael back.

Energy and purpose. Control.

Tonight, with Wally, she'd felt only powerlessness, a lack of control. It was how it had been for so many years in so many areas of her life. She'd been pushed into a career she hadn't sought and didn't particularly enjoy, moved into a marriage that appeared fine on the outside but was rotten at the core. Widowhood and childlessness had been thrust on her in one shattering moment.

As she slipped on her ivory nightgown, she faced the fact that she had never been in control, not one moment of her life. She had never *taken* control. It was time to do just that. So…what could she do about getting Michael back?

She climbed into bed and closed her eyes. Think, she ordered her mind. Come up with something concrete. Dom was dealing with identifying Wally. Wally's sister was Myra. Myra had been one of Reynolds's girlfriends. How could Jordan find out more about Myra?

She sat up straight in bed. Of course! Hal! Hal Cooper, Reynolds's oldest and closest friend. He would know all about Reynolds's girlfriends. Maybe he'd even met Myra. Yes, Jordan thought with building excitement, as she turned on her light and reached for the phone. She'd punched in most of Cooper's number when she happened to glance at the clock.

Midnight. No, she couldn't call Hal, not now. It would have to wait till the morning. Replacing the receiver, she lay against the pillow, eyes wide open.

Hal would want to know why she was asking about Myra. How much could she tell him? Not much at all, was the answer. At this point, only one other human being, Dom, knew about the possibility of Michael being alive. Even if she swore Hal to silence, she knew he would honor it only until he felt like it. It might be public in a matter of hours. Nothing was to be public, *nothing,* not until Michael was safe.

As she finished that thought, another flicker of disquiet assailed her. What about Cynthia? New considerations and questions rushed through her feverish brain nonstop. Shouldn't her mother-in-law know what was going on? Michael was her grandson, after all.

And the hard cold fact remained that Jordan might have to pay more money, lots of it, to get Michael back, especially if efforts to trace Wally's family were unsuccessful. Cynthia was wealthy. She wrote five- and ten-thousand-dollar checks to her favorite causes all the time.

Every instinct rebelled at the thought of asking her mother-in-law for money, but again, when it came to getting Michael back, there was no room for pride.

Yes, Jordan decided, in the morning she would tell Cynthia, prepare her. It was the right thing to do. Then she would call Hal. These were concrete, specific tasks. She was taking action. Finally.

Standing at the kitchen sink, Dom took a sip of instant coffee and stared out the window. The new day was coming in cloudy and overcast, but there was supposed to be plenty of sunshine by afternoon. He was showered, shaved and dressed, and it was only six o'clock. This not sleeping bit was going to take its toll one of these days, but he didn't feel a thing now except anxious to get on with his day. He had the money belt wrapped in plastic, and he wanted to get to the bureau early and set the wheels in motion.

Still, six was too early. His contact at the Scientific Services Bureau, the SSB, wouldn't be in till eight.

Was it too early to call Jordan? he wondered. Probably, but he picked up his phone anyway and punched in her numbers.

"Yes?" She answered on the second ring.

He felt a small lightening in his chest at the sound of her voice. "Hi," he said gruffly, to mask his sudden mood upswing.

"Oh, Dom." Two words, that was all she said, but he got how keyed up she was.

"How are you holding up this morning?"

"Running on sheer nerves. And you?"

"Hey, you know me—Mr. Serenity."

His sarcasm made her laugh. God, he loved her laugh. It was a full-throated yet husky, low-pitched sound, and it immediately activated his groin area. One day soon, he promised himself, he would have her in his bed. And it better be soon, he thought. She was a good part of his sleeplessness.

"What happened with Nick?" Jordan asked him.

"Nothing. He lost the guy."

The message had been on Dom's machine when he'd gotten home. The blond kid had ducked into an alley. Nick had watched him go a few steps and turn down an alley that ran in back of the buildings. Dom had told Nick to be super careful not to be spotted, so he hadn't given chase. By the time Nick had hurried around the block to head him off, he'd lost him. He'd seen a car—silver Honda, maybe ten years old, hatchback model—driving away, but he wasn't even sure it was the kid at the wheel. Nick had been too far away to make out the license plate number.

"So," he told Jordan, "we're not any further along than we were last night."

"Oh." She expelled a breath of disappointment. "What about the money belt? Did you get it?"

"Yeah. But leather doesn't take prints too well, so I'll need the letters for backup."

"I'll drop them off to you today—where is your office? Or station, or whatever you call it?"

"Office, station, bureau, HQ. Doesn't matter," he told her as he considered. The investigation so far was still unofficial, and it would be best for all concerned if it stayed that way. For now. "Better not bring them there," he told her. "I don't want to draw any attention. How about I pick them up from you?"

"No," Jordan said firmly. "You've done more than enough for me, Dom. Let me do something for a change."

"Well, I'll be here at home for another hour or so."

"Tell me where you live."

As he reeled off his address, he decided to include his home phone and pager number while he was at it. She might as well have all his numbers. She might need them.

"I'll be there in half an hour, forty-five minutes," Jordan said, "tops. Oh, Dom," she went on, her voice a notch lighter than it had been a moment ago, "talking to you has made me feel more hopeful."

"Yeah?" Should he tell her not to waste the energy, that all this might come to nothing? Should he tell her that from now on they would be playing a waiting game, one that involved footwork and patience and a lot of dependence on other people's schedules? Not to mention luck and maybe some prayer?

Nah, why spoil her mood. Let her have her optimistic outlook, for a while anyway. "You know how to get here?" he asked her. "Venice is filled with dead ends. It's just off Abbot Kinney Boulevard."

Jordan smiled into the phone, grateful for the small, upward turn of her spirits. She'd been pretty anxious before Dom called. "I'll find it. Don't worry."

Cynthia chose that moment to come into the breakfast alcove, and she raised her eyebrows at the sight of Jordan on the telephone so early in the morning.

"I have to go now," Jordan told Dom, and pushed the off button.

Cynthia sat down and rang the small porcelain bell in front of her. She wore a long green silk dressing gown, and without her careful makeup and hairdo, which she always attended to after breakfast, she seemed tired. With a start Jordan realized that although her mother-in-law was close to seventy—no longer considered old—her heart condition made her appear fragile, even elderly.

Maybe, Jordan considered, she needed to rethink last night's decision to let her in on the current situation.

"Who were you talking to?" Cynthia asked.

Jordan almost lied but didn't like herself for the impulse. "Detective D'Annunzio."

"That policeman?"

"Yes."

Cynthia sniffed as Sofia appeared in the doorway, her broad, peasant's body clad in a cotton print dress and apron, her hair off her face in a neat bun. The housekeeper glanced at the half-eaten piece of melon on Jordan's plate, then at her. "Will you be wanting anything else, Mrs. Jordan?" she asked in her Eastern European accent.

"No, thank you, Sofia." Her appetite, never hearty, had been practically nonexistent lately.

"And you, madame?" she asked Cynthia.

"Just some toast and tea, Sofia, thank you."

After the housekeeper had left, Cynthia picked up the newspaper folded by her place and opened it to the obituaries, as she did each morning. Jordan took another sip of her coffee, cold now, and glanced at her watch. She had time to talk to Cynthia for a few moments and still make it to Dom's house before he had to leave.

As she got up to pour herself a fresh cup at the sideboard, Cynthia spoke from behind her newspaper. "Are you working today?"

"I think I'll drop by the shop for a couple of hours."

"Did you happen to remember that we have the myasthenia gravis dinner tonight at the Bel-Air?" The way the question was phrased made Jordan realize that her mother-in-law was sure she did not remember. Which was correct—she had completely forgotten.

Seating herself again, Jordan took another sip of coffee, hot and welcome. "I'm not sure I can go."

"Will you be seeing that policeman instead?"

Jordan's defensiveness clicked in, but she counseled herself not to let the remark get to her. She had nothing to apologize for, nothing to be ashamed of. "Not tonight," she said truthfully. "But I do like him," she added, "so I expect I'll be seeing more of him."

Setting the paper down, Cynthia stared at her, her mouth pursed in disapproval. "So, you're going to that shop today—" she made *shop* sound like a piece of sour fruit "—you're going to renege on an obligation you made, and you're involved with that policeman."

"That policeman," Jordan said, trying not to show her irritation, "has a name. It's Dominic D'Annunzio, and he's been very good to me. Really, Cynthia, I—"

She cut the sentence off as Sofia entered the room, carrying a tray with Cynthia's toast and tea. In the Carlisle house, one never discussed personal matters in front of the servants. Her mother-in-law glanced at the housekeeper and smiled. "Thank you, Sofia."

After Sofia disappeared into the kitchen, Cynthia stirred two sugar cubes into her tea, arched an eyebrow and said, "You were saying?"

She would not discuss Dom with her mother-in-law, Jordan decided. Nor would she tell her about Michael. In truth, she could not impart anything of importance to her. They shared a house, but it was as if they came from different planets, spoke untranslatable languages.

Over the years, Jordan had yearned to be a part of a loving family. Her parents had died in a flu epidemic five years earlier, and Jordan rarely spoke to her younger brother, whose life as a Wyoming rancher kept him overworked and closed-minded. But Cynthia would not fill the void.

The older woman went on, her tone clipped and condescending. "Jordan, I find myself mystified by your behavior. I hope I have provided a good home and a reasonable allowance for my son's widow. I hope I have done my duty by you. But, in all candor, I do not understand you. I expected—"

Jordan cut her off. "Your duty?" she repeated, surprised by the deep well of bitter sadness this discussion was tapping into. "That's all I am to you, isn't it? Your duty."

Cynthia seemed taken aback by Jordan's response. "Well, I didn't really mean that."

"What *did* you mean?" she asked, again surprised at her strong reaction—hadn't she just admitted to herself that she and Cynthia were worlds apart?—but unable to mask the hurt anyway. "What *did* you expect? That I would go on behaving as I did when Reynolds was alive? The perfect trophy wife? The gracious hostess? The perfect mouse?"

On the verge of tears, Jordan bit her lower lip to keep them in. She was too raw to be having this discussion. "Cynthia," she went on more quietly, "I thank you for all you've done for me, really I do. And I'm sorry about tonight. I've had a lot on my mind lately."

The older woman sniffed, her expression remaining stiff and unyielding.

Jordan gave up. *You're not enough,* a voice inside mocked her, but she knew it was an old voice. Old tapes. She was enough, she told herself, just not for this frail, set-in-her-ways woman. A woman who was not her mother and didn't want to be considered for the job.

So she would manage without her. As Jordan rose from the table, the phone rang. Cynthia picked it up. "Hello?... Oh, Mabel. Hold on just a moment." Putting her hand over the mouthpiece, she said, "I'm not sure what we decided. Are you going tonight or aren't you?"

At the doorway, Jordan stared at her. A sense of responsibility came with being beholden to another person. "I'll go," she said. "We'll go together, okay?"

Her mother-in-law nodded, then spoke into the phone. "Mabel, what in the world has you up at this ungodly hour?" Her tone was warm and chatty, but Jordan would not torture herself again with wondering why her mother-in-law never spoke to her that way.

She left the room, the sound of Cynthia's dry laugh trailing after her.

When Jordan knocked on the door, Dom opened it right away. Her face lit up in a smile at the sight of him, and he answered with one of his own. They'd parted only hours ago, but the two of them stood in his doorway now, grinning at each other like idiots. Damn, he thought, she looked good today in a sleek, short dress and heels. Her legs were long and perfect, and he really wanted to know how they would feel wrapped around his waist.

Remembering his manners, Dom said, "Should I invite you in?" then added warningly, "the place is a mess."

Laughing, she handed him the plastic bag with Wally's three letters and shook her head.

"No, it's okay. I know you have to leave."

He grabbed another plastic bag, containing her money belt, from a table just inside the door, then closed the front door and locked it. "Come. I'll walk you to your car."

On either side of the walkway there were patches of faded grass and two rows of sad-looking bushes. No flowers. Theresa had kept the garden up. Today, as he and Jordan approached her car, he wished he were more of a gardener.

His musings almost made him miss what she was saying. "So I've thought of a way to help out." With one hand on the Rover's door handle, she told him about her planned meeting with Hal.

"The guy you were with at Bistro Rodeo?"

"I wasn't with him, I ran into him."

"He a good friend of yours?" Dom knew he sounded prickly.

"He was a good friend of Reynolds's. Why?"

"He's a creep," he told her bluntly.

Chuckling, Jordan looked at her car keys, playing with them. "You two didn't like each other on sight, I could tell."

He rested a hand on the roof of the Rover. "I can smell creeps a mile off. How about I talk to him instead of you?"

"Why do I get the sense that talking to someone is a little different for you than it is for me? What are you going to do?" Cocking her head, she went on in a mock tough-guy accent, "Make him an offer he can't refuse?"

''Nah—that's not my style.'' He paused, then added, only half-kidding, ''Not unless it's necessary.''

''How about you let me handle this one?'' She placed a hand on his arm. ''It will be all right, I promise.''

He didn't like it, but then, who was he to forbid her to talk to anyone? ''Just be careful,'' he said gruffly. ''Okay?''

With a soft laugh, she opened her car door. ''I promise.'' Then she turned, glanced up and down the street and gave him a quick kiss on the mouth.

His lips burned after she had driven off. He ran his tongue over them and nodded. Soon, he promised himself. Real soon.

Jordan called Hal at his office on her morning coffee break. She'd been looking through a few of Reynolds's old suits, she told Hal, before giving them to charity, and had found a diamond pin with Myra inscribed on it. Did Hal know this Myra? When he hedged, Jordan said, ''It's all right, Hal. I knew about his mistresses. He used to tell me.''

''No way.''

''Oh, yes,'' Jordan said smoothly, playing with the phone cord in the shop's office. ''It was part of our agreement. We went our separate ways. Hal—'' she made her voice sound confidential ''—I really didn't care, and that's the truth. This Myra, I thought she might want the pin.''

''Toss it.''

''I considered that,'' Jordan said quickly, ''but, it doesn't feel right. Maybe she'd want something from him, to remember him by. Did he mention her?''

''Who? Myra? Sure. She was around those last couple months, before he—'' He cleared his throat. ''Well, you know.''

She reined in the sudden burst of exhilaration. Hal knew Myra! Careful, she told herself. Keep it casual. ''Good. So then, do you know where she lives? Her last name?''

After a moment of silence, Hal came back on the line with a sly, insinuating tone. ''What are you willing to give me in return?''

"My gratitude."

"How grateful will you be?"

Even as her stomach churned with disgust, she knew she had to play along. "That depends on what you tell me," she said silkily. "For instance, her last name?"

"I don't know."

"Did you ever meet her?"

"Sure, yeah. I ran into him with her a couple of times. Blond, flashy, big boobs, you know. But who the hell can remember last names?"

The phone cord was getting more and more tangled as Jordan continued to twist it. "So," she persisted, "you don't know where she lived, anything about her."

Hal's low, intimate chuckle turned her stomach. "How 'bout if I make something up?"

Disappointed, she let the cord go limp. "That won't help, will it? If you remember anything, let me know, okay? I appreciate it." She hung up before Hal could offer up any more innuendos.

"Foster! Her name is Myra Foster!"

Jordan stood on Dom's doorstep under the porch light. She wore a straight floor-length black gown with a high neck. Her arms were bare; a long strand of pearls was her only jewelry, and she took his breath away.

She was like something out of a Paris fashion show, slim and elegant. But still Jordan, he thought. Real flesh and blood under that exterior.

He'd been watching "Letterman" and drinking a beer when his doorbell had rung. He was bare-chested, barefooted and wore the bottom half of some old gray sweats. She looked like royalty, he felt like Sylvester Stallone way before he beat the champ.

Even so, man, was he glad she was here.

"Come in," he said.

As she passed him he got a whiff of her perfume. It was

something made from roses, both subtle and provocative, and it started his senses humming.

As he walked over to turn off the TV, Jordan said, "I'm sorry, I know I shouldn't have come here like this, without calling, but I wanted to tell you about Myra."

"No problem." He kept his tone even. He knew instinctively that she was buzzed, with a lot of energy to expend, so needed him to be calm.

She threw a tiny purse onto a chair, then began to pace in front of his fireplace, back and forth, back and forth. Not just buzzed, he thought, agitated as hell.

"Maybe you want to sit down?" he suggested.

"No. I can't. I'm too jumpy. Hal told me her name, Myra's, I mean. I saw him tonight at this gala, this stupid big event." She rubbed her hands together as she walked. "I hate them. Everyone brags about who has the deepest pockets and the latest million-dollar toy." She glanced at him, smiled apologetically. "Of course, it's for a good cause and all that, I mean, they raise money for charity—"

"Hey, you want to bad-mouth something, you don't need to apologize. Sure you don't want to sit? You're pretty wired."

"Yes, I know. I'm sorry."

"Don't be. How about something to drink? It might settle you down."

"All right."

She followed him to the kitchen, her high heels clicking on the linoleum. Good thing he'd done the dishes, put things away when he got home tonight. Still, there was probably some grease on the countertop, and it had been a while since anyone had mopped the floor, so he didn't turn on the overhead light. There was plenty of illumination offered by a small night-light near the stove.

He opened another beer for himself, got some brandy for her, poured it into a juice glass. He handed it to her, watched her sip it, then he leaned against the sink, didn't touch her. Not yet. "Take a deep breath," he told her and watched her as she did. "Better?"

Holding the glass in both hands between her small, high breasts, Jordan made an effort to smile. "Better." Then she frowned and shuddered, as though some unpleasant thought had just entered her head.

"What?"

She shook her head. "Nothing."

He reached a hand to her. "Tell me."

She met his gaze, then lowered hers, took his hand and moved to stand next to him at the counter. "Hal," she said. "You're right, he is a creep."

Dom felt his jaw tensing. "What did he do to you?"

"Just a little heavy breathing and an attempt at groping. Not that I let him, I didn't. I wouldn't." She shook her head. "He disgusts me," she said quietly, then took another sip of her brandy, set it down on the tile counter.

Dropping Dom's hand, she moved away from him, her hands on her hips, pacing again. "I had no tolerance tonight for all the shallowness. You know how you can put up with something for a while, then you just can't any more? It made me think of all those years, being on display, for photographers, the public, on Reynolds's arm. An object, men wanting to possess me because my picture was on the cover of a magazine." She rubbed her hands up and down her arms. "Undressing me with their eyes everywhere I went. So many lost years. Too many."

She stopped moving, gazed at him out of deeply troubled eyes. "I didn't want to be there. All I was doing was waiting. All day, I've been waiting, to hear from you about the fingerprints, to hear from Hal if he remembered Myra's last name, to get another note from Wally. Waiting, waiting, waiting. To be with my son again." Her eyes filled.

He pushed himself away from the sink, pulled her into the living room, put his arms around her. She smelled like brandy and old roses. "Yeah, waiting's tough."

She sank into him, rested her head and hands on his chest for a few moments and let him hold her. She was so thin, he thought. And so tense. He laid his cheek on the top of her head and closed his eyes as they stood there.

After a while, Jordan raised her head, looked at him and grimaced ruefully. "Here I am, falling apart on you again. It's a pattern. I never do this. This is terrible. Just awful." She tried to step away from him. "I'm sorry. I don't even know why I'm here. I need—"

"Shh," he said, cupping her face in his hands. "I know exactly what you need."

Chapter 9

He kissed her then, his action a surprise yet not a surprise, his mouth soft yet not soft. Shocked, Jordan froze for a moment, then she pulled away. "Dom, I can't," she said. "We shouldn't."

He kissed her neck. "We can and should."

"But Michael—" she began.

"Shh," he said again, licking behind and around her ear, setting up a new kind of hum in her bloodstream. Closing her eyes, Jordan threw her head back, allowing his mouth and tongue further access to the area beneath her chin.

Dom reached behind her for the dress's zipper and slowly drew it down. "We can't go after Michael right now, can we? Let it happen, Jordan. Let it go. Just for tonight."

Her eyes were still closed, and she tried to come up with more reasons they couldn't do this. Then she felt her dress slide from her and onto the floor and heard Dom's gasp. Her eyes opened to see that he'd taken a step back and was staring at her. Beneath the dress, she'd worn a black lace demibra, matching bikini pants and garter belt and black silk stockings.

His hands were clenched into fists by his side. His eyes devoured her. "God," he breathed. "You're like a dream."

She had to fight the urge to cover herself with her hands. The desire in Dom's eyes was so potent, she felt more than a small amount of trepidation. Would she please him? Or would he be disappointed with her? The worry stayed with her even as he unhooked her bra and removed it slowly, taking his time. He suckled her bared breasts—were they too small for him? she worried even as her nipples hardened into diamond-hard points.

His mouth and hands skimmed over her rib cage. She watched him, heard herself groan as he played all around her garter belt but didn't remove it. Kneeling, he kissed the inside of her thighs. That was when her knees began to shake.

"I need to sit down, Dom," she gasped.

"Not yet," he murmured. "Brace yourself on my shoulders."

She dug her fingers into the muscles of his shoulders as he kissed and tongued all around that most sensitive area, closer and closer to the junction of her thighs. Her panties were wet, and most of her self-consciousness was gone. He pulled off her panties, discarded them, cupped her buttocks and buried his face between her legs. At that point, she stopped thinking at all. A long groan ripped from the back of her throat as his tongue found all her secret crevices.

He was amazingly tuned to her, his hands and tongue all-knowing about what she needed. As he tended to the small bud that was the center of desire, Jordan's shuddering spread from her knees all over her body. He had a tight grip on her so she wouldn't fall, but she was shaking so hard she thought she might break apart.

Up, up, up she went, spiraling toward some peak she couldn't see but knew was there. As he urged her on, her groans mixed with Dom's, her sighs became moans as she neared the apex of sensation. When she found it, she let out a long scream and began to buck in Dom's embrace, pushing against his face like a wild bronco.

But he stayed where he was, firm and in control, holding her, kissing and caressing her, until she began her descent.

Dom didn't give Jordan any time to come down. His body was insane with need. He lowered her onto the carpet, tore off his sweatpants. Remembered about protection just in time. He reached for his wallet, which was—lucky for both of them— on the table right here in the living room. He reached in, found a condom and slipped it on.

He took a moment to gaze at her. Jordan lay panting on the carpet, her loud sighs music to his ears. She'd been so wired, he'd wanted her to have the relief of an orgasm right away. What surprised him was the power of her release. She'd come apart like she'd been waiting for him all her life.

"Jordan?"

She opened her eyes, saw him above her, ready for her. There was a brief flash of concern in her eyes, then she smiled, opened her arms. "Yes," she said. "Please, I want you in me."

Without waiting for any other invitation, Dom plunged into her to the hilt. "God!" he cried out. The fit was perfect, she was so tight, she was everything he'd fantasized. It was an effort, but he forced himself to hold still just for a little while longer. She had more to give him, more pleasure to take.

Leaning over, he thrust his tongue in her mouth, rubbed her nipples with his thumbs, heard her gasp with surprise. Her hips rotated beneath him, as though urging him to move in her. Still he held back. Gathering her hands, he held them over her head, then moved his mouth from hers and over the column of her neck, sucking as though drawing life blood from her.

Jordan's body began to writhe with impatience, so he gave her what she wanted. Slowly he withdrew partway, then pushed into her with all the force of the first time. Out again, then in, the intensity of his movements increasing each time.

He watched her face as more surprise, then ecstasy shone on it, and he pumped in and out, waited till she reached the crest. This time, as her muscles clenched around him, as every one of his muscles tightened into unbearable tension, he roared his release into her. The sound he made was primal. He poured it all into her, everything he'd been saving for her since the day he'd first set eyes on Jordan Carlisle.

When it was over, Jordan somehow found herself lying on top of Dom. As she fought to catch her breath, she wasn't sure how she'd wound up in this position or if she remembered how to breathe. Wonder filled her. And awe. Had that really happened? Had that been Jordan Carlisle—the same woman her husband used to call boring and unexciting—who had given herself up so totally to sensuality, moaning and writhing all over the floor, even screaming in passion? How, Jordan wondered, had she gone so long without experiencing this total, no-holds-barred, *voluptuous* experience?

Her cheek lay against Dom's sweat-slick chest. His struggle for breath made her head rise and fall. Was she hurting him? she wondered. Instead of asking him, she rolled off him and onto the carpet. Just that effort cost her dearly, and for the next moments she lay on her back, totally depleted, her eyes closed.

''Oh,'' she said finally, dragging the word out.

''Mmm,'' she heard Dom say in reply.

Twice, she'd exploded with powerful orgasms. If she'd died the first time, she'd been reborn with the second. If her body was thoroughly, totally relaxed, her mind was adrift with hazy, delicious memories of sensations.

Dom's steady, even breathing made her wonder if he was asleep.

Opening her eyes, she gazed around the part of the small living room she could see from her position on the rug. Burnt orange corduroy-covered sofa, two paisley-patterned armchairs, pastoral scenes and family pictures on the walls. The room was cozy. Theresa, Jordan imagined, had put it all together, and her taste had been good.

Jordan turned her head to gaze at Dom. His eyes were closed, one arm slung above his head, the other resting loosely by his side. His chest hair and underarm hair was black and curly, as were all the other thatches of hair on his body. And she was in the position to know.

She raked his form with her gaze. Tawny skin, thick muscles, strength of body. He was perfect.

"Are you asleep?" she asked him.

He grunted noncommittally. He'd probably hate it if she tried to discuss what had just happened between them. But she wanted to talk about it, needed to tell him what it had meant to her. "You know," she began, "I thought I wasn't going to be very good at this."

He frowned but didn't open his eyes. "You're kidding."

She turned onto her side, crooked her elbow and rested her cheek on it. "Well, I'm a little out of practice," she said with a smile. "There hasn't been anyone since Reynolds's death. And," she added with candor, "there wasn't much of him before then."

Dom's eyes popped open, and he angled his head to look at her. "I don't understand."

"In case you haven't gotten it yet," Jordan said ruefully, "my husband wasn't a very nice man. Oh, he could be charming and thoughtful, when it was convenient, when he wanted something. He came after me, got me, then didn't want me anymore."

As her body temperature returned to normal, she felt a chill. She spied a crocheted afghan draped over an ottoman, so she grabbed it and covered herself with it, then resumed. "Anyway, I lived with him for ten years, and until then I don't think I ever realized the extent to which one human being can bring down another. It was subtle, I think, gradual, like Chinese water torture."

"How?"

"Oh, a little comment here, a small dig there. He made me feel awful about myself, and of course I played a part in it— the partner always does in these things. I let him. I hardly ever defended myself or stood up for myself. I don't think I knew how."

His mouth thinned. "Did he treat you badly in bed?"

"No, it was more like neglect. All the lovers he had, all his conquests—he would tell me about them and explain it was because I didn't satisfy him.''

Dom's nostrils flared, and he turned his head so he was gazing upward. ''Another creep. If he were still alive, I'd take him and his buddy Hal into an alley.'' He shot her a glance. ''You didn't believe that bull, did you?''

She lifted her shoulder. ''Remember, I was eighteen when I met him, and not real experienced, so yes, I believed him.''

He turned onto his side so he was facing her. Leaning on one elbow, he studied her, then reached over to adjust the afghan so it covered her more completely. She wondered if he was aware of that unconscious caretaking gesture, of the several unconscious caretaking gestures he'd shown her since the day they'd met. She wondered if he knew how much goodness he had under that tough-guy exterior.

Dom regarded her. ''You started modeling at, what? Fifteen? What was that like?''

She was in a talkative mood, as though something had been released from prison and needed the air. ''I was scared a lot of the time. I think I was still unable to believe that my career was anything other than a fluke and that one day someone would come along, snap his fingers and say, okay, it's over. Back to the Wyoming dust. I used to huddle in my hotel rooms and watch old movies on TV.''

She reached over and smoothed a lock of hair off his forehead. ''All of which goes back to the fact that I was a blank slate when I met Reynolds, and spent the next ten years of my life feeling like an insignificant carpet. Not a pretty picture, huh?''

His nostrils flared again, and she knew he was on the verge of saying something crude about her late husband. She put her fingertips on his mouth to hush him. ''Don't,'' she said. ''It's over, I got past it, I'm a grown-up now, no longer a child.''

He took her hand in his and kissed the palm. ''Amen to that,'' he murmured.

His mouth on her skin made her feel all warm inside. ''And

besides, when Michael came along, I changed. Motherhood can change you.''

Dom's gaze flickered to a point above her head, and he brought her hand to the carpet. A frown creased his brow, ending the brief moment of sensuality. ''So can lack of motherhood.''

Jordan angled her head to glance behind her, following the direction of his gaze toward the fireplace mantel. A framed portrait of a woman was placed there. She was round-faced, with sandy colored hair and freckles and an open, sweet smile. Jordan turned to face Dom. ''I take it that's Theresa.''

Dom nodded, unable to speak. Theresa had been staring at him and Jordan the whole time they'd been making love, had been witness to all the acrobatics, the tastes, the smells, the sighs and the screams.

Not that he actually believed Theresa was there, in that picture. But the spirit of her haunted him still in a vague, unsettling way.

''Hey, Dom.''

Jordan's voice brought him to the present. She lay on her side, her straightened arm serving as a pillow for her head. She gazed at him, her expression filled with a sweet, trusting tenderness that about broke his heart.

''Are you all right?'' Her concern for him was obvious.

''Yeah, I'm okay.''

''I did what you told me, you know. Put away my worries about Michael for tonight, let myself go. Are you having trouble doing the same thing? I mean—'' He watched her fumble for the words, waited.

''This must be hard for you,'' she said finally. ''We both have spouses who are gone, but my memories are, well, not exactly fond ones. Yours are the good kind. Do you feel— I mean, is it like you're being unfaithful to Theresa or something, making love with me?''

''Don't, Jordan,'' he warned, as his defensive hackles rose. She was trying to get into his head again, in that way she had, and he wasn't sure this was a good time to let her. ''This has nothing to do with Theresa. You have nothing to do with Theresa, nothing at all.''

"I know that. But these things are complicated," she persisted. "I mean, we can tell ourselves we should be feeling a certain way, but—" She left the sentence unfinished, then shrugged. "Okay, you'll talk to me when you want to. I won't pry."

She yawned, then pulled the afghan a little more tightly around herself.

"Are you cold?"

"I wouldn't mind moving to the bedroom."

Again, he felt his back stiffen at what was a perfectly reasonable suggestion. In the three years since Theresa's death, he'd never brought another woman to the house. He'd always gone to their place. But he'd broken that little tradition tonight, hadn't he? Another woman was most definitely on the premises. Was he ready to bring that other woman to his marriage bed?

Marriage bed? The phrase echoed in his head. Old-fashioned nonsense. He was a single man, his wife had been gone for three years, he slept in a bed, he could do in that bed as he pleased. But even as he told himself how he should be feeling—there was that word again, *should*—turmoil raged in his gut.

Did he think Theresa would judge or punish him for having sex? Nah. Hell, she'd have told him to take care of his needs as best he could. Yeah, Theresa would have understood. But it felt as though she was judging him for *something*.

No, he realized. He was judging himself and laying it on Theresa. He could screw his brains out with a hundred faceless women and no problem. But with Jordan, it was more than screwing, and that made it different. It meant giving and receiving promises he couldn't keep. He might mean them at the time, but they wouldn't stick, and his late wife's picture was there to remind him of that very fact.

But Jordan was here and she was cold and he needed to take care of her. He scrambled to his feet, pulling her up with him.

He adjusted the afghan so it was draped around her more tightly, then led her past the guest bedroom that had, one time or another, housed various members of his and Theresa's large families. The door was open, and a night-light burned brightly enough to reveal cartons and papers scattered on the floor, stacks of files on the bed.

He grimaced. "The place is a mess, but it's not dirty. Someone comes in to clean twice a month."

His bedroom was only slightly better. At least he'd pulled the covers up that morning, and he'd changed the sheets a few days before. A table lamp was on, so it was impossible to miss the clothing draped over the small armchair in the corner. Dresser drawers were open, a trash basket was filled with gum wrappers and old newspapers, and there was a general feeling of disorderliness.

"I'm not much good around the house, you know, domestically. Or is that obvious?"

Jordan offered a wry smile. "I'm not here to grade you on your housekeeping skills. You have other gifts." With a laugh, she climbed into his bed, then opened her arms to him.

He wanted to laugh with her, but somehow he couldn't. Instead, he sat on the edge of the bed, his back to her. A cigarette. Damn, how he wanted a cigarette. For some reason, the words of an old greeting card he'd seen when he was about nine popped into his head. Something about lifting a glass to the three greatest pleasures in life—a cocktail before and a cigarette after. He'd brought the card to school—he'd just discovered the facts of life, and he and his buddies had found the suggestive message uproariously funny. Sister Mary Magdalena hadn't agreed, and for days after, his knuckles were raw from her punishment.

"Hey," Jordan said softly.

Her voice zoomed him to the present. He looked at her.

"Where were you?" she asked, her fingertips stroking his back.

Her touch felt so good, so real. "Thinking about the nuns."

"Excuse me?"

He lay on his back, his head resting on his bent arms, and stared at the ceiling. "There was one who had a face like a prune, and she made my life hell."

"Why? I mean, how did a nun come up?"

"I guess I am a little guilty," he said, feeling he owed Jordan honesty. "Like I said, it has nothing to do with you, but…"

He struggled to find the right words, and to her credit, Jordan didn't prompt him. She waited until he began to speak. "See," he began without making eye contact, "we had a bargain, Theresa and I. She wanted marriage, a large family, a home with a garden—we didn't have gardens in my part of Brooklyn—and I would give her those things."

"What was her part of the bargain?"

"To be a good cop's wife, which is a rough thing to be. She never complained, rarely nagged. Put up with my moods. There were always hot meals when I got home. And…she loved me unconditionally."

"How lucky you were," she murmured, "to have had that."

Saint Theresa, Jordan thought, and she sounded too good to be true. Too darned perfect. For the first time, Jordan wondered if—in memory—Dom had placed his late wife on a pedestal, if his view of her was unrealistic, if he'd glossed over the bad times.

"Yeah, I was lucky," he said.

"So what's the guilt about?"

"About the night she died, for starters."

"I know you weren't there, and it was a horrible death, I'm not minimizing that. But you were working. How could you work—how could anyone work—and be with her twenty-four hours a day?"

"You don't know the whole story. It was this motherhood thing. She wanted babies. God, she wanted them so much. You should have seen her with her sister's kids, she went nuts with the little ones. And we kept getting pregnant, and she kept having miscarriages. Finally the doctor said no more, that it was dangerous for her. So I said fine, we'll adopt, but she wanted to give me a child.'' He angled his head, and his troubled brown eyes met hers. "I swear, it wasn't that important to me.''

"I believe you.''

He was *talking* to her, Jordan thought, rejoicing silently. He was letting her in without fighting, without his tough-it-out attitude toward confidences. She felt honored and a little scared, too. She didn't want to say the wrong thing, didn't want to shut off the spigot of his confession.

"Then, those last couple of years,'' he went on more slowly, "it was all she could think about. I would come home and find her crying, and she'd wipe her eyes and lie and say she'd just been watching a sad movie. She was depressed, real depressed. I tried to get her to get some help, but she pooh-poohed it. I didn't push it.''

"Then she got pregnant again.''

"Yeah, and she didn't tell me this time. I had no idea about that last one. Her sister Patty told me about it afterward. Theresa had been so happy, she knew this one was going to be okay. She was going to wait, Patty said, until she got past the fourth month and then surprise me with the news.'' He closed his eyes, and she saw him fighting for control.

She laid her hand on his arm, compassion for him filling her. Let it out, she told him silently, all of it. Jordan, of all people, knew how important it was to exorcise ghosts. If a painful secret was kept inside, it festered like an untreated wound. It invaded the rest of your mind, your brain, your personality. It changed you.

"Do you know what happened that last night?'' she asked gently.

He opened his eyes, stared at the ceiling. "We reconstructed it later. She probably woke up with real bad stomach pain. The tube had burst, the doctor said. She went to the bathroom, fell to the floor. Either she was hurting so bad she couldn't crawl to the phone or she just passed out and bled to death.''

Tears of sympathy for a woman she'd never met gathered in Jordan's eyes. She removed her hand from his arm to wipe under her lids, and that movement drew Dom's attention. An expression of sheer misery on his face, he turned onto his side, away from her. She watched his ribs move up and down with his breathing.

Several moments went by before he spoke again, and she stared at his back as he did. "You want to know why I'm guilty?" he said, his voice hoarse with feeling. "It wasn't just that I wasn't here the night of her death. I didn't push her to get help for her depression. I didn't keep tabs on our birth control, didn't wear a condom or even get a vasectomy. I didn't make sure she was protected, didn't convince her that adoption was a fine thing to do. We had a bargain, Theresa and I, and I didn't keep my end of it. I didn't keep her safe. My mind wasn't on the home front—it was on my job. I was the bread-winner, yeah. Good cop, lousy husband. I wasn't there for her. I wasn't there for Theresa."

Dom's shoulders shook with emotion, but he kept himself angled away from her. Jordan moved closer, curving her body against his, slung her arm over his ribs and hugged him as tightly as she could. She felt his thick chest hair against her palm, felt the rapid beating of his heart. If he was crying, he did it soundlessly, and it was obvious he didn't want her to see his face as he did.

Still, she told herself, he was letting her in, allowing her to be present while his insides ached with grief. It was a start, a good one.

They lay like that for a while, then she felt his hand cover hers and press it tightly to his chest. Cuddling even closer to him, she kissed his back. "Would you like to hear my guilt story?" she murmured.

She felt Dom go still, then he turned onto his other side and faced her. His eyes were dry but slightly reddened, and she wondered idly if men's tears were somehow thicker than women's so that less of them escaped the tear ducts.

"You?" When she nodded, he said, "Tell me."

"For months, I thought Michael's death was my fault. You see, I shouldn't have let Reynolds take him for the day. I knew he was in one of his foul moods and that his driving could be erratic. I was going to go with them, but I had a bad headache that day, and Reynolds said he would take him without me. I wanted Michael to have a close relationship with his father, so I let him go. I made Reynolds promise he would be extra careful with his son in the car, which annoyed him, I know it, maybe even made him drive carelessly, on purpose, to get back at me. Afterward, I kept saying if only I hadn't let him go, if only I'd been along, if only I hadn't had that headache.''

Dom nodded. ''If only I'd called in during the night she died, if only I'd had a phone in the bathroom for her.''

''If only, if only.''

There was silence as they gazed at each other. It was a moment of perfect communication, Jordan thought, no walls, no attitude. Keeping her attention fixed on his serious face, she traced the curve of stubble on his chin with her thumb. He grabbed her hand and kissed the palm. ''I had a Catholic childhood,'' he said with a mocking smile. ''What's your excuse?''

''Just garden-variety insecurity, I guess.''

He kissed her palm again, then used the tip of his tongue to trace the lines that told the story of her life.

In an instant, Jordan felt a flash of heat between her legs, followed by an ache of longing. Again? she thought. Should I be doing this again? It seemed her body had the answer to her question. Already it was throbbing with need just from one small contact with Dom's tongue.

''You're very good at this,'' she said, lowering her eyelids suggestively. ''Did it take a lot of practice?''

''Nah, I think I had a natural bent.''

Was this really her? Jordan wondered again, as Dom lowered his mouth to hers. This woman making sexual innuendos and feeling and acting confident about her attractiveness—was this really Jordan Carlisle? Sure was, she answered herself. Most definitely. And she liked this Jordan, liked her a lot.

''I agree,'' she murmured a while later, ''you do have a gift. Better watch it. I think I could get used to this.''

"Fine with me," he murmured.

As soon as she'd said the words, she'd wanted to recall them. She'd meant them as light pillow talk, a joke to counteract the heavy emotion she was feeling. But the words sounded possessive, as though she were making plans for the future.

Was that what she was doing? Was this mixture of emotions she felt when she was with him—trust, gratitude, intense and fulfilling passion and a craving for intimacy—was this what was meant by love? If so, she had never experienced it before.

Get off this, she told herself, as a familiar anxiety started up. The one that said she wasn't worthy of feeling or being loved. No. Stop. Old tapes.

And besides, this was way too soon. With mounting horror, she realized she was being a typical woman. Meet a man you click with, in bed and out, and that first night you begin planning the honeymoon.

Honeymoon? What was she getting herself into here? Way, way too soon, probably not even in the cards. Dom had a lot of inner demons, and she couldn't possibly be feeling love, not yet.

No, no, no, she told herself silently. Too heavy. She was ruining a delicious afterglow with old voices and introspection.

Opening her eyes, Jordan found herself looking right into Dom's. He lay on his stomach, his hands underneath his pillow, his head turned toward her. She wondered how long he'd been staring at her and what he was thinking about.

"Your husband was nuts," he said. "You are one hell of a passionate woman."

His words made her blush. "With you," she said, smiling into his warm brown eyes. "With you," she repeated softly.

As the expression on Jordan's face registered in Dom's fuzzy brain, a faint alarm sounded. There was satisfaction, affection, admiration in the way she looked at him. And the soft glow of a woman on the verge of falling in love.

He felt warmed, flattered, moved...at first.

Then the opposite reaction set in, and he felt threatened. What had he gotten himself into here?

There was no doubt the woman got to him, touched deep parts of him that hadn't been touched since the early years with Theresa, before the baby insanity took her over and he'd erected a wall of protection around himself. He liked his wall, damn it. It got him through the days and nights.

But Jordan's very existence seemed to be nibbling at the edges of his wall. He'd opened up to her, shared his deepest pain. She brought out a tender side of him he would have denied he possessed, would have laughed at only a few weeks before.

Something about this woman, especially tonight, made his trustworthy, hard-as-nails cynicism shut off, get put on hold. Tonight, he'd made love to her and with her. Tonight he'd *felt*.

It scared the piss out of him.

Dom shifted his focus around the room and let it stop at the old oak dresser on the far wall. There, in a silver frame, stood another picture of Theresa, this time as she'd been in high school. Braces, hair in pigtails. She hadn't wanted him to display that picture of her, but he'd insisted. He'd loved the spunky kid she'd been back then, loved being reminded of how she looked just before her metamorphosis into womanhood.

He returned his gaze to Jordan. Her eyes were closed, her breathing even, a gentle, satisfied smile on her face. Don't, he wanted to tell her. Don't. I can't make you happy, he wanted to say.

He would say it. He owed her that. "Jordan?"

Her eyes opened with a start. "What time is it?"

Glancing at the bedside clock, he said, "Three."

"I have to go." She threw back the covers and scrambled to her feet.

"Why?"

"Cynthia will worry."

"So what?"

Dom might have been on the verge of warning her off him, but now that she seemed eager to leave his bed, he didn't like it, didn't like it at all. She hurried from the room, made a quick stop in the bathroom, then headed toward the living room, where her clothing was.

Grumbling, he got out of bed, found his robe and put it on. Scratching his head, he followed Jordan into the living room. What he needed was some sleep, but damn it, he wanted Jordan there with him, sleeping alongside him.

She sat on the faded ottoman, pulling on one sheer black stocking and hooking it to the lace garter belt. She wore nothing else at the moment—the pose was like something on a naughty French postcard—and the sight of her long legs and bare breasts had the undeniable effect of making him hard all over again. He was like a randy kid around her—couldn't get enough, always ready for more.

His resentment dissipated as he leaned on the door frame and crossed his arms over his chest. "You sure you have to go? I could make it worth your while to stay."

She glanced at him, caught the meaning of his words and smiled regretfully. "I'm sure."

"Why do you live with her?" he asked, then winced. "Stupid question. I mean, you probably love living in that big house. Most people would."

She cocked her head. "But not you?"

"Nah," he said honestly. "All that room, it would make me nervous. I'm used to ten people and one bathroom."

"Yes," she said thoughtfully, "there is a lot of room in that house. And it's the emptiest, coldest place I've ever been in."

She pulled on the other stocking, then rose, picked up her gown and lowered it over her head. It fell in soft folds over her body. He didn't like seeing her covered up again, all elegant and unattainable. Of course, he reminded himself, she only seemed unattainable. He knew differently.

"So, seriously," he asked, "why do you live there?"

"It's temporary. I can't afford to live anywhere else at the moment," Jordan told him. "There's nothing left of my modeling money, and Reynolds's estate was tied up in a family trust, so I didn't inherit anything. After the tragedy, I had nowhere else to go, and Cynthia wanted me to live there. I was in pretty bad shape, had no inner resources left. So I live with my mother-in-law. For now, anyway. If all goes well, I'll be moving out in a few more months.''

"Do you two…get along?"

He tried to sound neutral, but she read between the lines and smiled grimly. "She wasn't very pleasant or welcoming to you, was she?"

He shrugged. "I figure she's a snob. You got a lot of them in Beverly Hills. Goes with the territory."

"Yes, she is a snob," Jordan said thoughtfully. "Also vain and shallow. And she has a bad heart and is terrified of dying. But, funnily enough, once in a while, when she's a human being, when she forgets to be a Carlisle, I do get along with her. I even sometimes like her, although I don't think the feeling is mutual." She sighed, looked around the room. "However, at the moment, I'm all she has."

"Guilt again."

"Some. But I'm working on it." She found her earrings on a side table, put them on. "I guess when I get Michael back, I'll—"

"If," he interrupted.

"Excuse me?" Both hands were at her earlobe, adjusting the clasp as she looked up.

"*If* you get Michael back," he explained, emphasizing the first word.

"What do you mean, if?"

Aware that he was destroying the nice afterglow, but unable to see any way around it, Dom pushed himself away from the door frame, walked toward her, stood facing her. "Hey, Jordan, you're assuming all kinds of stuff. First, that the kid in the picture is Michael."

"It is."

He took a beat, let her see his doubt. "Okay. Then you're assuming we'll find him."

"We will," she said forcefully, obviously upset with his attitude. "No matter how long it takes. *I* will."

Her intensity was one hundred percent real. She believed with all her heart. Dom could see it, could smell it on her skin.

Not just intensity, but obsessiveness. That powerful maternal urge that kept the race going but could also destroy women who had that urge frustrated. Theresa with no babies, Jordan with hopes that her baby had risen from the dead.

He grabbed her by the shoulders and lowered her onto the ottoman. She stared at him, confusion written across her face. "Listen to me," he said firmly. "I want you to promise me something."

"What?"

"Don't do anything more about meeting Wally's demands without me. If you get another note, if he sets up another little get-together, you call me immediately. If you find out any other information, you tell me right away. You let me handle things. But most of all, please stop kidding yourself, stop building up false expectations."

Shaking her head, she put both hands over her ears. "Why are you doing this? Why are you being so negative?"

He sat down on the nearby chair, pulled her hands away from her ears and held them between his. "This is not being negative, Jordan. This is being realistic. The guy could be conning you, probably is. I'm just trying to prepare you, keep you from getting your hopes up too much."

She ripped her hands from his grip. "This is not some missing child on a milk carton," she said with intensity, "this is my little boy, and through some strange twist of fate, he is alive and living elsewhere. I know you don't believe me, but I don't care. So, no, I will not leave everything to you. I have to help, have to play a part. I was the one who found out Myra's last name. I know I can find out more about her."

"How?"

"I'll go through Reynolds's records, his checkbooks." She ripped a hand through her hair, looked around the room wildly. "I'll call up his friends—surely one of them will know something."

"The more people you let in on this, the quicker Wally will disappear."

"But you're going to find Wally! You said you would. You have his fingerprints."

"And unless he's an ex-con, there may not be any fingerprints on file. Then it's a dead end. Again."

Her agitation grew. "Then we'll have to look for Wally Foster. We'll track down all Wally Fosters."

One more time, Dom took her hands, squeezed them to get his point across. They were ice cold and achingly slender. He put them against his chest to warm them. "Jordan," he said firmly. "Are you sure that's his last name? It's Myra's, or so Hal says. What if Foster was a married name or a stage name? Wasn't she planning to break into Hollywood? Wouldn't she have changed her name?"

"You have to stop this," she said, twisting away, trying to free her hands.

He held tight. "And you have to hear me. I want to get this guy, Jordan, but if you get too involved it might get screwed up."

"And who's to say if you get too involved it won't get screwed up?" she challenged.

"This is my job—it's what I do."

"Being a mother is what I do."

"Damn it, you're more than just a mother, and you know it."

"But not right now, Dom, not while each day passes without my son."

He started to counter, then changed his mind. Inhaling a deep, frustrated breath, he held it, then blew it out of his mouth impatiently. Dropping her hands, he rose, walked over to a window, looked out. Nowhere, he was getting nowhere with Jordan. Butting heads with an obsession.

Turning once more, he locked gazes with her, straight on. "I want your promise not to do anything on your own. I'm asking you. Please."

"Dom," she said, rising from the ottoman. "I'm going to cooperate the best I can. But you need to know that I will do anything, and I mean anything, to get my son back!'' She picked up her purse, fumbled for her keys and found them.

''Good night,'' she said tightly as she walked to the door and pulled it open. Then she paused, turned and offered him a wan smile. ''I know I'm sounding unreasonable and I'm sorry. But—'' she shrugged ''—there's nothing I can do about it. Please, Dom, try to understand.'' She chuckled then, but it was a weak, half-hearted, tired chuckle. ''Believe it or not, I had a lovely time tonight.''

Then she turned and walked out the door.

Dom watched her as she got into the Rover and drove down the block. As her taillights disappeared, he felt an ominous sinking in his gut.

Moments before, they'd been so close, sharing confidences and—despite his ambivalence and inner struggle—strengthening that connection they seemed to have together. But now, like a puff of smoke in a windstorm, it was gone.

Jordan was on her quest again. What, he wondered, would happen to the two of them along the way?

Chapter 10

Dom showed up at his desk early the next morning to attack the piles of paperwork that continued to multiply, one on top of the other, like the piggyback plants his mother used to nourish in the small kitchen window box. For a change, he'd woken up with Jordan in his head and on his mind, but this time with the taste of her in his mouth. Still, he was determined, this one morning, to put her on hold and to pay attention to his job.

He stared with disgust at the manila file folders, notebooks and loose sheets spread out on the desktop. As the bureaucracy grew, it created more and more forms to fill out—requisition forms, case status forms, unsolved, solved and pending, duty schedules, subpoenas currently tucked into his calendar pages. Every time a crime was committed, every time someone was questioned about that crime, a new mountain of paperwork was created. Paperwork was not his strong suit, never had been.

And even with all his cases staring accusingly at him, the one that was taking up most of his head was an unopened one—it didn't even have its own paperwork yet.

Jordan Carlisle's son was officially deceased—case closed.

To open it up again would involve a hell of a lot more than a mother's notion that a snapshot of some kid was her son one year after he was supposed to have died.

Muttering with disgust at how easily he'd gotten distracted from his vow to clear off his desk, Dom called to check on the status of Wally's fingerprint search—nothing yet—then walked himself over to records, where he finagled a readout on Reynolds Carlisle's death without having to deal with the computer himself, another non-strong suit.

As he stood there and leafed through the various forms, he ascertained that it was pretty much as Jordan had told him. Two burned bodies, adult male and child, no alcohol or drugs in Carlisle's system, no explanation of why the car had swerved and gone over the embankment. No witnesses, nothing. The coroner's report revealed that due to extensive damage, there had been no positive physical ID of the kid, but there was no doubt Michael Carlisle was the dead child in the back seat.

No positive physical ID. That small fact, Dom supposed, meant there was some chance, some possibility, however minuscule, that Jordan's hope was justified. Like one in a million.

Mulling it over, he headed to his desk. What else could he do? There were police artists, of course, computer specialists who could take a picture of the eighteen-month-old Michael and come up with what his face would look like a year later. Dom could probably call in a favor and get one of them to do a workup, see if it matched the picture Jordan had been sent. But he'd already asked Nick to follow Jordan, asked a contact in SSB to "unofficially" run the fingerprints for him, gotten records to access a file that had nothing to do with any of his cases. How many more favors could he ask on this one?

All law-enforcement officials did things under the table—if they didn't, nothing would get done. But he knew he was skirting the boundaries here, maybe even placing his job in jeopardy by using his status, his contacts, for a noncase, a purely personal matter. Jordan Carlisle.

Clear that desk, he admonished himself. Put her away. There was work to be done.

However, he finally admitted an hour later, leaning back in his desk chair and stretching his arms over his head, the work on his desk was not getting done. Not when he was so preoccupied with Jordan's situation.

Myra Foster. She was the link, and he needed to find her. She'd wanted to be an actress, so he'd start there. He hit the phones, called Screen Actor's Guild, Screen Extra's Guild, American Federation of Television and Radio Artists and Actor's Equity. The only Myra Foster registered was an extra, and she was seventy-two years old. There was also a Myra Ann Foster, age eight.

So, if she'd done any acting, she was nonunion, which meant she might have done some independent films, and there was no one central place to call for that kind of information.

How had Hal described her? Blond, big boobs, flashy. Maybe she'd done some porn, Dom thought. Possible. A lot of wannabe actresses who came to town went that road. Dom had a snitch, Manny McCabe, in the porn video field, from when he'd worked vice, so he called him up and asked him to find out what he could about Myra Foster, ASAP.

What else? Frowning, he stared again at the chaos on his desk. Man, oh, man, he did not want to be here.

At that moment, Steve came down the aisle between the cubicles, whistling. Throwing his sports jacket over his chair, he asked, ''How long you been here, my man?''

''Too long.''

''So why doesn't it look any neater than it did yesterday?'' Steve was the orderly type and loved to rag Dom about his clutter.

''That's because I was thinking about setting fire to the whole pile.''

The brown-skinned man nodded solemnly. ''It's a solution.''

A uniformed deputy hurried up to Steve's desk and dropped a sheaf of papers in his in basket. He plucked them up, read them.

''What?'' Dom asked.

"Our new assignment. Possible jewelry smuggling ring being run out of a pawnshop on Melrose."

Dom nodded, took the papers, checked them over, tossed them back to Steve. His partner sat and studied Dom for a moment, a furrow between his dark brows. "Hey, what's going on?"

"Huh?"

"You're not on the job. Your head is taking trips to some other planet."

"Yeah."

"So? What's up?"

Dom rubbed his hands over his face, then shook his head, hoping that might reassemble his scrambled brains into paying attention to his job. "Just some personal stuff. But you're right," he agreed, as more disgust heaped itself on top of the previous load. "I'm not present."

"Anything I can help with?"

Steve didn't know about the whole Jordan Wally Michael thing. Dom hadn't told his partner about his romantic involvement with Jordan. Hell, it was so new, had happened so fast, even he wasn't sure what to call it.

Besides, Dom figured, it was better to play this one close to the vest. Steve was a little more of a by-the-book type than Dom was, and he didn't want to jeopardize their working relationship. "Nah," he said, answering Steve's question. "I'm just beat, that's all. My bones ache."

"Yeah, you haven't been yourself for a while now. Know what I think? You need to take a little time off. What do you say? We get sick days—take 'em. Go somewhere. Or get into bed, watch some TV. You've been working way too hard."

Dom glanced at his partner, who nodded encouragingly. What Steve said was not a bad idea. He could take a couple of days, get this whole Carlisle affair cleaned up, close the file, then get back to what he did best. Nabbing the bad guys.

"What about the jewelry ring?" he asked Steve.

"I'll clear it with the commander, get him to give me Santos. The kid's ready. It's no problem. Really."

Dom considered some more. The idea was making sense. "Maybe you're right."

The phone rang, and he picked it up. "D'Annunzio," he said.

"Hey, this is Manny. I got what you wanted."

The porn snitch had hit paydirt. Myra Foster had done a couple of low-level porn flicks a few years back, then had disappeared from that end of show biz. He had an address on her, on Martel in Hollywood.

A phone call revealed she was no longer living there, and there was no forwarding address, but Dom drove over there anyway, to see what he could find.

Last night with Dom had been a lovely respite, but today Jordan was back to fretting about Michael. She was so glad to have her job. It kept her hands busy and her mind occupied. Still, when Lisa tapped her on the shoulder, she jumped.

"He's here again," Lisa said.

Jordan grabbed a size seven blouse that had found its way to the larges and walked it over to the smalls. "Who?" The moment it came out of her mouth, she knew.

"Your detective. This is getting to be a habit."

Jordan turned her head and saw Dom. He was at the front of the shop, one hip leaning against the counter, his elbow resting on the countertop. His gaze was focused in her direction, and even yards away from him, she could swear his eyes were boring into her very soul.

The sight of him made her breath hitch in her chest. He seemed to have that effect on her all the time, but it was worse today, ten times worse. Because today she had intimate knowledge of him, *all* of him. In the brief moment before she waved hello, she found herself mentally undressing him. Then she had to bite her bottom lip to suppress the nervous giggle that threatened to erupt.

He lifted his hand to acknowledge her wave, but she could have sworn he was aware of the picture in her head, because one side of his mouth curved up in a knowing smile.

''Be right there,'' Jordan said, smoothing her sweater over her hips, wondering if she had any lipstick on, experiencing all those self-conscious, preparing-for-a-lover feelings. Her lover. Yes. Dom was, most definitely, her lover.

Behind her, Lisa said in a low voice, ''So, how was it?''

''Hmm?'' Jordan said, distracted, unable to take her eyes off him.

''Between the sheets. One to ten.''

Turning, she glared at Lisa, but her friend's grin was too sweetly impudent to get angry at. In fact, Jordan couldn't stop herself from grinning. Then she turned and walked toward Dom, tossing words over her shoulder as she did. ''None of your business.''

''Darn.''

Oh, that face, Jordan thought as she approached Dom. All those hard, tough planes, those heavy-lidded brown eyes that remained steady on hers, that mouth with those full Roman lips that knew every which way to reduce her to a shivering, quaking, needy woman.

But if, after last night, he knew her all too well, she was onto him also. An outsider would see no expression on Dominic D'Annunzio's face, but she knew better now—lord, yes, she knew him—and underneath that poker face was the same hunger for her that she felt for him.

''I keep doing this to you,'' he said, straightening as she came toward him. ''I should have called first.''

When she'd been in the blouse section, his impact on her had been formidable. Close to him, it was as though she'd walked into pure hot sun from a fog-enshrouded cave. Heat came off him in waves that soaked into her skin. ''No, it's all right.''

As she came to a stop in front of him, he reached for her hands, and she placed them in his and squeezed. God, it was good to touch him.

''Do you have some news?'' she asked hopefully.

''Bits and pieces, yeah.''

Her heart rate jumped up a notch. She glanced around. She

couldn't leave Lisa to cope on her own, but at present there were only a couple of customers browsing through the mer- chandise. Jordan led Dom to the rear of the shop, where a pair of folding chairs sat outside the single dressing room. "Tell me," she said, sitting down and patting the seat next to hers.

He turned the chair around and straddled it, folding his arms over the chair back. "I got some info on Myra Foster."

"Oh, Dom, that's wonderful."

She hung on his every word as he recounted the details of the morning, his phone calls for information, his visit to a courtyard of thirties-era bungalows in Hollywood, the neighbor who remembered Myra and how she'd moved out a couple of years ago, saying something about hooking up with a rich guy. This neighbor had never heard about a brother, nor did she know Myra's hometown, but she did mention her little boy.

He'd been nearly a year old when Myra had moved, and his name had been Rory. "Sweetest little boy," the neighbor lady had told Dom. "Blond, like her. Never cried."

As she took in this last bit of news, Jordan's hand flew to her chest with shock. "Oh, my God," she said, her mind racing furiously. "Myra had a child, too. Almost the same age as Michael. Could he be the little boy who died? Dom? What do you think?"

Dom narrowed his eyes. "What I think is that you need to use some logic, Jordan, okay? The picture you saw? It was probably of Rory."

"No, it was Michael."

"How can you be sure? What if Reynolds was that kid's father, too? That might explain the resemblance."

"Oh," she said, her spirits plummeting. Weeks of hope plummeted with them. She was wrong, had been wrong all along, had been stupid to think she'd been blessed with a mir- acle.

"I suppose you're right," she said slowly, but then a re- membered snippet of conversation came to her that reversed the direction of her hopes once more. "I don't think so, Dom.

From what Hal said, Reynolds hadn't known Myra more than a few months.''

"But you don't know that, do you? Not for sure."

"No, of course I don't. I won't know, will I, until I see him." Closing her eyes, she took in a deep breath and let it out again. Her mind was still whirling, a free-for-all jumble of possibilities and explanations. "This is all so confusing. It makes my head spin."

Dom edged his chair closer, unfolded an arm and reached for one of her hands. He stared at their joined hands, rubbed her knuckles with his thumb, nodded. "Yeah, it's not an open and shut thing, not yet, anyway. But it'll all come together." Emitting a brief, humorless chuckle, he added darkly, "I hope."

Jordan could sense herself drifting into Dom's pessimism, so she fought against it. "Tell me, did you find out anything else?"

"No prints on the letters or pictures, but we got a couple of partials on the money belt. I sent it right through. I'll be paged when that comes in—later today, I hope."

Placing her other hand on top of his, she offered a worried smile. "I feel awful. You're taking so much time away from your own work."

"Right now, my work is this case. I want to get it resolved. I'm taking a couple of days off." Without releasing her hands, he got up from his chair and pulled her up with him. "I can't concentrate on anything else, so I might as well be doing this, anyway."

He placed her hands around his waist, released them and cupped her face. "Correction," he said, his voice becoming more intimate, "I'd much rather be doing this."

"But Dom," she began, "you shouldn't—"

He stopped her protest by kissing her quickly. "Hey, did you hear me? I *want* to." His voice was hoarse, and softer. He moved closer to her, backed her gently against the wall next to the dressing room. "I want *you*."

His back was to the rest of the store, and his broad body

shielded her from view, but even so, Jordan felt embarrassed by how public they were. "Dom, I don't think this is such a great idea—" The hunger in his eyes made her stop talking.

She watched as his gaze roamed every inch of her face, exploring her, making love to her with his eyes. Finally it settled on her mouth, which he stared at for several breath-robbing moments. "I knew it," he murmured.

"What did you know?" she managed to say, then licked her dry mouth.

She felt his body tense up, tighten against hers, heard him make a low, guttural sound in the back of his throat. "That once we got started I wouldn't be able to stop. I want you as bad as I did last night."

"I'm…getting the message." And the feeling was, most definitely, mutual.

He glanced around, noticed the dressing room and backed her into it, against the single wall mirror. He closed the door behind them, pushed in the lock and hugged her, hard. The bulge of his arousal pressed against her lower stomach, and she felt moist heat pooling between her thighs.

"Being with you—" He stopped, pulled his head back and stared at her. "You're like a drug, Jordan. I can't get you out of my head."

"You don't seem very happy about that."

"I'm not. I don't know how to deal with this craving."

Her nipples were rock hard as she pressed her body into his. "By giving in to it, I guess."

"When? I'd like to take you—" he breathed warmth into her ear "—right here, right now—"

The distant jangle of the shop's bell signaled new customers, followed by female laughter. Wincing, Dom pulled his head back and observed her through half-lidded eyes that promised sensual pleasures above and beyond anything she had experienced before.

"Can you get away?" he asked. "Come home with me?"

"Not right now. I'm sorry. I'm the only one here to help Lisa."

He raised an arm and rested it on the wall next to her head. Leaning in, he sniffed her hair, ran the tip of his tongue around the whorls and crevices of her ear. Her legs trembled. She wasn't sure how long it would be before her knees gave out, as they nearly had last night.

"I'm not good with words, Jordan," he murmured.

"You're doing fine."

He brought his mouth over hers, insinuated his tongue between her lips and slowly, teasingly stroked and tasted her. With a groan, she felt her knees buckle, and she sank onto the small stool set in the corner.

Seated, Jordan wound up face-to-face with Dom's zipper. She glanced at him, saw him watching her, a knowing smile on his face. His nostrils flared as he waited to see what she would do next.

"Excuse me?" a woman's voice said from right outside the dressing room door. "Is anyone in there?"

Jordan's hand flew to her mouth in horror. In the semi-drugged state of arousal that happened in Dom's presence, she had forgotten where she was, what she was supposed to be doing. She could barely remember her name.

"One moment," she called, then struggled to her feet.

Dom continued to trap her with his body. "I'll take a rain check on that," he whispered. "When are you through?"

"Five o'clock."

"I'll be here. My place or yours?"

"Yours." The conversation might have been over, but he continued to mesmerize her with his gaze. The look on his face held such intensity, such erotic heat, promise and, yes, tenderness, that she felt overwhelmed with an emotion she was still hesitant to name. He was amazing, a man of many colors and emotional layers. How had she ever thought him only what he seemed on the surface—a cynical tough guy?

Finally, Dom nodded, moved away from her, adjusted his crotch, straightened his tie, winked at her and opened the dressing room door.

A short, plump woman stood there, several dresses draped

over her arm. At the sight of Dom, her eyes widened and her mouth formed a perfect *O*. He nodded to her, said, "Hi," and ambled away, leaving Jordan to deal with the woman.

Aware that her face had turned beet red, she attempted to smile brightly at the customer while she racked her brain for something casual and offhand to say. But nothing came to mind. Nothing at all.

At five, Dom hurried into the shop, his pulses racing with excitement. He had news for Jordan that he couldn't wait to deliver, to see the expression on her face. He spotted her coming out of the back office, her purse tucked under her arm.

"Got him," he told her, reaching her with several long strides.

"Who?"

"We got a hit on Wally's prints." He stood facing her. "The guy's name is Walter Kaczmarak. His rap sheet says he's an ex-con, still on parole. He was in for burglary, robbed a video store. Did time in state prison. Last known address was in Chatsworth," he went on, naming a community in the San Fernando Valley. "I already called the parole officer. Wally does live in Bakersfield like he said, but with a new address, new parole officer. He's working up there at a hardware store. Reports in regularly. Keeps his nose clean. Model parolee, his new officer said."

"Bakersfield." Jordan gripped his arm, a glow of excitement in her eyes. "Could that be the town up north he was talking about?"

"Maybe."

"Where do his parents live—do you have that information?"

"No, that's on his original file, which, it turns out, is not on computer, so I had to approach it back door. I got a friend in records working on it, but it might take a day or two. Still, we might get lucky in Bakersfield, you never know." He glanced at his watch. "Anyhow, I have to cancel our date, much as I hate to. I'm taking off for Bakersfield now."

She tightened her grip on his arm. "Don't even think about not taking me along."

He paused, stared at her. "Hey, Jordan, no."

"Hey, Dom, yes." Her jaw was stuck out stubbornly, a woman determined to have her way.

Every instinct screamed against letting her come with him. It was never a good idea to get a civilian involved in law-enforcement matters. Too many potentials for disaster. It wasn't good for the two of them to be seen together, not when they might come across Wally. No, it was not a good idea for Jordan to come along, and he knew it.

Knew it and didn't follow through. This was her kid they were talking about. "Okay," he said, "but I call the shots."

"When we get there," Dom told Jordan, as he battled rush hour traffic north over the Sepulveda Pass, "you stay in the car, out of sight."

"But what if he—?"

"He won't find out I have any connection to you," he said grimly. "I won't let him."

As Jordan watched trucks lumbering by, impatience built inside with each mile. They passed through the valley, past Magic Mountain, climbed up and over the Grapevine, after which green trees and shrubbery gave way to flat, bare, colorless terrain. And all the while, her head was filled with thoughts, plans, hope. Most of all, hope.

"Tell me something," she said, turning to face Dom. "Why haven't you pushed me harder to do this officially? Why haven't you said, 'Jordan Carlisle, let's go in, file charges against Walter Kaczmarak for extortion, let's get the case of your son's death reopened, let's get it taken care of all legal and proper. Let's do it by the book'?"

Dom shot her a look, then smiled. "Yeah. Funny, I've been thinking about that today—what would have happened if that night, when I came to your place and you showed me the letter, what if I'd told you to do just that."

"And?"

Looking in his side mirror, he pulled out to pass a driver who was foolish enough to be observing the speed laws. "Here's how it would go down. You walk into a police station and say, 'I think my son is still alive and there's some guy trying to get money out of me to find him. Here's the letter he sent and a fuzzy picture of my little boy. Please investigate.' What do you think they do?"

"Not much, I guess. At that point."

"They probably brush you off. Or, if you get lucky and get someone more conscientious, they talk to you a while, see if you're a loony. Maybe if they're thorough, run a quick check, find out your kid is officially dead, case closed, assume you're grasping at straws or still grieving, tell you to ignore the letter and talk to your minister or get some therapy."

"Get a life, in other words."

"Something like that."

The sun had disappeared, but the western sky outside Dom's window was still streaked with pink light. The view on Jordan's side, however, showed night setting in. She opened her window and let the cool evening breeze into the car while she pursued the topic she'd introduced.

"So then what if I'd brought in the second letter, with the picture of Michael?"

"Then they might have to take you more seriously. Ask if you want to cooperate with them. Maybe set up an undercover guy on the night you met Wally at the bar, nab him. You press charges. But it's slippery, legalwise. You were paying for information, no one forced you to go there. It's not, strictly speaking, extortion."

"It's not?"

"Nah. It's like going to a psychic, saying, 'Here's a bunch of money to put me in contact with my late husband.' She guarantees nothing, only information. Wally did give you information, lots of it, just not enough to put you in contact with this kid, who you hope is your son, but there's a ninety-nine-point-nine-percent chance isn't. See?"

''Yes. All right, then, say we got past that part and knew where Myra and my son—''

''If he is your son.''

''All right,'' she snapped, annoyed that he kept doing that, ''if he's my son.''

''Let's get this straight, Jordan,'' Dom said firmly. ''I know you don't like it when I remind you of that, but I'm scared for you. You're setting yourself up here, and you may take a real dive if you're wrong.''

Frowning, she studied his serious face for a moment, wishing there were some way to make him see what she knew. ''Dom, I know that if I'm wrong, it will be devastating. But I'm not wrong, and there is no way I can impress on you how sure I am. I feel it, in here—'' She placed a curled fist over her heart. ''Michael's alive. I know he is. I accept your doubt. In your place, I'd have the same doubt. But I'm one-hundred-percent sure.''

He pursed his lips, seemed about to say something, then raised his shoulders, lowered them. ''Okay, I tried.''

''Yes, you did. Can we continue?'' With obvious reluctance, he nodded. ''So now say we know where Michael is. What do we do then, officially?''

''They would look up the record, see the case is closed. But you would push to reopen it, and with some Carlisle influence, maybe a friend or two in high places, someone would get the assignment. It probably wouldn't be a priority. What they'd do, they'd get a picture of Michael at eighteen months, let one of the computer guys work up how he'd look a year later. If it's a ballpark match to that second photo, run up to wherever Myra is, ask some questions. That would be assuming she would cooperate. Check the kid's birth certificate, identifying marks, stuff like that.''

''Michael has a strawberry mark on his left shoulder,'' she said excitedly.

Had a strawberry mark, Dom almost said, but didn't. Obviously, nothing he said or did would dampen her belief. He *was* afraid for her, that was the truth, afraid of what would happen to her if, one more time, her son was proved to be no longer alive. But Dom had done all he could. He only hoped she had the strength to get through it again and come out whole. He'd be there to help.

Or would he? He had no idea where the two of them were going...

One thing at a time, D'Annunzio, he told himself. Get through this, then see.

He retrieved a stick of gum from his pocket, offered it to Jordan, who turned it down, then popped it into his mouth. "Okay," he said, "so now we have a problem. We ask Myra to voluntarily submit to having the kid's blood drawn for a match. If she decides not to cooperate, you have to go the legal route. Which means she goes legal, too, puts up a fight. Child services would get involved, too, maybe put the kid in foster care for a while. So you got lawyers, social workers, paperwork up the kazoo and some guy assigned to it who has fifty-five other pending cases. Might take a long time. I work for the system, but I know how it can get bogged down. None of us like that it's that way, but it is that way. That's reality."

To her credit, Jordan seemed to take it all in without getting bent out of shape, and nodded her understanding. "So that's why you've never recommended we do this officially."

"Yeah, well, part of me wishes we'd done it that way from the first. But, to be honest, if you came in with this story—" He shrugged. "I'd be out of the picture. It's not my department. Not to mention the fact that I'm too personally involved with the complainant, so I'd never get the case. And, the truth is, I don't want to let some other cop run with it—not that he might not do a good job, but this is my case. I feel responsible. You brought me in, I'm not leaving till it's done. However it works out."

Jordan smiled at him. "Thank you, Dom. Really. I—"

He raised a hand to cut her off. "If you start getting grateful on me again, I'm turning this car right around."

Two and a half hours after they left West L.A., they entered Bakersfield. It took a while to find the right street, then to make out the addresses in the dark, but finally they pulled up in front of an old wood-framed house with a neglected yard. The porch was lit by a single yellow bug light.

Jordan stared out the window for a moment, then turned to Dom. "Are you sure I shouldn't be the one to go in?"

"If Wally's there, he'll want to know how you managed to get his address, then he'll figure out you had some official help, which meant you didn't listen to his instructions. Better if I do it. Trust me."

"But—"

"I said to trust me, Jordan. Do you?"

She stared at him for a moment, then nodded and slumped down in the passenger seat.

He felt her eyes watching him as he walked up the concrete pathway, climbed three steps onto a narrow porch and faced a screen door with several rips in it. He pulled on it, but it was locked. He rang the bell, and a moment later, a woman in late middle age, her hair gray and wispy, wearing a long robe, came to the door. A lit cigarette dangled from her mouth.

Dom said, "I'm looking for Walter Kaczmarak."

In the background he could hear the blare of a TV set. The woman took a drag off her cigarette, blew the smoke in his direction and looked him up and down warily. "Wally's not here."

"Where is he?"

"Who wants to know?"

Dom flashed his badge. The sullen, suspicious look on the woman's face didn't change much. "I don't want no trouble."

Dom reached into his jacket pocket, took out a notepad and pen and made a great show of turning pages to find what he was looking for. "This is the address of Walter Kaczmarak, isn't it? His file says it is."

"Yes, he lives here. He boards. I get money from the state. He done something? This is my place, I don't want no trouble," she repeated.

"No, it's nothing like that. We may need him as a witness to something, that's all."

"Oh, well—" she leaned against the door frame, but didn't invite him in "—he's just not here right now. He's a good boy, Wally is. Not trouble like some of them."

"Is he at work?"

"I don't think so. He just rooms here, see, and I—"

"Do you have any idea where he is?"

"Well, he mentioned something about heading down to L.A. for a few days."

"Do you have an address?"

"Nope. Just L.A., that's all he said."

He jotted a couple of notes. "Are his parents nearby? They might know where he is."

Shrugging, the woman inhaled and once again blew smoke in his face. He wished he could say he hated the smell, but the truth was, it had been four months since he'd last lit up, and he still missed the stupid habit something awful. "He's never mentioned his folks," the woman told him.

"Brothers? Sisters?"

"Nope."

Dom thought about asking if he could come in and check Wally's room, but this woman wouldn't buy that, not without a warrant. "All right," he said. "Thank you for your time." He closed the notebook and began to walk away.

"Hey," the landlady called after him, "if Wally comes back, what should I say?"

"I'll be in touch."

He got into the car and drove off before he filled Jordan in on the interview. As he spoke, Dom searched for a public phone booth with an existing directory. When he found one, he pulled up, got out of the car and turned to the Ks. There were three Kaczmaraks listed. He called them all, asked for Myra. No one knew anyone of that name, and he was pretty sure all three were sincere.

In the car, he turned to Jordan and smiled ruefully. "No luck."

"Not your fault," she said, but he could see the glow of hope they'd started out with had just about faded.

Meanwhile, it was past eight and he was starving. They stopped at a drive-through fast food place, picked up dinner and eased onto the highway that led home.

"A few days in L.A. was what she said," Dom mused out loud. Steering with his left hand, he bit into his hamburger. "L.A. covers a lot of space. But Wally picked a bar downtown, and Union Station is in that area too, so odds are he's probably staying close by. Where, I have no idea."

Jordan bit into one of her French fries. It had been so long since she'd had fast food, she'd forgotten how tasty it was. Not good for you, but delicious. She popped two more fries in her mouth, chewed on them and wiped her salty, greasy fingers on a napkin. "Maybe you could trace his car. Didn't Nick say he had a silver Honda?"

Dom swallowed his mouthful of burger. "He wasn't sure it was him. According to Wally's sheet, he drives a purple Mercury, so either that wasn't him in the Honda or he borrowed a car that night."

Several trucks roared by in the opposite direction, their powerful lights blazing. Traffic was much lighter now, but as the night was overcast, with clouds that hid the moon, the highway's only illumination was from passing vehicles.

They ate a while longer in silence. When they were done, Jordan gathered all the debris into one bag and set it by her feet. Dom reached for her hand and held it on the seat between them.

Closing her eyes, Jordan leaned back. Her anxiety about Michael was a constant, but right now all she felt was drained. All that traveling, all that hope, and now another setback. Dom rubbed his thumb lightly over the back of her hand, as though he knew the direction of her thoughts and wanted to offer comfort. And, indeed, the touch of Dom's fingers, his skin on hers, set her senses to stirring, the way they had that afternoon at the shop. She was hooked on his touch.

"What else can we do?" she asked him.

"Not much. Put it away till we get more answers—another note, the info from records on his parents, something we don't know about because it hasn't happened yet. I know this waiting is the pits, Jordan, but I'm used to it. Most of police work is about waiting."

"I hate waiting. I don't know what to do with myself."

"I have an idea or two...." He drew her hand toward the junction of his thighs.

He was rock hard, and as she cupped her hand over the bulge of his manhood, a shiver of sensation went through her like quicksilver. "Oh, my. What do we have here?"

"We had a date, remember? Come to my place. I guarantee we can find a way to make time pass."

Chapter 11

It was five in the morning when Dom drove Jordan to the shop to pick up her car, then followed her home. After he walked her to her front door, she was reluctant to say good-night, so she put her arms around him. Dom maneuvered their bodies away from the well-lit area and into a dark corner where they exchanged easy, lazy kisses. Her nostrils filled with the heady, musky smell of him. Her senses reeled from the new sensual dimension this man had introduced into her life.

"You should have spent the night," Dom murmured into her ear. "I want to wake up next to you, have you first thing in the morning, before you're awake."

"While I'm unconscious? Hmm. Kinky." She groaned as he glided his tongue along her collarbone. They had made love twice at his place, and she had thought both of them thoroughly sated, depleted of all energy, sexual or otherwise.

Apparently, she spoke for herself. She was in awe of the man—how could there be anything left?

"Think about it," he said, moving his hips against hers, kissing her eyelids, running his tongue over her brows. "There you are, all warm and sleepy and maybe even in the middle of a dream, and I slip inside you and you think it's still a dream, and I move some more and get harder and harder, and then you move, too. And you realize it isn't a dream.''

She moved her head languidly, offering new areas for his tongue to explore. ''Who is this man whispering sweet nothings in my ear? Who is this man with all this imagination, this man who said he wasn't good with words? What have you done with Dom?''

He kissed the bridge of her nose, her cheeks. ''When you find out, let me know, too.''

When he found her mouth, they kissed for a long, lovely time. Finally, and with reluctance, Jordan broke away. Smoothing her palms over his bristly cheeks, she said, ''If I don't get some sleep, I'm going to be no good to anyone. You, too.''

''Yeah.''

He walked her to the door. After inserting her key into the lock, she turned to face him once more. She felt dreamy and delicious, filled with an emotion that she was growing more and more sure of with each passing moment in Dom's presence. Love. The word was love.

She was in love with her tough-guy, hard-as-nails-on-the-outside-but-marshmallow-inside Detective Sergeant Dominic D'Annunzio. There would be lots of time to explore the sensation, after she had Michael back...

''Good night,'' she said softly.

He smiled, touched a fingertip to her nose, then walked away.

''Let me know when you have any news,'' she called softly after him.

''You know I will.''

''And get some sleep.''

He shrugged, as though sleep was the farthest thing from his mind, and she watched as he continued down the long driveway and disappeared into the blackness. She waited till she heard his door open and close, heard the sound of the engine, then swept into the house on a lovely wave of afterglow.

In the hallway, she caught her reflection in the antique mirror over the mail table. Her face was soft, all the tension gone from around her mouth and eyes. This, she told herself, was the face of a woman in love. Smiling, she glanced at the table.

A special delivery letter lay there, addressed to her, and in the space of a heartbeat, her dream-misted mood vanished.

It all came back—her anxiety about Michael, the tension of waiting—but at least this time, her heart didn't race quite as much. This time she wasn't in territory as foreign as it had been in the beginning.

It was too late to run after Dom. He'd already driven away. Jordan opened the letter and read the enclosed note. *Ten thousand more,* he demanded. In two days' time. There were instructions on where to drop the money, and he assured her she'd have all the answers to her questions once he received his "reward." Again, he said she was being watched, and again it warned her against bringing in the law. This time it was signed, *Your friend, Wally.*

Friend. Anger rose from somewhere deep inside. Friend, indeed. We're close to getting you, *friend,* Jordan said silently, we *will* get you, you miserable excuse for a human being.

She read the instructions a second time. In two days, either Dom would have found where Wally's parents lived or she, Jordan, would have to come up with ten thousand dollars. She folded the letter, put it in the envelope and climbed the stairs to her room.

When Dom dropped Jordan off, he was still too hyped to sleep. So he took himself for a drive west along Sunset Boulevard, past U.C.L.A. and through Brentwood, winding up at the Santa Monica Pier. As he stood at the railing, he ran his tongue over his lips, tasting Jordan, even smelling her subtle perfume on his clothing. He felt filled with her, oddly peaceful and contented.

He watched the sky change colors while the sun rose behind him, observed the homeless crawling out from under the wooden pilings, where many of them had found shelter during the night. Finally, he found himself thinking about Myra Foster and how to find her. He made his mind a blank, the way he often did when working on a case, letting it wander along whatever paths it chose to go.

Myra's brother Wally was somewhere in L.A., the landlady in Bakersfield had said. Dom had assumed that meant downtown L.A., near the bar where Wally had arranged to meet Jordan. It was a reasonable assumption. But Wally, from what he could tell, was the kind of guy to work all the angles. Maybe he'd chosen a place far away from where he was staying, in case Jordan decided to have him followed. What if he was staying, say, in Chatsworth, at his former address?

The parole officer had said it was where his ex-girlfriend, a waitress at a nearby Denny's, lived. The two of them had broken up when he'd moved to Bakersfield. Old girlfriends were always good sources, every cop knew that. And although Chatsworth wasn't really in L.A., most out-of-towners didn't know that.

Following his hunch, he headed out there, taking the 405 north for the second time in twelve hours, then hitting the 118 west, till he arrived at his destination. He parked across the street from a three-story stucco apartment-building complex that took up the entire block, then got out of his car to study the layout.

The complex had subterranean parking but wasn't gated, so Dom went around to the back alley and walked down a flight of steps to the garage. He made his way up and down the aisles, on the lookout for either a silver Honda or Wally's Mercury, not really expecting to see it, but hoping. When he reached the parking space for apartment #206, he stopped and stared. Hard.

Both cars were there, the Honda behind the Merc.

Yes! Dom thought, his fists clenched by his side. Gotcha.

Now he had to think through his options. What he needed to do was check out the guy, size him up—something Dom had gotten real good at in all his years on the force—see if Wally was the kind who'd break easily. If he was, Dom would bring him in, grill him in an interrogation room, get to the bottom of the story and find out just how much of it was real and how much was bull.

Myra existed, that much Dom knew, but much of the rest of the complicated tale Wally had told Jordan could be pure fabrication—the breakdown, the return to the parents' hometown. Who knew where Myra was, and if there was a little boy with her? If Wally cracked, Dom would detain him in lockup, head up to wherever the kid was, check it out.

If, on the other hand, Wally wasn't the kind to break easily, then Dom had to approach him from an entirely different direction. Wait for the information from records, get the parents' address and go there, wherever there was. With this second option, though, it was crucial that he take extreme care not to set off any warning bells in Walter Kaczmarak. Should he knock on the door of the girlfriend's apartment? he wondered. No, she might do something stupid; besides, he needed to talk to Wally alone.

After moving his car into an empty space in the garage, across from the Honda, Dom settled himself in for however long it took.

Morning sunshine poured in from the open terrace windows as Jordan knocked on the door. From within, Cynthia's voice responded, "Come in."

Jordan pushed open the door, carrying the tray with a teapot, a cup, sugar cubes, the way her mother-in-law liked it. She set it on the table in front of the small couch in the sitting room. More light streamed in through the French doors that connected Cynthia's suite to the pool area. Jordan sat and smiled as Cynthia came out of her dressing room tying the sash of her robe.

"Well, you're up bright and early," the older woman said. "How nice. You brought me tea."

"Yes, I wanted to talk to you."

She watched as Cynthia sank onto the couch, poured the tea into the china cup, lifted one cube of sugar, then another, with the small silver tongs, dropped them into her cup and stirred the mixture with a spoon. "Yes?" she said.

Jordan thought of the small talk she should be engaging in now, "chatting" about friends, gossip, and so on, before getting to the purpose of her visit. But to do so would feel manipulative. She had news for Cynthia of great importance and had decided to come right out with it.

She paused, took a deep breath and said, "Something's happened that I think you ought to know about."

Her mother-in-law glanced up, took in Jordan's serious face, then put her hand over her heart, as though to protect that fragile organ. "What?"

"It's not bad news, I promise," Jordan said quickly. "In fact, it's good news."

"Oh, well, that's better." She lifted her cup and took a sip of her tea. "Yes?"

"I…have reason to believe that Michael may still be alive."

Cynthia went still, then she lowered the cup to its saucer. At first her face registered puzzlement. This quickly turned into a look of disbelief, followed by cold fury. She sat up straight. "How dare you?"

Jordan was taken aback. "Excuse me?"

"How dare you say that to me? Michael is dead, as is my son. There is no possible way either of them could be alive. Are you delusional?"

Jordan hadn't expected this. Possibly she hadn't thought it through, hadn't considered this reaction, so caught up had she been in the recent events of her own world. Gently, she put her hand on her mother-in-law's wrist. The skin was thin, a layer of expensive oil over parchment.

"Cynthia, please listen," she said carefully. "I'm not imagining any of this, I promise. A man has sent me a picture of a little boy, and I'm sure it's Michael. There must have been some mix-up during the car crash, and he's—"

"Picture?" the older woman interrupted. "What picture? Let me see it."

Dom had the pictures, as well as the letters. "I don't have it with me. I'm sorry. Dom, Detective D'Annunzio, has it as part of an evidence file. We might have to—"

"You've brought in the police?" As Cynthia interrupted again, an expression of horror showed on her face. "Are we going to be bombarded by all that media attention again?"

Jordan shrank back, feeling as though she'd been smacked. Obviously, she'd approached this all wrong. She'd managed to push a couple of Cynthia's very sensitive buttons. Temporarily at a loss for words, she watched as her mother-in-law's agitated facial expression deepened.

But there was no way to sweeten the facts, not now that she'd begun, so she plunged ahead. Forcing herself to keep a calm, reasonable tone, Jordan said, "I've done nothing, Cynthia. I'm just trying to make you understand the situation. Will you listen?"

Mistrust hung in the air between the two women like heavy vapor. "Michael is dead, Jordan. What sort of fantasy are you involved in? Why are you saying these things? Why are you telling me this?"

"Because this man, the one who sent the pictures, he wants money. I'm hoping we'll find Michael before we have to pay him any more, but I'm not sure just how it will turn out."

Again, Cynthia went totally still, then her expression turned cold. "Oh. I see. So that's what this is about. Money."

Button number three, Jordan thought as she shook her head. "No, Cynthia, that's not what this is about, this is not an attempt to get money from you for my own personal use. Have I ever done that? In all the time we've lived together, have I ever asked you for money, or acted as though I expected it?"

Pausing, she counseled herself not to let any more resentment show. "This is about my little boy," she continued as calmly as she could, "your grandson. It's about doing all I—" Catching herself, she went on, "all *we* can. I've already pawned my engagement ring." She raised her left hand to show Cynthia her ring finger.

Her mother-in-law's eyes went wide with horror. "But Reynolds gave you that—"

It was about the only thing he did give me, Jordan wanted to fire back, with the exception of Michael. But, holding her tongue, she lowered her eyes to her lap while the elderly woman continued. "How dare you? How dare you pawn the ring my son gave you?" Tears filled the weak, gray-blue eyes. "He was precious to me, and I miss him more than I can say."

Awkward and uncomfortable as she felt, nevertheless Jordan couldn't help feeling sorry for the older woman. She, of all people, understood Cynthia's pain. Her only child, gone—a horrid, irreversible tragedy. It was the way Jordan had felt this whole past year. They had so much in common, she observed silently, not for the first time. What a waste that they couldn't talk to each other.

"I'm sorry," Jordan said, rising slowly. "Sorry I brought it up. It was wrong of me. I'll take care of it. I won't bother you again." She walked to the door, then turned as she heard Cynthia gasp. She waited for her mother-in-law to speak, but she sat there, her tears making narrow wet trails in her recently applied facial powder.

"Are you all right?" Jordan asked. "Shall I get your medicine?"

Cynthia shook her head and made a gesture with her hand indicating that Jordan should leave. She did so, and made her way to the breakfast alcove, where she poured herself a cup of black coffee from the silver pot on the sideboard.

She sank into a chair and sipped her coffee. The chat had been an unmitigated disaster, and she felt awful. What she could have done differently escaped her, but it didn't matter; she felt responsible anyway. Cynthia had a way of bringing that out in her.

Last night, after receiving Wally's latest demand, Jordan had called Dom's home and left word on his machine, telling him all about the letter and requesting that he speak to her first thing in the morning. He hadn't called yet. They had to tread carefully now, that much she knew. Things were coming to a head, and the slightest misstep could upset everything.

Exhausted, she sat back in her chair and closed her eyes. As she did, a kaleidoscope of images from the past week flashed in her mind's eye.

Friday night with Dom at Bistro Rodeo and Morgan R's, returning home to see the second letter from Wally. Working at the shop on Saturday, Sunday spent in a state of nervous agitation, Sunday night at the train station, Monday morning pawning her ring, meeting with Wally that evening.

Tuesday night—the charity dinner and making love with Dom. Wednesday night—last night—the fruitless trip to Bakersfield, followed by more lovemaking.

Days blended into each other, as did all the events: demands for money, secret meetings, waiting for Dom's contacts to come through with information, the widening of the chasm between her mother-in-law and herself. Her son—the promise of seeing him again dangled in front of her. Dom—the promise of falling in love, deeply in love, for the first time in her life, with a complicated man who was married to his job and who felt guilty about his first wife, a man who had given her the gift of sexual ecstasy but who, even now, didn't really believe her gut instinct about Michael.

Add to that the hours at the shop and the sleepless nights. She wondered how she was still upright. What she felt like doing was going to sleep for a week. Better yet, she'd like to have a breakdown and let someone else handle all this. Wake her when it was over.

Smiling ruefully, Jordan took another sip of coffee. Time enough for that later, she told herself. After Michael was back. No, as a matter of fact, she would postpone her nervous breakdown till after he graduated college. Again, she smiled, then shook her head. Enough silliness and mental meandering, she told herself. Time to pull back and reassess.

Dom was working the police angle, but Jordan needed to continue working hers. She had to come up with ten thousand dollars in case Dom's sources didn't come through in time. She could sell the wedding ring or the Rover. She'd prefer selling the huge diamond engagement ring, but it would take five thousand dollars to get it out of hock first.

What else? She trusted Dom to do all he could, but this was her little boy she was talking about. What if Wally got spooked and disappeared before revealing Michael's whereabouts? What if Michael had to spend the rest of his childhood with an unstable woman who called herself his mother?

No, Jordan said, her spine stiffening with resolve. That would not happen. She would not allow it.

After sitting in his car for two hours, Dom was rewarded when a youngish man with prematurely thinning blond hair approached the Honda, keys in hand.

Dom was out of his car in an instant. "Hold it," he called out.

"Huh?" The man looked up.

"Walter Kaczmarak?" As he advanced, flashing his badge, Dom studied Wally's face and body language. Dom wore his gun in a shoulder holster and, should it become necessary, could whip it out in under a second.

"Yes." Wally stood still, hands at his side, and looked him right in the eye. As he came nearer, Dom thought he saw something in his expression shift: Both awareness and hostility flashed briefly, but in the blink of an eye they were gone.

Any officer of the law was allowed to question any parolee at any time. Again, Dom flashed his badge, then said "Okay, up against the car, spread 'em."

Wally did as he was told. He was all cooperation as Dom patted him down. Clean as a whistle.

"What's this all about?" Wally asked pleasantly. "If you don't mind my asking."

"Just checking you out." Turning Wally around, Dom stood right in his face, stared hard at him. He knew how to intimidate perps, had used his rough looks and bulky posture quite effectively in the past.

Wally stared back, didn't flinch for a second. "For what?"

"Possible parole violation, for starters. You're supposed to be in Bakersfield."

He was all surprised innocence. "Just taking a couple of days to visit my girl, that's all. I check in regular."

Again, Dom picked up on the hostility in Wally's eyes, but

again, it was gone as quickly as before. Then his thin mouth curved into a good-natured smile, one that contained a hint of smugness. "Is it a crime to visit my girl?"

The guy was good, Dom had to admit. Real good.

What Dom wanted to do was to smash his nose, wipe that smug smile off it. But that was, as Steve would say, counterproductive, especially in an open parking lot where there might be witnesses. And Dom had a feeling the guy would stand up to whatever good cop-bad cop stuff he and Steve would throw at him.

Not that he could, anyway. Hell, there wasn't even a case opened yet, no accusation, no charges filed, no reason to bring him in.

"Then there's the matter of a couple of video store robberies," Dom told him, still an inch from his face, "last week. They had your MO stamped all over them."

Wally raised his hands, palms out. "Hey, not me. Like I said, I'm innocent as a twelve-year-old virgin." He smiled again. "But, if you need to take me in, Officer, let's do it. I need to call my lawyer."

The son of a bitch was calling his bluff. Dom glared at him, moved in a little closer, again saw the instant of hostility, this time accompanied by a touch of fear in the eyes. "That's your right," Dom growled.

"Hey, listen. I didn't do a thing. And there's no way I'm going back there. I didn't like it in state prison."

"Yeah, I can understand that."

"But I want to cooperate, Detective, so whatever you need to do, I guess you'd better do it." He held up his hands, wrists together, inviting Dom to cuff him.

He wanted to put his fingers around the guy's throat, say, "Cut the crap, where's the kid?" He wanted to haul him in, get him in an interrogation room and go to work on him, get the lowdown on whatever scam he was running. But his instinct told him he was in danger of crossing a line. He'd crossed a lot of lines since Jordan had come into his life.

So he held back, stepped away, his mind working furiously,

making sure nothing showed on his face. He was at option two: Perp not intimidated, so do nothing to set off any alarms.

"Okay this time," he told Wally. "But I may be back. And next time, be sure to tell your parole officer where you are. Or you'll find your sorry ass back in the slammer."

"Jordan, phone," Lisa called from the front counter.

She hurried to where Lisa was balancing the receiver between her cheek and her shoulder while she rang up a sale. "Is it Dom?"

"I don't think so."

Jordan smiled at the customer, then grabbed the receiver. "This is Jordan."

"You screwed up, Mrs. Carlisle."

She recognized the voice instantly. It was Wally, and he was seething with enough anger to melt the phone line. "What are you talking about?"

"I got a little visit this morning, that's what I'm talking about. From your cop friend."

Jordan's mind was racing, trying to make sense of what he meant. "Who? I don't know what you're talking about."

"Don't play innocent with me. You brought in the cops, which means our deal is off."

Both Lisa and her customer were watching her intently, so Jordan angled her head away from them and kept her voice low. Her heart raced with panic. "I'm sorry. I don't understand."

"Then let me lay it out for you. A guy with a badge came to see me. And it's the same guy that's been hanging around your shop, paying you visits. Your friend, get it?"

She was struck dumb. Dom had found Wally? Had met him face to face?

"No answer, right?" Wally sneered. "Yes, Detective D'Annunzio was kind enough to introduce himself to me. Not that he mentioned your name or your connection with him. He's not totally stupid, is he? But I'm smarter, Mrs. Carlisle, a lot smarter. I told you I'd be watching you, so I had no trouble recognizing him. Which is why I've already called my sister and told her to take the kid and scram.''

''No!''

''Yes. By the way, you can ignore the latest note. I withdraw my offer. I guess Myra's little boy will stay just that, Myra's little boy. You'll never see him again.'' He hung up with a loud finality that made Jordan jump.

In a state of shock, she stared at the receiver.

''Jordan?'' Lisa came from behind the counter. ''Hey, are you all right?''

She turned and looked at Lisa, then shook her head. ''No, I'm not. I have to leave. I'm sorry.''

As she headed for the office, Lisa ran after her. ''Wait, Jordan, what's the matter? Can I help?''

''I'll call you later.''

She threw open the door of the office, grabbed her purse, got her car keys and made for the back door.

''Jordan,'' Lisa called after her, but Jordan had nothing to say.

Not to Lisa, at least. To Dominic D'Annunzio, she had a lot to say.

The pounding on his door woke him out of a deep sleep. He hadn't meant to conk out, had come back from Chatsworth to shower and change and get moving again, but had passed out on the couch on the way to the bedroom. He awoke with a start and sat up straight, waiting for the world to come into focus.

The pounding continued. ''Dom?'' he heard Jordan call. ''Open up!''

She sounded agitated, that much registered. Stiffly, he pushed himself from the couch, limbs aching, head pounding, and made for the door. He wished his brain wasn't so foggy, wished he could gather his wits enough to form a coherent thought.

When he opened the door, bright sunlight hit him like a bombshell, making him wince. Jordan barreled past him. It was obvious that she was furious, over-the-top pissed off. He hadn't a clue why. As he closed the door behind her, she whipped around to face him.

"What in God's name have you done?"

His brain could hardly take in her words. Rubbing his eyes, he walked to the sofa and sank onto the cushion. He scratched his head, yawned. "What?"

"He called me!"

"Who called you?"

"Wally. Walter Kaczmarak." Rubbing her hands in agitation, she began to pace in front of the small fireplace the way she had the other night. "It's off, the deal's off, he said. Because a certain cop paid him a visit this morning, and he's seen that certain cop at the shop where I work, has seen that certain cop *with* me, several times."

She stopped pacing, turned and faced him, hands outstretched. "He's been watching me. Did you know that?" Jordan walked toward him. "Did you happen to observe the fact that we were under surveillance? Apparently not. But now, Wally's called his sister and told her to take my son and make a run for it. Did you know that?"

She stood looking at him, hands propped on her hips, sarcasm, rage and pain in her expression. "Oh, I can see by the look on your face that this is all news to you. Didn't you get my message? I put it on your machine right after you left last night. I got another note, I told you. We had to be more careful than ever, I said. Didn't you pay any attention, or is my opinion not important here just because I'm not part of your stupid lawman fraternity?"

He shook his head, mumbled, "I didn't listen to my machine."

"Well, let me tell you, Detective, you blew it. You blew it, do you hear me?"

With tears of rage streaming down her face, she came at him, falling to her knees and punching him several times in the chest before he grabbed hold of her clenched fists to restrain her. "Jordan, stop. Please, stop."

She continued to struggle for a few moments, then sagged against him, weeping. He tried to put his arms around her, to hold her, but she shook him off. Cutting off all physical contact, she turned her back to him and curled up in a ball of despair.

As Dom stared at Jordan, his brain finally cleared. All she'd said to him, and all it meant, registered. That morning, Wally had known who he was. That was the reason for the look of hostility in his eyes, the reason for his smugness. The son of a bitch had made him, and Dom had walked into it completely ignorant.

Resting his elbows on his knees, he covered his face with his hands as self-loathing filled every part of him. How could he have been so stupid? Why hadn't he taken more precautions, thought it through? He'd had a hunch about Chatsworth, had rushed over there like a rookie, like some hotshot recruit instead of a seasoned professional.

Everything Jordan said about him was right on the money. He'd blown it big-time, and he had no excuse except that he'd failed to honor the line between professional and personal business. His thinking had been fuzzy. He hadn't considered all the angles from a detached viewpoint. As a result, Jordan was enraged at him, for which he didn't blame her. He was a washout, both as a cop and a man.

Lowering his hands from his face, he stared at the top of her head, misery sitting in his gut like an undigested meal. Weary, he rose to his feet. "Give me five minutes."

She looked up at him, her pain-ravaged face beautiful even in despair. "For what?"

"I need to shower. Then we're going down to the bureau."

He reached out a hand to help her up, then drew it back and let his arm fall to his side. She didn't want him touching her. Hell, she'd probably never let him touch her again. "I swear to you, Jordan, on my wife's grave, that if Michael is still alive, we'll find him. If it's the last thing I ever do."

She continued to gaze at him, doubt and hopelessness in her

expression. Then she shrugged listlessly and leaned her head against the couch cushion. "What choice do I have?"

As they walked through the detectives' room, one of the others called out, "Hey, D'Annunzio, I thought you were on sick leave."

"I am on sick leave," he replied. "This is what sick leave looks like."

The detective's gaze shifted to Jordan, and he seemed about to follow up with another remark. However, the look on Dom's face made him shut his mouth.

They'd better keep their mouths shut, he thought, all of them. It wasn't common for a civilian to be here, much less a looker like Jordan, but damn it, if any of them said word one, he'd rearrange their face.

Dom was angry. At himself, for sure, but that didn't matter. Anger could be a kind of fuel, and he would use it to propel him through whatever barriers were put in his way.

When he reached his desk, he pulled up an empty chair, indicated that Jordan should sit, then pushed away the pile of crap on his desk as he lowered himself into his chair. He'd been waiting for an unofficial favor from State Prison Records, but he no longer had time to wait.

He picked up the phone, punched in the number for the state prison. When the operator came on, he requested records. A woman answered, and he identified himself. "I got an emergency here," he said. "I need you to pull up a file, and it's not on computer."

When she started asking him things like case numbers and authorization codes, he barked, "I'll fax it all to you ASAP. Right now it's a kid's life we're talking about." He gave her Wally's name, spelled it for her, told her he needed the parents' home address and phone number, and no, he would not wait for her to call him back, he would hold on.

He kept his gaze averted from Jordan, who sat still and unsmiling next to him, her hands folded in her lap. His threatening tone seemed to have the desired effect, because the lady from records was back on the line in three minutes. The Kaczmaraks were listed as living in Buttonhollow, a tiny town in central California, no phone number given.

Dom slammed down the phone, rose and went to Santos's desk. The young Hispanic detective eyed Dom's approach with a mixture of awe and trepidation.

"Santos, I need you to do me a favor. Steve usually does the computer stuff because I suck at it, but he's not here. Will you look something up for me?"

Santos let out a relieved breath. "Sure, Dom."

"Check out the name Kaczmarak in Buttonhollow, see if they're still there." He spelled it for him.

"Sure, Dom," the young detective said again, then swiveled his chair so it faced his computer screen and pressed a lot of keys. In the two minutes, he had the information. "George Kaczmarak, 529 Whetstone Lane. No phone."

"What the hell kind of people don't have a phone?" Dom muttered, then remembered to thank the kid, saying he owed him one. At least the address was the same one as in the state prison file. At least they still lived there.

He walked to Jordan and offered his hand. She looked at it, then at him without taking it. "Where are we going?" she asked.

"To Buttonhollow."

"But Wally told me he contacted Myra and told her to run. He said—"

"I know what Wally said, Jordan. And maybe he meant it. But maybe he lied. Whatever. But we got to start somewhere. Coming?"

Chapter 12

On the road again, Jordan thought. The seemingly never-ending journey, searching for her son.

She and Dom didn't speak much on the trip to Buttonhollow. They'd decided to take the Rover, which was in much better shape than Dom's car, but he drove while Jordan studied the scenery. They took the coast route up to Santa Barbara, then inland along a two-lane highway through farm country. Groves of fruit trees, acres of crops stretched as far as the eye could see.

An hour went by. Two. Dom's mouth was set in a hard, firm line. He wore his wraparound sunglasses and stared straight ahead, never at her, only shifting his gaze to pass another car. For herself, Jordan wouldn't have thought it possible, but her anxiety level had been cranked up to new heights. Every muscle in her body felt tight, her stomach was filled with acid, the expression "jumping out of your skin" made more sense to her than it ever had.

None of this was helped by the barrier between her and Dom. She had unloaded on him because she'd had no option.

She had been livid, more filled with rage than she ever remembered feeling in her entire life.

Had she vented her anger disproportionately? Had he deserved to be yelled at that way? Was it really his fault that Wally had gotten so bitter and cut off contact?

Jordan had no idea whose fault it was. Maybe hers. Maybe no one's. What she did know was that she was so wound up, she had no objectivity left. Her brain seemed incapable of rational thinking.

Maybe it was her fault for not making sure Dom got her message about the new note demanding ten thousand dollars. Maybe she should have known that she was being followed. But shouldn't Dom have known it? Wasn't that his job?

And was she expecting too much of one person so he couldn't help but fail?

If she kept this up, Jordan knew, she would crack. Instead, she decided to break the silence. "How did you find him?" she asked.

"Who?"

"Wally. This morning—how did you know where to look?"

Dom scratched his cheek. "He was at his previous address, in Chatsworth, which is often a good place to start. SOP. Standard operating procedure."

"I see. And what did you say to him?" It came out like an accusation. She heard it, but couldn't seem to help it. Her anger had yet to dissipate.

Predictably, Dom bristled, and she saw his jaw muscles working a few times before he responded. "Nothing about you, nothing at all. A parole violation, I told him. It wasn't that big a deal, most parolees are used to it. I didn't know he'd made me. If I had I would never have gone there in person, would have sent someone else."

She nodded. He hadn't known, of course he hadn't. Still, she couldn't apologize for her anger, couldn't make it all right between them. Not yet. She was still too wound up.

She wanted to urge him to drive faster, but when she glanced at the speedometer, she noticed it hovered between eight-five and ninety. More than fast enough. Dom's face remained a hard, taut mask. Again, she had to ask herself if she'd expected too much of him. Should she have brought him in in the first place, and would it have turned out differently if she hadn't?

Had she? Should she? Would it?

All the self-doubts, crowding around her like a circling chorus of taunters. Stop, please, Jordan begged the old tapes. Give me a break. She closed her eyes, felt the rocking motion of the car, let it soothe her. Lord, how she needed soothing.

Somewhere in there, she fell asleep and had a dream, the same one she'd had for several months after the car crash. Michael, his face staring at her from the rear window of a car, saying something, his lips moving, but she can't make out what it is. Then somehow, the window widening to show Michael's arms raised, as though asking to be picked up. She can't move toward him, but he doesn't get any closer either. The two of them remain like that, suspended, for a time. Then he disappears, poof! Just like that. Gone.

Jordan awoke with a start, her heart pounding, her mouth foul-tasting. She looked around wildly until she remembered where she was.

"You okay?" Dom asked.

"How long have I been asleep?"

"Five minutes."

"Oh." She ran her tongue over her teeth, then her eye was caught by a movement. Dom was holding out a piece of his wintergreen gum, of which he had an apparently endless supply in his pocket.

"Thank you," she said, taking it and unwrapping it and putting it into her mouth. It tasted delicious, its flavor almost too sharply sweet. But it did the trick.

That last image before the poof—Michael with his arms raised. It had been one of his signature gestures. Michael had been slow to talk but had managed a small vocabulary by eighteen months. "Mommy, hug," had been two of his words. He would say them in that sweet-little-boy voice of his while he raised his arms. Whenever he did, she would always scoop him up and say, "Michael, hug." She would cradle him in her arms while he rested his head on her shoulder, one small hand around her neck. Then she would growl into his neck and he would giggle, then squirm to be let down. That happened once or twice a day—it had been their little ritual, their special moment.

On that first day of Michael's life, when she looked at him, her heart had been so full it hurt. That sense of closeness had never really diminished. The dream was about the last day of his life. Or so she'd thought.

"You okay?"

Dom's voice startled her. She'd almost forgotten where she was and why she was there, so lost had she been in memory. She glanced at him. His face was still set in the same harsh lines, but she detected a slight undercurrent of concern for her that he might not admit, but she knew he felt. "Yes."

He nodded, then returned to concentrating on the drive.

Was she still angry at him? No. In the deep five-minute sleep, her rage at him had disappeared. The incident with Wally hadn't been his fault. Any one of a number of things could have gone wrong.

"Dom?" She angled her head to face him.

"Hmm?"

"I'm sorry I yelled at you like that. I was out of line."

He glanced at her. His sunglasses made his expression hard to read. Then he returned his attention to the road and shrugged. "No you weren't. It's okay."

She stared at him a while longer, but it was plain he didn't want to talk, which was fine with her.

No, Jordan would not punish Dom any more. As she admitted that to herself, another strong image came to mind. Yesterday—had it been just yesterday? No, this morning—she had realized she was falling in love with this man. Even now, in her rage at him, warranted or not, even in the middle of her anxiety about Michael, that feeling of love was still there.

Strange, she thought. Blossoming love in the midst of a nightmare.

* * *

The town of Buttonhollow was a small one. Farms dotted the outskirts, then closer in, modest homes took over. The business district consisted of three square blocks of two-story buildings, storefronts on the first floor, offices or apartments upstairs. It was a community that was large enough to have a convenience store and a grocery store plus two gas stations, but there was no chain supermarket, no franchised fast food.

The place reminded Jordan of the nearby town of her Wyoming childhood. A tired place, not yet quaint or on the verge of becoming gentrified. Just old. It had come into existence post World War Two, and hadn't changed much since.

Whetstone Lane was part of the business district, and 529 turned out to be K's Laundromat, just on the edge of town before the paved sidewalk ended. The laundromat had twenty machines and dryers. The Kaczmaraks, the owners, lived above.

As Jordan followed Dom up the outside staircase, she was aware of constant vibrations from the machinery below. "I'll bet that goes on all the time," Jordan told Dom.

"During the day, yeah."

Dom knocked, and a woman opened the door. Her face was broad, and her small eyes seemed lost in the surrounding flesh. She was a big woman, almost as tall as Jordan, and she probably weighed twice as much. She wore a velour sweat suit that had seen repeated washings. Her faded blond hair was streaked with gray and was pulled off her face in an unflattering ponytail. She was probably not yet fifty, Jordan thought, but had long ago stopped fighting the aging process.

Dom flashed his badge and ID. "Mrs. Kaczmarak?"

Considering her bulkiness, it was a surprise when the woman spoke in a girlish, high-pitched voice. "What do you want?"

"Are you Mrs. George Kaczmarak?"

"Yes."

"I'm Sergeant Dominic D'Annunzio, a detective with the Los Angeles Sheriff's Department. May we come in?"

Flustered, she said in that incongruous little-girl voice, "Of course, yes, of course. My husband's in the living room."

They followed her through an old but clean kitchen. On the wall above the table hung an embroidered homily that read There are no shortcuts to God.

The living room was claustrophobic, with old furniture way too large for the room's dimensions. A couple of narrow windows, their blinds drawn against the fading afternoon sun, faced the street. Doilies covered the back and arms of a faded couch. There were two overstuffed armchairs, one positioned in front of a TV. A man sat in it, glued to the set.

"George, turn it off," the woman said.

"It's the last quarter," he grunted.

"These people are from the police."

Jordan didn't bother to correct the woman's impression, nor, she was glad to see, did Dom. It was better that they think she worked with him rather than discover her identity as a woman who had come to take their grandson away from them. If she felt a small twinge of guilt at the thought, she quickly brushed it away.

The man reached for the remote, turned off the TV, then stood. He was four or five inches shorter than his wife, and small-boned. Jordan recognized Wally in his father, but as Mr. Kaczmarak had thirty years or so on his son, his face had hardened into a look of perpetual suspicion. "Police, huh?"

Again, Dom brought out his badge and ID. The man studied it longer than his wife had. Then he nodded. "What do you want?"

"Would you like to sit?" the woman asked.

"We'd like to talk to your daughter," Dom said.

"She's not here."

"When will she be back?"

"I don't know," Mrs. Kaczmarak said.

"I see. Then, yes, I guess we will sit."

The man nodded, indicating that Dom and Jordan should take the armchairs while he and his wife sat on the couch. After they were settled, Dom began. "We're making routine inquiries about your daughter, Myra Foster."

"That's her stage n—" the woman began to explain.

Her husband said, "Hush," then turned to Dom. "What do you mean, routine? What's she done?"

"We're not sure she's done anything, but we need to talk to her. Just to ask her a couple of questions about something that happened in L.A. An old case."

"And I'm afraid," Jordan found herself adding smoothly, "we can't reveal the nature of our inquiry, not until we've talked to your daughter."

Half-expecting Dom to signal her to be quiet, she was surprised when he leveled her a look and cocked an eyebrow but indicated nothing about her shutting up. So she went on. "Myra has a child, is that correct?"

The woman nodded. "Yes. Rory."

Jordan opened her purse, took out her small notepad and silver pencil. "That's right. Rory Foster?"

"Yes."

"Is Foster your daughter's married name?"

"No," Mrs. Kaczmarak said, "it's her stage name."

"She never did marry the father," her husband said sourly. "Myra wanted to be an actress."

"Not the way she looks now, she can't be no actress."

The woman rose and walked to the piano, a small upright in the corner. From there, she took a color picture in a brass frame and showed it to her visitors, a hint of pride on her face. "That's her."

"Was," her husband amended.

Jordan took the picture and studied it. Myra had been given the full glamour treatment at her photo session. Lots of wavy tumbling blond hair, a low-necked, tight-fitting top that showed off an abundance of cleavage. Her eyes were made up heavily, her lips glossy, slightly parted in invitation.

Definitely Reynolds's taste in bed partners, Jordan admitted, if not in wives. Myra was an attractive young woman without being really pretty. In the broad cheekbones and wide nose, Jordan could see the same Slavic background as her mother.

"She's very pretty," Jordan murmured, handing the photo to Dom.

"Used to be," said the father gruffly. "Add fifty pounds to that, and that's what she looks like now."

"Don't, George."

"Well, it's the truth."

"Do you have any recent pictures of her?" Dom asked. "Say, with the little boy?"

The woman shook her head sadly. "No, Myra doesn't like to have her picture taken now. She says it depresses her." Sighing loudly, she lowered herself onto the couch. "Just about everything depresses her, seems like."

The father snorted disdainfully. "Can't keep a job, goes off for days at a time, we have to look after the child."

"He's a good little boy," the woman interjected. "Doesn't talk much, but—" She shrugged.

"Where are they now, Mrs. Kaczmarak?" Dom asked.

"I have no idea. Her brother, Walter, called, is all I know, and said to put her on the phone quick. Whatever he said to her, Myra just climbed in the truck and drove off."

"How long ago?" Dom asked.

At the same moment Jordan asked, "Alone?"

The man answered. "About five hours or so, I guess. Just after lunch. No, not alone. She had the kid with her."

"I suspect she'll turn up soon," Mrs. Kaczmarak said. "Sometimes she takes these drives, says they relax her. Our daughter is kind of, well, unstable, Detectives. It breaks my heart to say it, we raised her proper and all, with manners and church, but she always had these crazy ideas."

"And you have no idea where she went?" Jordan asked, trying to keep her voice from betraying her mounting concern. "It's really important that we talk to her."

"No. Sorry."

"What kind of car is she driving, Mrs. Kaczmarak?" Dom asked.

The man looked from Dom to Jordan and back again. "Hey, this isn't some routine thing, not if you're trying to track her down."

"It's time-sensitive," Jordan blurted, then looked at Dom.

He continued smoothly. "We're on a deadline and although your daughter isn't directly involved, there are lives at stake. That's about as much as we can say."

Mrs. Kaczmarak shot her husband a look, her eyes widening slightly. "Tell them, George."

"She drives my old truck. An old beat-up pickup, used to be red, now it's mostly rust. Seventy-two Ford," he added, and gave them the license plate number.

Jordan scribbled it down, then wrote her car phone number on a separate piece of paper. This she tore off, then stood and handed it to Mrs. Kaczmarak. "If you hear from your daughter, will you call us? Oh, that's right, you don't have a phone."

"We use the pay phone downstairs."

"We don't want any trouble," her husband said.

"And we hope there won't be any," Jordan replied.

Dom stood, too. "We'd appreciate the names of a couple of her close friends. People she might go to?"

The woman looked doubtful. "Well, they were high school friends, she hasn't kept up much contact with them."

"Every little bit of information helps."

All four of them trooped into the kitchen, where Mrs. Kaczmarak kept her address book. After leafing through the pages, she read off three names and phone numbers, which Jordan wrote down.

Thanking the Kaczmaraks for their cooperation, Jordan and Dom took their leave. They didn't speak to each other until they'd walked down the stairs and gotten into the Rover and Dom had driven away from the laundromat.

Jordan glanced at Dom. "I hope I didn't talk too much. Did I ruin anything?"

"Nah." He smiled in admiration. "I take back what I said about you being a lousy liar. You're a champ."

"In the right circumstances, I guess I can be."

As night descended over the small town, a cool mist filtered in. As the street lamps came on, they seemed like ghost lights. Jordan peered anxiously out the window. "Where do you think the police station is?" she asked him.

Dom shrugged. "Town this size may not have one."

"Well, then, what do we do now? Put out a—what do you call it? An APB?"

"For Myra's truck?"

"Yes. For my little boy."

How many times, he wondered, would they have this discussion before she got her answer and, most probably, got her heart broken all over again? "Jordan, you don't know if Rory is Michael. I can't go to the local cops based on your gut feeling and some ex-con's story he came up with to get money from you."

"But Myra's been gone—"

"For five hours. She's an adult," he continued with as much patience as he could muster. "As far as we know, she's gone for a drive with her little boy. Taken him to the zoo."

"After a phone call from Wally—"

"Who might have said any number of things to her. Let's give it some time."

"Time?" She glared at him as though she couldn't believe what she was hearing. "We don't have time. Wally called five hours ago. Myra could be halfway to Mexico or Canada by now."

"Jordan," Dom said, "please, try to—"

The car phone rang. Jordan snatched it up, said, "Yes?" and listened, then nodded and said, "we'll be right there."

Disconnecting, she said to Dom, "We have to go back to the Laundromat. It seems Myra ran off so quickly, she forgot to take her purse. It's still there. Do you think that'll help?"

"Can't hurt to check it out."

They were at the Kaczmaraks within minutes. Jordan ran up the stairs ahead of him, and when Mrs. Kaczmarak opened the door, she said, "Thanks for calling. May we look through Myra's purse?"

Dom winced. Jordan had been a champ so far, but in this instance, the direct approach might not be the best one. If the Kaczmaraks knew their rights, they could refuse.

As though he'd had a pipeline to Dom's thoughts, the husband said, "I don't think we should let you—"

Jordan jumped in. "But—"

Dom put a restraining hand on her arm, and she seemed to catch his signal because she clammed up. He stepped in with a little hardball.

"Mr. Kaczmarak," he said, with a small warning smile that he knew was not a pleasant thing to see, "if I remember correctly, your son served some time, didn't he? Let's all work together so your daughter doesn't have to do the same. Okay?"

The husband and wife looked at each other, then nodded.

At the kitchen table, while the Kaczmaraks hovered anxiously, Dom emptied out Myra's purse. Inside were used tissues, a pack of cigarettes, a disposable lighter, several lipsticks, sunglasses, two candy bars and a cheap plastic wallet, which he opened.

Apart from her driver's license, which said Myra Kaczmarak, there were three pictures—a wallet-size version of Myra's glamour shot, a photograph of Myra and a man Dom recognized as Reynolds Carlisle, and an infant wrapped in a blanket.

"Not Michael," Jordan told him under her breath.

The wallet also contained seven dollars and some change.

"Did she take a credit card with her?" Dom asked Myra's father.

"She doesn't have any credit cards."

From the purse's side pocket, Jordan brought out a yellow flyer, which she read, then told Dom, "It's an invitation to a school art sale. Does Myra go to school?" she asked Mrs. Kaczmarak.

"No, Rory does. Day care, over at the Methodist church."

"Where is it?"

"Two blocks south, on Broad."

Dom and Jordan said their thanks one more time, then headed for the church. It was seven-thirty at night and the mist had become a light fog. Businesses were closed, the streets were empty and lamps were lit in living room windows. The church was closed and locked, there were no inside lights visible, and repeated rattling at the back gate didn't produce a janitor or night watchman.

Jordan scowled in disappointment. "I remember when churches were open all the time, you know, to offer sanctuary."

"Not any more. Too many homeless, too much robbery, too little respect for tradition, not enough members to pay the electricity. Come on."

They got in the Rover, and Dom circled the grounds, looking for an old red pickup truck, but to no avail. After that, he drove up one street and down the other, slowly—it was difficult to make out the details in the fog—on the lookout for the vehicle, while Jordan called Myra's old friends.

The story she came up with was a pretty good one. She claimed to be an agent calling from Hollywood, trying to contact Myra Foster, whose parents had given this number. There was a chance for a small part on an afternoon soap opera.

Two of the women said they had run into Myra in town in the past year but hadn't renewed any kind of friendship or knew who her current friends were. The third one was more emphatic, saying she wouldn't go near her. "Myra's always been weird," she told Jordan, "and since she's back, she's *really* weird."

"Another dead end," Jordan said at the end of the third phone call.

"She can't get far without money. She can't buy any food or gas."

"Tell me again why we're not going to the police? I mean, you're an L.A. sheriff, you're a detective, for heaven's sake. Don't they have to listen if you tell them to?"

Dom turned onto one more side street and checked the vehicles parked there. "Depends—sometimes they resent us guys from the big city. But apart from that, say they accept what I tell them, that I'm looking for Myra Foster, aka Myra Kaczmarak, license number etcetera. They call down to my bureau to verify, which they always do, and when they do, they'll find

I'm out on sick leave, that there is no open case having to do with Michael Carlisle or Myra Foster or Myra Kaczmarak or Wally Foster, that I'm not working on anything like that, and I get hauled in on charges of abusing my power.''

Turning left into an alleyway that ran behind a row of houses, he continued, ''Not that I wouldn't gladly do that, Jordan, I'd abuse the hell out of my power if it would do any good, but it won't. Myra's not missing, can't be reported missing for days. Best-case scenario? They decide to help us. What a small-town police department would do is this—they send out a patrol car to look for the truck. Which is what we're doing right now. I'm sorry, Jordan, but that's how it goes.''

Her long sigh told him he'd accomplished what he'd meant to. Worn her down with words because he was tired of explaining himself to a woman too frantic to hear him.

Jordan said nothing for a little while, then she shook her head sadly. ''I'll bet you're sorry you ever met me.''

''Sometimes I am,'' he said truthfully. ''Yeah, sometimes. Mostly not, though.''

The barrier between them, he observed, erected when she had burst in on him today, was way diminished, but it was still there. She'd apologized for her anger, but he was still angry at himself and frustrated with her. She was frustrated with waiting. Neither of them could offer the other the comfort they needed, he concluded, which was the pits.

They were in farm country, on the outskirts of town. Up and down dirt roads and side streets they drove, looking for Myra's truck, but they had no luck.

The fog had diminished, but that didn't mean visibility was any better. The three-quarter moon was about the only illumination available this far from town.

Dom glanced at Jordan. In the moonlight, her face looked so drawn, her cheekbones more prominent than ever.

In the time he'd known her—two and a half or three weeks, he figured—she must have dropped five or six pounds. On her, that didn't look good.

Coming to a decision, he wrenched the wheel to the left and made a U-turn, found the highway and headed toward town.

"Where are we going?" Jordan asked sharply.

"To get something to eat."

"But Michael—"

"You have to eat, and after that, you have to sleep."

She shook her head adamantly. "No, I can't."

"You'll fall apart if you don't."

"How can I sleep when my child is out there with a mad-woman? Did you hear what they said? She's unstable, gets crazy ideas. Her friends say she's weird."

"And if it is Michael, he's been with her for a whole year, so whatever crazy ideas Myra's had, he's still all right."

"How do you know that?"

"I don't, but tell me this. What good are you going to be to him if you pass out, get sick? Because you're on the way, Jordan. I'm watching it happen," he continued grimly, "right in front of my eyes."

It was all too familiar to him, that motherhood thing again. With Theresa, she couldn't have babies, so she got crazy. With Jordan, she was positive her kid was in danger, and that led to another kind of insanity. Couldn't she see it?

As though in answer to his unspoken question, Jordan closed her eyes and seemed to concentrate on steadying her nerves. Then she nodded. "You're right. I'm close to the edge and I don't know how to stop it. Sorry," she added in a small, apologetic voice.

Maybe he should feel good that she'd heard him, but it almost broke his heart, seeing her so defeated. However, he couldn't afford to let down. One of them had to remain strong here, and as he was the professional, he got the job.

He found a run-down coffee shop, scarfed down a hamburger and a cup of coffee and kept watch over her while she ate some oversalted soup and a small roll. Then he checked them into a motel. She was so exhausted, the moment they walked into the room, she sank onto a chair and closed her eyes.

"Come on," he said, "take off your clothes."

Jordan's eyelids lifted halfway. "Tell me you don't mean what I think you mean."

"I'm not going to jump your bones. I'm going to run you a bath."

She struggled to sit up. "Did you bring the phone in from the car? In case the Kaczmaraks call?"

"Yes." He went into the bathroom and started the hot water running into the tub. Then he returned to Jordan, who hadn't moved from the chair. When he undressed her, she didn't protest, just went along like a rag doll. He carried her into the tub, set her in it, soaped a washcloth, washed her all over.

The automatic male part of him was aroused by her nakedness—thin as she was, his body remembered the pleasure she had given him—but he ignored his reaction. As he gazed at her, all soapy and sad, he felt moved in another, decidedly unsexual way. Tenderness toward her filled him. She was so tired, so worn down with stress, and yet that fire still burned fiercely in her, that fire for her son.

As he rinsed her off, Dom couldn't help smiling ruefully at the direction of his thoughts. *Way to go, D'Annunzio,* he told himself, *you're just a little bit jealous, aren't you? Of a toddler. You want all that attention, all that fire, for yourself.*

By the time he'd finished rinsing her off, Jordan was sound asleep. Dom let the water run out, rubbed her as dry as he could, wrapped her in a towel and carried her to bed. After pulling the covers up to her chin, he arranged the pillows so her neck was comfortable, then sat in the armchair near the foot of the bed, propped his feet on the coffee table and gazed at her while she slept.

His thoughts were not peaceful ones. For the first time that day, he allowed them free rein, and they did not go toward self-love.

He'd screwed up, he told himself, all down the line, by not taking the first letter seriously, then by not insisting Jordan get her son's case reopened. If he had, at least now he'd have backup instead of feeling like some rogue cop on his own, surrounded by the bad guys, who were calling all the shots.

And because he hadn't taken the letter seriously, he hadn't been on the lookout, hadn't been checking his rearview mirror, hadn't observed the passersby when he visited Jordan at her shop. Had given Wally ammunition.

The list of screwups could go on and on, a bottomless well of lists, but that was enough for now. On the professional front, anyway. Because then there were the personal screwups, beginning with Jordan.

He watched her as she slept, deep purple shadows under her lower lids, her hands twitching in sleep. It was almost as if her body was insisting on resting, but her mind didn't know how to turn off. He wanted to do something wonderful for her, but he was just a man, and an imperfect one at that.

He'd pursued the woman, despite a strong inner voice telling him not to. He'd set something in motion when he couldn't offer what she needed and deserved. Her husband had ignored her, belittled her. Maybe Dom would never belittle her, but eventually he would ignore her, in subtle, soul-killing ways. It was who he was, a cop first, a person second. Jordan needed someone who would put her first.

Hell, Jordan needed someone who loved her. Dom didn't love her, wouldn't allow himself to love her. He didn't even like to think of that word.

Love.

He'd loved once, married her, let her down, maybe even destroyed her. He was a lousy love candidate. There was no room for it in his life. He was committed to his career, always barreled ahead, always did it his way, didn't know how to do it any other way. Maybe the fact that he followed no one's agenda but his own was what made him a good cop—or used to, anyway.

But because he lacked the ability to compromise, to let anyone else in his life in any kind of meaningful way, he made a lousy life partner. Hadn't he proven that with Theresa?

Now here was Jordan in his life just in time to prove something else. He used to say he was a good cop but a bad man. Now even the good cop part was wrong.

Jordan turned onto her side, muttered something. Dom moved to the edge of the bed, adjusted her blanket so she wouldn't get chilled. He stayed there, gazing at her.

If he sometimes felt a strange stirring of emotion when he looked at Jordan, if when they made love he experienced a newer, deeper level of sensation than he ever had before, that didn't mean he was in love. It only meant that, if he were a different person, she might be someone he could love.

That was all it meant.

He lay next to her and nodded off, but the moment the morning light came in through the blinds, he was up. He showered, got into his clothes, went out and got two cups of coffee and several doughnuts, then sat on the edge of the bed, waving a plastic cup under her nose.

She stirred, then opened her eyes. She was groggy, unfocused, her lids heavy. "Where are we?"

"In what passes for a motel in Buttonhollow. Come on, we got some investigating to do."

Their first stop was at the Kaczmaraks, who informed them that no, they had not heard from Myra. Dom and Jordan were at the church day-care center when it opened at seven. When they found the woman who ran the program, Dom questioned her about Myra. Had she ever mentioned any favorite places? Hobbies?

Jordan stood next to Dom but let him do all the talking. Even with a few hours of sleep, her energy was nearly depleted. She was running on sheer raw nerve, and knew it. If she tried to assume the persona of female officer she'd managed yesterday, she might very well scream at someone, "Listen to me! We have to ask you these questions! My little boy's life depends on it!" So she kept quiet.

They needed a break, Jordan thought. Someone somewhere had to know something, had to have seen something. Someone…

"Excuse me?" a woman said, tapping Jordan on the shoulder.

She turned. "Yes?"

Jordan found herself facing a friendly-looking woman with freckles and short red hair holding a child in her arms. "You're asking about Myra Kaczmarak, aren't you?"

Jordan was instantly alert. "Yes."

"I saw her truck last night, parked in the woods near my house. Just the truck, not her."

The woman lived twenty miles out of town, in a tract of homes that had been built in the seventies. Myra's truck was parked, as she had said, near a wooded area adjacent to a double-size lot where two houses were under construction. There were no workmen at the site.

A quick perusal of the trees told Dom that no one was hiding among them, so he turned his attention to the construction. A high chain link fence, woven with barbed wire for extra security, surrounded the two homes, each in a different stage of completion. A stucco machine and a tractor were parked inside the fence, and piles of brown dirt were pushed to the perimeter.

Dom walked quickly around the fence, looking for a way in. He'd gone about a third of the way and had found the padlock and chain that connected two sections of fence when he heard Jordan call softly, "Michael?"

He turned to see her staring at something in the construction area, but his line of vision was blocked by one of the homes. Quickly, he made his way around the fence to where she stood, transfixed. Again, she said, "Michael?"

And then Dom saw him. A little boy, standing in the dirt in front of one of the wood-framed structures. His hair was white-blond. One index finger was in his mouth. With his other hand, he held a small teddy bear to his chest. He wore shorts and a T-shirt, and his legs, bare arms and face were smudged with dirt.

The child stood very still, staring at Jordan as, again, she whispered, "Michael?"

He cocked his head, then moved slowly toward her, a puzzled look on his face. He stopped about a foot away from the fence that separated them. Dom watched while Jordan put her finger through the fence, wiggled it at him and smiled softly. Tears streamed down her cheeks.

Dom came closer, put his hand on her shoulder, stared at the little boy. His movement caught the child's attention, and he shifted his gaze from Jordan to Dom.

From this distance, Dom had no trouble making out the details of his face. It was thinner now, more mature. The nose, the mouth—yes, he'd seen those before.

And, of course, he'd seen the eyes, which were a pale, eerie green color. They were achingly familiar. They were Jordan's eyes.

Dom was staring at Michael Carlisle.

Chapter 13

Her heart was so full, Jordan could barely contain it within the boundaries of her chest. Her son, her beautiful, darling little boy—he was not only alive, but he was right in front of her looking at her. And looking at her as though he almost recognized her. Her voice seemed familiar to him, that much she could tell from the way he cocked his head each time she spoke.

"Hello, Michael," she said again. "Remember me? It's all right if you don't, we have lots of time."

"Jordan," Dom whispered warningly as, seemingly from out of nowhere, a woman appeared.

Myra, Jordan knew at once, but a completely different Myra from the woman in the glamour shot. If at one time she'd been blond, curvaceous and flashy, now she looked like a slightly younger version of her mother. Not only was she considerably heavier than in her picture, but her dry-as-straw blond hair was almost eclipsed by brown roots, and her face had angry red blotches all over it. Myra wore a large white overblouse, black pedal pushers and scuffed loafers, and her clothing and her face were smudged with dirt. Obviously Myra and Michael had spent the night at the construction site.

Myra grabbed the little boy's hand. "Rory, come here," she said as she began to pull him away.

"Michael, no!" Jordan cried.

Stopping dead in her tracks, Myra turned and stared at Jordan with a look of dawning realization. Gripping the child's shoulders possessively, she raised her head defiantly. "His name is Rory."

"No, it's Michael."

"Rory, I said. I know who you are, and you, too," she added with a quick glance at Dom. Then she turned the boy and picked him up in her arms. Unprotesting, he went to her. "You can't have him," she told Jordan. "He's mine."

As she backed up, her eyes darted from left to right as though seeking an escape route. Her gaze landed on the house on the farthest edge of the lot. It stood on a concrete foundation and had been framed and bolted. Electrical wiring ran along its beams, its roof rafters and ceiling joists were in place, but there were no walls, no floors, no windows yet.

Myra dashed for it. With amazing agility for a woman of her size, she began to climb a thirty-foot ladder propped against the side of the structure, holding Michael in the curve of one arm and using the other to pull herself up.

Dom, in the meantime, attempted to climb the chain link fence, but his progress was hindered by the barbed wire threaded through the links. By the time he was halfway to the top, his hands were bleeding. Myra was nearly at the roofline.

Holding a ladder rung with one hand, she turned to face Dom and Jordan, shifting her weight enough to make the ladder wobble. "Stop!" she screamed. "You come over that fence, mister, I jump. Remember, I got Rory!"

Dom—one leg slung over the top of the fence, his pants ripped, his hands streaked with blood—froze in place. Horrified, Jordan looked from Myra to Dom and to Myra again. The woman was extremely far off the ground, and if she did as she threatened, it could be catastrophic. No, no, no, Jordan thought, her heart in her throat. To be this close to her child and have him snatched from her again. No, it was not acceptable.

"Dom," she called. "Come down."

"I mean it, mister," Myra shouted. "Climb right back down, or I'll do it, I swear I will."

"Dom," Jordan said again, tugging at his pants leg. "Please, do as she says."

"She's bluffing," he said through clenched teeth. "She won't jump."

"You don't know that."

He glared at Myra, a look of fury on his face. Then, with obvious reluctance, he climbed down the outside of the fence, cursing under his breath as he did.

Triumphant, Myra climbed the next two rungs, then maneuvered herself so she sat on the roofline between two rafters. After she set Michael on her lap, both their legs dangled.

Panting from her exertions and scowling at Dom and Jordan, Myra kicked the ladder away. It fell with a loud clatter against the adjacent house frame. The board she sat on creaked warningly beneath her weight, but she froze in place, and it continued to hold her.

"He's mine," she screamed. "You can't have him."

Jordan bit her knuckles to keep from screaming at the woman. The roof was high enough off the ground so if the wooden beam broke, if Myra fell off or jumped, if she dropped Michael, he could be injured seriously. Scattered about the concrete foundation were all kinds of debris—wood chips, nails, tools—all of them potential dangers.

Jordan bit harder on her knuckle, tried to summon up a plan or at least some rational thought instead of the nightmare scenarios that were popping around in her head like grasshoppers. Her son. She needed to focus on her son.

His gaze kept alternating between Myra and her, and although he didn't make a sound, he was obviously confused and frightened. Who could blame him?

Moderating her voice so the child wouldn't pick up on her terror, she called, "Myra? Can we talk about this, at least?"

She tried to sound friendly and upbeat, but she heard the way her voice quivered.

Dom whispered in her ear. "Distract her, then keep her talking."

Nodding to let him know she'd heard him, Jordan inhaled a deep breath and began to climb the chain link fence herself. The barbed wire cut into her palms, and it was difficult getting a solid foothold, but she managed to make it a third of the way up before Myra screamed, "Hey! Don't you come over that fence! I told you, I'll jump off and take Rory with me."

Out of the corner of her eye, Jordan observed Dom move away and slip quietly into the copse of trees next to the construction site. Clinging to the fence, Jordan called out, "Please, Myra, all I'm trying to do is talk to you."

"He's my Rory."

"Yes, of course he is. I just want to hear all about him, that's all."

"Climb down first. And no tricks or nothing. His name is Rory."

The repetition of the name seemed to give the woman comfort. Wally had said his sister was in and out of reality. Her mother had called her unstable. Jordan had no doubt that what she was seeing now was a woman on the perimeter of insanity, which meant she had to be very careful not to push her over to the other side. Not while Michael was a hostage.

As Jordan jumped off the fence, she said, "Okay, no tricks." Wiping her bloodied palms on her pants, she looked at her son. "Hi, Rory. That's a great name. Is he named after anyone, Myra?"

Michael, firmly held by Myra, stared at Jordan with that puzzled expression on his face, but said nothing.

"Can Rory talk, Myra? I'd love to hear him talk." There hadn't been a sound out of him so far. Had his vocal cords been injured? Or, traumatized by the switch in mothers a year ago, had he stopped speaking completely?

"Myra," Jordan went on, "I mean you no harm, I promise. In fact, I understand how difficult this must be for you. Your child, our children, they mean the world to us, don't they? I know mine did, and it broke my heart to lose him.''

A movement behind Myra caught Jordan's attention, but she made sure her gaze didn't shift in the slightest. Dom had made it to the other side of the lot and was quietly easing the two sections of gate apart, proceeding very slowly so as not to make any noise. Jordan moved a little to her left so Dom was completely out of Myra's line of vision.

And all the while, she watched the face of the little boy who had her eyes.

''Tell me about that day, will you, Myra?'' Jordan said conversationally. ''That last day?''

''What day?''

''When Reynolds was in the car with Michael? Or was it Rory?''

''My son is Rory.''

''Of course, your son is named Rory. Mine was named Michael.''

''Michael's dead.''

''Yes, I know. I was so sad when that happened, I wanted to die myself.''

Suspicion mixed with confusion were in Myra's expression, as though she wasn't sure how to respond. Dom had said to keep talking, so Jordan had been trying a little mother-to-mother bonding. However, Myra was probably too far gone to allow any kind of connection between the two of them.

Dom had made it through the gate and was moving slowly and stealthily toward the framed house. Jordan schooled her face not to reveal anything.

''So, will you tell me about that day?'' she repeated. ''Who was in the car that day with Reynolds? Were you there? And Rory, too? Where was Michael?''

With another look of triumph on her face, Myra announced, ''No. All four of us were in the car. Ray honked the horn—I called him Ray, you know—he honked the horn, said let's go, the kids, too.'' As she continued with her story, she seemed to become distracted, and her dangling legs kicked back and forth

nervously. "He never did that, never brought Michael along
never invited Rory to come with us. It was the first time."

"Really?" Jordan said. "How nice." It was thoroughly lu
dicrous to be talking pleasantly about a ride in the car with th
woman who held her son's life in her hands. But if that's wha
it took, Jordan would chitchat, sing, tap dance, whatever, til
her face turned blue.

"Yeah," Myra went on dreamily, "me and Ray and Ror
and Michael, just like a family, we all went for a drive to lool
at the ocean. It was a real pretty day."

With each movement of her legs, her grip on Michae
seemed to loosen. When he grabbed at her knees for purchase
Jordan screamed, "Myra! Don't let him go!"

"Huh?" Myra snapped awake, then pulled Michael close
to her, wrapping him in her embrace. "I...I was just shifting,'
she said petulantly. "My back hurt."

Willing Dom to hurry, Jordan reminded herself not to let th
conversational ball drop. Keep talking, keep breathing. "O
course. So, you were going to look at the ocean?"

Dom was grateful that a stack of drywall leaning against th
house kept his progress masked. Even though he was directl
behind her, Myra could still turn around. If she did, sh
wouldn't see him. Not until, that is, he began the final part o
his climb to get the kid.

Listening to the two women's conversation and keeping ai
ear cocked for any inflection in Myra's voice that she wai
aware of him, he carefully propped a small ladder against th
side of the house, climbed it slowly and evenly, so as not to
set off any vibrations in the wood structure. Then he used a
second-story window frame to boost himself up. The top of hi
head was at the roofline.

Bracing his hands on the beam, Dom was on the point o
pulling himself up when he heard Myra say to Jordan, "Don'
think you can fool me. You're trying to keep me talking—
Hey! Where's the other one? The cop?" She looked aroune
wildly. "Where is he?"

"I honestly don't know, Myra," Jordan replied.

"You're lying." Holding Michael to her with one arm around his waist, Myra used a rafter beam to help her get to her feet. "The two of you have this plan to take Rory from me. Never. You'll never get him."

Knees bent, she clutched at the beam and stared measuringly at it as though deciding whether to climb its deeply pitched angle. All of a sudden, the little boy began to kick wildly, which made it difficult for Myra to maintain her balance. She slung an arm around the rafter and held on tightly while Michael struggled.

"Myra," Jordan screamed. "Please don't move. From the bottom of my heart, all I care about is his safety, not who has him or who doesn't, what his name is or isn't. Only that he's safe!"

Jordan's plea died away and from a distance, sirens sounded, heading in their direction.

"What's that?" Myra shouted, her head bobbing wildly, trying to see where the sounds were coming from. "He called the cops, that's where he went. He called them."

Letting go of the rafter for an instant, she grabbed Michael's kicking legs. "I told you," she said, teetering on the edge of the roof, "I warned you...."

One, two, three, Dom said silently, then hoisted himself onto the beam. In no time, he had hopped from joist to joist. Balancing himself by hanging onto a rafter, he grabbed Myra and Michael from behind.

Jordan, in the meantime, ran along the fence, squeezed through the opening and stood directly under the three struggling figures. "I'm here," she shouted to Dom.

Sirens blaring, two patrol cars pulled up to the fence, lights flashing.

Dom used all his strength to contain Myra's angry efforts to push him away. She was strong, but he was stronger. Finger by finger, he released her hold on the child, then he pulled the little boy away from her. Tucking Michael under one arm like a football, he took off, vaulting from ceiling beam to ceiling beam until he was on the opposite side of the house. Below, a hill of brown earth backed into the chain link fence.

"Jordan," Dom called out. "Over here."

The police car doors slammed. A voice called out, "Halt, or I'll shoot!"

"Don't shoot!" Dom yelled. "I'm L.A. Sheriff's Department. The woman behind me is a 5150 and I've just removed the child from danger. Jordan," Dom called again. "Open your arms, catch him and fall into the dirt. Got it?"

Her answering shout came from directly below. "Got it."

As an enraged Myra struggled to reach them, Dom released the little boy and watched him fall, down, down, down, right into his mother's embrace. The impact threw them both into the dirt pile, but all the while, Jordan shielded him from harm by holding him tightly to her.

Dom heaved a sigh of relief. Michael was safe. Now it was time to deal with Myra and the local cops.

Resting her head against Dom's shoulder, Jordan held onto his hand a little more tightly. Soon, she thought, soon it would all be over.

The bench they sat on was cool, as was the hallway outside the judge's chambers, with its marble columns and stone floor. But Jordan felt almost feverish. It was so close, so near, the moment she would have her son back for good.

The last few days had gone by in a blur. After Myra, still screaming, had been led away in handcuffs, Jordan had wanted to take Michael home, but the police—who had been called by a neighbor—had detained her. No, they told her, she could not take him out of the county, not until the local department of children's services had investigated the case.

She'd protested, but Dom's assurances and a talk with the social worker had settled her into accepting reality—Jordan might know beyond a shadow of a doubt that this small boy was hers, but it had to be proved and sanctioned by the State of California.

From there, Dom had taken care of everything. Arranged for

tetanus shots for all of them. Gotten on the phone, made sure the hospital records from Michael's birth—including his new-born footprints, blood type and the record of the strawberry mark on his shoulder—were faxed to them in two hours instead of two days. It was Dom who harried, nagged, bullied the social worker, doctor, lab technician, local police, lawyers, paper pushers, Dom who'd burned up phone and fax lines, twisting arms, calling in favors. Getting results.

Because of Dom, she was sitting outside the judge's chambers only days after her reunion with Michael, instead of the weeks or even months that a child dispute case could take.

Cynthia sat on the adjoining bench next to the high-powered lawyer she'd brought with her from L.A. She seemed collected and calm, as she usually did. She had offered a stiff apology to Jordan for doubting her, which Jordan had accepted. Still, their relationship was strained and probably always would be.

Jordan clutched Dom's hand again—she felt much closer to this man she'd known only for weeks than the woman with whom she'd shared a house for twelve years.

"You've given me so much support," she told him. "What would I have done without you?"

"Don't, Jordan."

"I have to. You've earned my undying gratitude for the rest of my life."

Gratitude. Again.

If he went the rest of his life without hearing that damn word, Dom figured it would be too soon.

He'd done what had to be done, that was all. He'd extended his sick leave so he could be with Jordan these past few days. While she visited with Michael, he kept tabs on all the paperwork and legalities necessary to make sure Jordan's case was handled right.

At night, they'd eaten dinner together, slept together, made love. As if by mutual agreement, they hadn't talked about the future, hadn't spoken of feelings. She'd needed distraction, he figured, not more emotional burden; he'd needed to see her through this, to make up for his missteps.

Jordan snuggled into him, as though seeking warmth and protection. Oh yeah, she was grateful as hell.

But how did she feel, deep down, about him? he wondered. He wasn't blind, she got that look on her face each time they made love, that shining glow of satisfaction and trust that looked like love. But was it? Or was it gratitude?

Jordan was basically alone, no family to speak off, and Cynthia with her arrogant sniffs was no support. So Dom had come into her life, and she'd glommed onto him like a drowning woman needing rescue. Not that he blamed her. Hey, if you needed help, you took it wherever you could find it.

But he didn't want Jordan's gratitude. Hell, he didn't deserve it. Here she was thanking him right and left for making this day possible, when with a slight turn of the coin, it could have come out differently. Myra could have jumped before he got to her. The kid could have been proven to be Rory Foster, not Michael Carlisle. Any one of a number of things could have gotten in the way of a happy ending, and it was only sheer luck that had made it turn out all right.

So he was here today, by her side, finishing up what he'd begun. He was ready to close the file on Michael Carlisle…and Jordan Carlisle. It was better that way. Let her return to L.A. with her little boy, start a new life with him. And without Dom. Clean break. Best thing.

Then why did that thought make him feel as though his heart was being squeezed by a vise? Because sometimes you didn't get what you want. That was how life worked. And he was strong; he'd get over it. He just needed to tell her.

Jordan stirred beside him, then lifted her head from his shoulder and said, "Do you think this is all a dream?"

"Why are you asking that?"

"Because all this seems so strange, so impossible to believe. Myra's story, the fact that Michael is alive, that he's here. It's like something out of a fantasy."

Myra had broken down when led away, and was now hospitalized. In the past few days, her version of the car crash had come out in bits and pieces. That day, Michael was in his child safety seat in the rear right of the Mercedes. Rory was strapped into the regular seat belt behind Reynolds. In the back seat, the two little boys fought over Michael's stuffed dog. Rory grabbed it and threw it out the open window. When Michael sobbed for Pup-Pup, Reynolds lost his temper and turned to slap Rory. Myra blocked his arm, he lost control of the steering wheel, they veered off the embankment, rolled over twice and landed on the driver's side.

Reynolds and Rory were killed immediately. Myra and Michael, both on the passenger side, were miraculously spared. She managed to get her door open, dragged Michael with her, hauled him up the embankment and started running. Even when she heard the big explosion behind her, she kept on running. A truck driver stopped to pick them up, and gave them a ride to Santa Barbara. Her parents came to get her and the rest of the story was known.

Somewhere in there, both her grief and her mental instability had caused her to become confused about the child's identity, and she began to call the boy Rory.

She would probably be hospitalized the rest of her life.

"So, is it a dream?" Jordan asked again. "Because if it is, I don't want to wake up."

A uniformed bailiff approached. "Mrs. Carlisle?"

"Yes?"

"The judge sends his apologies. It will be another half hour before he can meet with you."

Jordan didn't want to wait any more, not even another half hour, but there wasn't much she could do about it. As though he'd read her mind, Dom rose from the bench and offered a hand. "Let's get some fresh air."

"Good idea. Cynthia?" she said, turning to her mother-in-law. "Feel like a walk?"

"No, thank you."

There was a little garden behind the courthouse, and the moment she and Dom got outside, Jordan lifted her face to the sun. "Oh, that feels good."

"Yeah."

She put her hand through Dom's bent arm and they strolled along the garden. Early spring flowers and bushes were in colorful bloom. Life, she thought. A fine thing. She was still edgy, would be until the papers were signed, but the fact was, she was so much better, so much clearer-headed at this moment than she'd been all the weeks preceding, that she could actually appreciate a garden.

She laughed with the sheer pleasure of being able to laugh again, then squeezed Dom's arm. "When we get back to L.A.," she told him, "Michael and I expect to be seeing a lot of you."

"Yeah, well, I need to get back to work. It's all piling up on my desk, waiting for me."

"Of course." Grinning, she reached up, pushed a few strands of hair off his forehead. One of these days, the man really needed to get a proper haircut. "Expect dinner invitations, then, lots of them."

He halted, which made her stop also. The sides of his mouth were turned down. "Don't, Jordan."

"Don't what?" she asked, puzzled by his attitude. "Invite you to dinner?"

"Don't expect anything of me."

The abruptness of his comment made her head jerk in surprise. "Is that what I'm doing?"

Without him answering, the frown line between his brows deepened. They stood near a white stone bench, beneath a shade tree, and shadows cast by the leaves made his face seem even darker than normal. "I need to talk to you," he said finally, and the way he said it made her stomach turn suddenly queasy with trepidation.

"All right." Slowly, she lowered herself onto the bench and looked up at him.

Propping a foot on the bench next to her, Dom grabbed at a narrow, low-hanging branch and stripped off a couple of leaves. He held them in his hand and stared at them. "From the beginning," he said, without looking at her, "there's been something in the back of my head that feels wrong, about you and me, you know, being together. I've thought about it and thought about it, and the way I figure, it's a big responsibility, loving someone. And deep down, I'm one of those old-fashioned types. The last time, the only time, I told a woman I loved her, I proposed marriage right away. That's what the word 'love' means to me—commitment, making it official in a church." Turning his troubled gaze on her, he added, "Following me so far?"

He was so serious, almost mournful, Jordan thought. And he was about to tell her he didn't love her. Oh, lord, she thought. What would she do? "So far," she said hesitantly.

Removing his foot from the bench, Dom sat down next to her and refocused his gaze on the ground. "I can't do that to you. Being a cop's wife is too damned hard for most women, and besides, I'm not good husband material. I've gone over this in my head for a while, and I can't get past it. No matter how I feel about you, I can't make any promises. I—" He paused, seemed about to say more, then shook his head. "Damn, this is hard."

"Dom?"

He looked at her. "Yeah?"

She thought she got it now, but she wasn't sure. "Forgive me, but I'm confused. Did you just say you don't love me, or that you do?"

"Well, yeah, I do, but I can't marry you."

A smile started at her toes and shot right up her body till it reached her mouth. He loved her! "Can we stay on the love thing for a minute?" she said, her eyes filling. "Because as it turns out, I happen to love you too,"

For an instant there, his expression softened and she thought he was going to smile back, but then he scowled again. "Don't, Jordan."

"Don't what?"

"Don't look at me that way. Damn it, I don't want to love you. Every time I'm with you, I feel guilty."

She had to tread lightly here. "Why is that, do you think?"

"I've already told you. It's something about Theresa."

"What about Theresa?"

He expelled an impatient breath. "I didn't take good enough care of her. I didn't protect her."

Jordan stared at her lap for a moment, wanting to be sure to choose her words carefully. "Dom, she was a grown woman. She was the one who chose to get pregnant, even knowing it could affect her health. It was her choice."

"She was obsessed."

"Yes, poor thing. And no one can make anyone else get over an obsession." She gave him a rueful smile. "I think I'm proof of that."

Why wasn't she getting it? Dom wondered, gritting his teeth, frustrated as all get-out. Finally, he turned and gripped her arms, not hard, just emphatically. "Jordan, you have to understand. I wasn't there for her, and I'm afraid I won't be there for you."

She smiled at him lovingly. "I can't speak for Theresa, but you've always been there for me. Always, from the beginning."

"Yeah," he said with disgust, "as a cop."

"No, as a man."

"Bull," he said, rising from the bench. Turning his back on her, he rested one hand against the tree trunk, filled with hearty dislike for himself. "I almost blew this case. You almost didn't get Michael back because of me."

"And I *did* get Michael back because of you," she answered him. He heard a rustling sound, then Jordan came around to face him. Propping a shoulder against the tree trunk, she crossed her arms over her chest. "You're beating yourself up over something that was not in your control, Dom," she said firmly, "crucifying yourself on your own, homemade cross." Her expression softened. "Theresa wanted a child, she got tunnel-visioned about it. It wasn't her fault, she wasn't a bad person, but neither are you. She wasn't perfect, and neither are you."

"You got that right," he muttered.

As she continued to stare at him, she seemed puzzled. Then her gaze narrowed. "Feeling sorry for yourself, are you?"

"Hey, Jordan, don't."

"Well, you know what? I'm getting angry. You say you love me, but you've done all the thinking for us and you've decided it's a dead end. Have you ever heard of taking a little time to work on a relationship? To explore some options? Have you ever heard about talking?"

"Mrs. Carlisle?" The bailiff had come outside and was trying to get Jordan's attention. But she wasn't done with Dom, not yet. Yeah, she was definitely working up a good head of steam.

"Whatever you want to do with your memories of your marriage," she went on, shoving her finger into his chest for punctuation, "get it through that thick skull of yours, D'Annunzio. I'm not Theresa. I refuse to stand here and let her memory interfere with us, with you and me. I refuse."

He threw his hands up in the air and walked away from her. "Fine. Refuse all you want, I'm not marrying you."

"You stupid, pig-headed man!" she shouted after him. "I don't recall asking you to!"

"Mrs. Carlisle?" the bailiff repeated.

She whipped around to face the young man. "What!"

He flinched, but went on bravely. "Sorry to interrupt you, but the judge is ready for you now."

Chapter 14

The hearing was over in minutes.

The Kaczmaraks were there, but they left before Jordan could talk to them. It was probably best that way, she thought. She had compassion for their situation and gratitude that Myra had saved Michael's life, but she also knew there was nothing she could say or do that would restore their daughter's mental health or return their real grandson to them.

As for the fourth Kaczmarak family member, Wally had been picked up two days before and charged with parole violation and extortion.

The social worker had explained to Jordan that Michael had been through a lot, that he was physically capable of speaking, but at present chose not to. Time and patience and love would repair most of the damage, but Jordan was not to expect anything from him for quite a while.

She didn't care how long it took, she thought, as she signed all the papers put in front of her. She had her son back. And when the social worker brought Michael to her, Jordan got down on her haunches to speak to him. Instinctively, she knew enough not to grab him and confuse him further.

"Michael," she said slowly, in a soft voice, "we're going home now. A different home than you've been living in. Maybe you'll remember this home and maybe you won't. Whatever happens, you are safe. I love you with all my heart."

He stared at her, his finger in his mouth.

"Do you remember," Jordan went on, "you used to raise your arms to me and say, 'Mommy, hug,' and I would lift you up and hug you very tightly? One day, when you're ready to do that again, I will be there."

With a smile, she stood, took his small hand in hers.

Dom, his arms crossed over his chest, watched the whole thing, most especially the look of mother love on Jordan's face as she gazed at her son. The back of Dom's throat got tight, and he had to swallow a couple of times before it loosened up.

When Jordan had Michael's hand, she looked directly at Dom. In her gaze was a question and not a little trepidation. So much always showed in those eyes of hers. She hadn't been too pleased with him a few moments ago; hell, he hadn't been too pleased with himself. He'd intended to lay it out for her and end it. It hadn't gone down anything like that clean, and both of them, he was sure, were feeling abandoned in limbo.

"Coming?" she asked him.

"Nah. I think it's better if I don't. Give you two a little time."

After a moment's hesitation, she smiled. "You're right. I'll talk to you soon?"

"Yeah. Sure."

The little boy gazed at his mother, then turned his unsmiling attention to Dom. Jordan's old soul was staring at him out of those eyes.

"You nervous?" Dom asked Nick as they stood adjusting their tuxedos in the chapel's anteroom mirror. "You're supposed to be a wreck by now."

"Sorry." Nick held one hand, fingers splayed, in front of him. "See? Steady as a rock."

"I can't believe you." Dom cursed as he fidgeted with the tie. It was a clip-on—why wouldn't it lie straight? "I mean, it's not as though you don't know what's ahead. It's hard work being married. You've been down that road before."

"But not with Carly. She's the right one, so I'm not nervous." Nick shrugged, adjusted his cuffs, turned to make sure the back of the jacket hung right. "Sorry, best man, I guess I'll have to leave all that nerves crap to you."

"Me?"

"Yeah, you. You're the one who's been falling apart this past month. Have you talked to Jordan?"

"Yeah, I called once and she was busy with the kid. Then she called me back and invited me to dinner, but who wants to sit there with that dragon lady sniffing at me?"

Chuckling, Nick shook his head. "When are you going to admit it?"

"Admit what?"

"You want the woman? Go after her."

"It's complicated."

"So's everything. So what? You're giving up? You're not going to see her?"

Dom shrugged.

"Ever again?"

"I don't know. I want to, but—" He shrugged again. "The whole thing is a hassle."

Nick nodded. "With Carly, I went through hassles, too."

"You kidding? You met Carly on a Saturday and you were living together by Wednesday. When did you have time for hassles?"

"You make time, trust me. Do you have the ring?"

Dom patted his pocket, brought out the ring and showed it to the groom-to-be. "Right here."

As Nick stared at the ring, his face lost its color, and his air of confidence evaporated. "You know what?"

"What?"

"I think I'm going to throw up."

Three hours later, as he sat in his living room, beer in hand, slightly drunk and still dressed in his tux, Dom recalled that last moment before Nick took the plunge. He chuckled loudly. "Macho man Nick, I salute you," Dom said to the empty room, raising his beer can. "Tough till the end."

It had been a nice wedding, as weddings went. Ceremony at ten, brunch immediately following, over by one so the bride and groom could head out for their honeymoon in the Caribbean.

You want the woman? Go after her. Nick's words had stuck in Dom's head throughout the ceremony and the hoopla afterward. They were in his head as he sat sprawled on his couch. Other words came back to him, words Jordan had said to him a month ago: *You've always been there for me. Always, from the beginning. You're beating yourself up over something that was not in your control, crucifying yourself on your own home-made cross.*

Jordan. Damn, but he missed her, missed her bad. He'd thought maybe she would diminish in importance if he didn't see her. Instead she'd grown larger and larger in his imagination until she took over most of his waking thoughts, and several of his sleeping ones, too.

What should he do about Jordan Carlisle?

Hell, he might not have a chance to do anything—she might have crossed him off her list weeks ago.

Dom found his gaze shifting toward the fireplace, then along the mantel to where Theresa's picture sat. As always, her smile was warm and loving.

"Hey, Theresa," Dom said. "Tell me what to do."

Silence greeted him, of course, but he decided to keep talking to her anyway.

"Jordan's nothing like you. No, that's not true. She loves fiercely and fights for what's hers. She's a hard worker. She gets insecure and has a temper and a sense of humor. Okay, she's not Irish-Catholic, and she's tall and thin, so in that way, she's nothing like you. She doesn't go on diets all the time. In fact, she's too skinny. But who the hell cares about the size of a body?''

Dom raised his beer to the portrait, took a sip and cradled the can between his hands. ''Was I a failure as a husband, Theresa? Jordan said I did the best I could. Did I?''

Theresa was still smiling. Dom shrugged. ''I don't know. But I love her, Theresa.'' As he said the words, there was a funny, tingly feeling in the back of his throat. ''I don't want to live the rest of my life without her. Do you mind that I fell in love again?''

Theresa smiled, so did Dom. ''Nah. I didn't think you would. You were always big on the falling in love department. Yeah, you don't mind. In fact, it's an honor to you, isn't it? An honor to your memory.''

As Dom said the words, he could have sworn Theresa's warm smile grew broader, but of course, that was the beer talking, and maybe a little emotion that slipped in there too.

Still, something that had been wound tightly around his gut, for years it seemed, released inside him, spreading softness and peace as it did.

Love.

Yeah, love. The word, the concept, here, now, today, it all resonated deeply within him. Jordan Carlisle was the woman Dom loved. And it was okay that he did. More than okay. It was terrific.

You want the woman? Go after her.

''How are you doing, sweetie?''

At the sound of Jordan's voice, Michael looked up from playing with his toys and offered his shy smile to let his mother know he was fine. She'd set him up in the corner of the shop this morning, and between Jordan, Lisa and the other two women who worked at Riches and Rags on Saturdays, he was never out of someone's vision. All of them loved him. His sweetness shone from his soul.

Perched on a stool near the cash register, Jordan watched her son at play.

In this past month, there had been some progress—a few words here and there, more and more smiles. Even though she hugged him occasionally, Jordan had been careful not to overwhelm him physically, contenting herself mostly with quick pats, a smoothing of his hair, holding his hand when crossing the street. Michael lavished most of his affection on his stuffed animals, especially Pup-Pup, which Jordan had saved and which was always with him.

Cynthia had tried to take Pup-Pup away, claiming it was filthy and that Michael needed all new, better, bigger toys. It had been an ugly scene, one among many ugly scenes since Michael had returned to their lives. Not content with the mere fact of his return, Jordan's mother-in-law had become more and more demanding, making all kinds of plans for Jordan and Michael, insisting she quit working at Riches and Rags, discussing how Michael would go to the "right" school, so he would have the "right" friends.

Yesterday morning, Jordan and Cynthia had had a showdown in which Jordan had informed her mother-in-law that she and Michael would be moving out. Jordan would raise the boy herself, without interference. She would like her son to have a relationship with his grandmother, she had added, but not one with strings attached, and it was up to Cynthia.

The older woman had been stunned by Jordan's attitude, but that had been nothing compared to Jordan's reaction to her own audacity. Sometime in the recent past—it had begun before Michael's miraculous return, and Dom's presence in her life had had a lot to do with moving it along—Jordan had finally decided, somewhere inside, that she was a deserving, worthy human being.

After yesterday morning, when she had stood up for herself proudly and fearlessly, she knew that it would be much harder in the future for anyone to manipulate her through guilt or through her own feelings of not being enough.

How she wished Dom could have been there.

Dom. Jordan fiddled with a fun pin they'd just gotten in. It was a fierce, scowling jeweled bumble bee, and it reminded her of Dom.

He'd played a huge part in her transformation. She missed him, wanted to be with him. Stupid, stubborn man, she thought. When are you coming back?

As though some higher power had been reading her thoughts, the bell over the shop's door rang, announcing a new arrival. When Jordan looked to see who it was, she had to prop her hand on the counter so she wouldn't fall off her stool.

Dom stood in the doorway, dressed, of all things, in a tuxedo and carrying a large fast-food take-out box. Her mouth dropped open with surprise. He looked good enough to eat.

Dom's gaze quickly scanned the shop till he found her, and she snapped her mouth shut. The man didn't look happy. In fact, he looked downright irritated. Dom at his most disgruntled. A wave of strong affection for the tough cop washed over her. God, she loved him, with all his brooding moods and cynical asides, loved him as she loved life.

He made his way to her, the frown line between his thick brows as deep as she'd ever seen it. When he stood in front of her, he nodded once. "Hi," was all he said.

"Hi back."

Lisa breezed by, carrying a pile of clothing to the cash register. "Take Michael," she told Jordan, "go to lunch with Dom."

Jordan did a double take at her friend's order. "Did you know he was coming?"

"He called to tell me he was on his way and to make sure you didn't take a lunch break till he got here."

"And you didn't tell me?"

"Are you kidding? And miss that look on your face? Go on, get out of here."

So Jordan gathered Michael, Pup-Pup and her purse and accompanied Dom out the door of the shop.

It was a beautiful, sunshiny April day, unseasonably warm, and people passed by on Santa Monica Boulevard wearing shorts and halter tops and thongs. Southern Californians in their element, Jordan thought with a smile.

Dom hadn't said another word, and she wasn't quite sure what to expect. In truth, not knowing made her a little jumpy inside, but she did her best to go along with whatever was on his agenda. Stupid, stubborn man. At least he was here. Thank God.

He herded Jordan and Michael to a small park a block away, one equipped with swings, a sandbox and a couple of picnic tables. He'd stopped at McDonald's and bought enough food for an army instead of one tuxedo-clad detective, one ex-model with an appetite that was anything but robust, and one small child. He plopped the box of food on a table beneath a towering tree.

Birds chattered and whistled above their heads, and the sound of children's laughter came from the play area. Jordan and Michael sat on one bench. Dom sat across from them. Jordan found some fries and a hamburger for her son and set them on a napkin in front of him. "Here's lunch, sweetie. Can you say thank-you to Dom?"

Michael studied Dom solemnly, then he whispered, "Thank you."

Beaming with pride, Jordan glanced at Dom for his reaction, which was one raised eyebrow. "So, he's talking, huh?"

"Here and there."

Now that their own silence was finally broken, Jordan rooted around in the take-out box and selected a cheeseburger. Amazed at how famished she was, she went to work on her lunch. The act of eating together seemed to ease whatever tension Dom felt, and he relaxed visibly.

On the grass nearby, a courting couple sat on a blanket, wrapped up in each other and totally oblivious to anything around them. Farther on, a grandfather and his granddaughter tossed a large plastic ball back and forth. It was nice here, Jordan thought. Peaceful. Her insides were not nearly as peaceful, but she counseled herself to be patient.

After her initial hunger was satisfied, Jordan wiped her mouth, smiled at Dom and said, "So, what's with the tux?"

Dom lifted a shoulder. "Nick got married this morning. I had to be his best man. Besides—" one side of his mouth quirked up "—I wanted you to see what a classy guy I can be."

"I'm impressed."

Michael poked her on the arm, and she turned to him. Pointing to the sandbox, he said, "Play."

After she wiped his mouth, she kissed his cheek and said, "Sure, honey, go on and play." Her gaze followed her son as he made his way to the small square of sand. Two other toddlers were there, as were shovels and pails and other toys. When Jordan saw that he was settled in, she turned her attention to Dom.

"It's hard to let him out of my sight," she said with a sheepish smile, "but I'm working on it. I don't want to be one of those clingy mothers."

"Hey, with all that you went through, no one would blame you if you were."

"Yes, but it's not good for him."

Dom nodded, glanced briefly at her son, then turned to her. "So, how's it going with Michael? With everything?"

He had his poker face on, Jordan observed, revealing nothing to her. Obviously, though, he wanted her to go first before he said whatever was on his mind. She would have preferred it the other way, thought of saying so, but decided against it. Dom did things when he was ready, and not before.

So she told him what had been happening, how she'd sold the rings and the Rover, was now driving a used Toyota, was in partnership discussions with Lisa and was about to go apartment shopping. Cynthia was paying for Michael's therapy, and there was a trust set up for his education, but everything else Jordan would be handling on her own. She was determined, she told Dom, to give her son a mother he could be proud of.

Dom listened, lifted an eyebrow, nodded his approval. But mostly, he let Jordan talk, which he was good at, and which she seemed to do a lot of when he was around. And when she'd finished catching him up, he nodded. "Good," he said. "You're doing great. I wish I could say the same for me," he added ruefully.

Concern made her reach across the table and cover his hand with hers. "Dom, are you all right?"

He gazed at her hand. "Sure, except that I'm miserable..." frowning, he raised his eyes to hers "...without you."

Her breath hitched, then her heart skittered in her chest. "Are you?" she said softly.

"I miss you something awful, Jordan. It pissed me off how much. And so—" he sighed loudly, made a disgusted face "—okay, I love you, and all that means."

"Excuse me?"

"I just said I love you. A lot damn it." He had the most sour look on his face. "You love me, I love you. Okay?"

Placing her hand over her wildly thudding heart, Jordan realized she was either going to break into sobs or roar with laughter. "Never, in all my years, have I heard anything as romantic as that," she said, laughter winning out and bubbling up from somewhere deep inside. "I mean, you take my breath away."

It was sarcasm, but with a twinkle, and he took it as such. "Okay," he said with a loud, resigned sigh, "you want me to get down on my knees—?"

"Not really—"

"—because if that's what it takes, you got it."

Sure enough, Dom rose from the bench, came around to Jordan's side of the table and sank onto his knees in front of her. The people nearby looked up from whatever they were involved with and watched.

Jordan's hand flew to her neckline, and she played with a gold button at the base of her throat. "What...what are you doing?"

"I'm proposing, damn it. Can't you tell?"

Her sharp inhalation of breath was enough to make her feel dizzy. Tears formed, began to flow. "Oh, Dom."

"Unless you don't want to marry me."

"Are you crazy? Of course I do."

He seemed startled by the vehemence of her response. "Yeah? You do?"

"Idiot," she said, tears streaming down her face. "Yes, yes, yes."

"Yeah?" he said again, then got off his knees, pulled her up from her seat and wrapped her in his arms.

Somewhere nearby a woman giggled. Jordan knew she and Dom were being observed by everyone in the park, but she didn't care.

"Yeah," she said, pulling her head back and grinning at him through the film of her tears. "I love you, and I want you."

She sniffled. Her face was probably a mess, her nose was most definitely running, but she went on. "But I also want a father for Michael, someone he can look up to. I want a home of my own, a business, more babies. All of it, even the life that goes with being married to a cop. That's what I want. Think you can give me all of that?"

Tenderly, Dom wiped the tears from under her lids with his thumb. The look on his face was one she'd never seen before. All the toughness, the cynicism, the bitterness, the guilt—they were all gone. In their place was a softness, a vulnerability, an expression that said he'd stopped fighting and was willing to believe in miracles.

He cupped her face in his hands. "Jordan, love—" he sighed, pressed his lips together tightly as though overcome "—if you and Michael can put up with my life, I will gladly come home to any house where you and Michael are waiting for me."

That elicited a whole new round of sobs from Jordan, and she buried her face in his neck while he rocked her back and forth. She thought she heard a few people applauding, but she didn't care. Dom was here, Dom was hers. At last.

She was so overcome with love and emotion, she almost didn't feel the tapping on her leg.

Pulling back from Dom's embrace, she looked down to see her son, staring solemnly at both of them. Then he raised his arms, smiled that sweet, shy smile, and said, "Mommy, hug."

Epilogue

A year and a half later

Dom turned the ribs and sprinkled a little more barbecue sauce on them. Then he glanced at the little boy who stood next to him, watching his every move. "So, what do you think, Mike? Are they almost done?"

"I hope so. I'm starving."

"Yeah, so is everybody else. Italians, they just love to eat."

"Daddy?" Michael said.

It killed Dom when the kid called him that, just killed him. "Yeah, Mike."

"Am I Italian?"

"Not blood Italian, but you can be Italian if you want to be."

The kid nodded. "Good," he said, then ran off to play with his cousins.

It was Mike's birthday, and most of Dom's family was in L.A. to celebrate. The family reunion had been his mother's idea. Jordan, in her eighth month, was not to travel to Brooklyn, Mama had declared, so they would all come to California. Most of his sisters and brothers were here, most of the kids. And of course Mom and Pop, looking proud and healthy.

The small yard was packed with D'Annunzios, their husbands and wives. And friends. Steve and his wife were here, Santos and his girl, Nick and Carly. Lisa was flirting with Dom's only unmarried brother, and the smell of ribs and chicken and burgers permeated the hot September air.

The loud yipping of a puppy caught Dom's attention. He watched while Mike and his cousin Bobby traded a rubber toy back and forth, which the puppy happily tried to snatch from their small hands. Pup-Pup, the dog's name was, and he was the latest member of the household. The little mutt had wandered into the precinct last week, and now he had a home.

Dom was at home a lot more these days. He'd transferred to a desk job while he studied for his lieutenant's exam. What he was aiming for was to be in command of a squad of detectives instead of being in the field. He had responsibilities now, and twelve-hour, seven-days-a-week work schedules no longer fit into his life.

He checked the ribs again, then found his gaze wandering to the woman who sat on a lounge chair, fanning herself and laughing loudly at something Dom's dad was saying to her.

Dom's heart turned over in his chest, even though he was careful not to let his face reveal anything in case anyone was looking. Jordan Carlisle D'Annunzio, his beautiful, beloved wife. Her hair was longer, and she wore it pulled off her face with barrettes. Her cheekbones were less prominent. Her face had become round with her pregnancy. His gaze shifted to his wife's stomach. How the hell did they do it, he wondered, not for the first time. Carry all that weight and still remain upright. It was a damned miracle, that was all.

Another miracle was the fact that Cynthia was here today. She had offered to have Mike's birthday party at her place, complete with clowns and pony rides and catered food. But Jordan had said she preferred a more casual party for Mike, so the old lady had backed down. She sat under an umbrella conversed politely with whoever stopped by to visit, but mostly observed all the happily chattering human beings scattered about the yard. It was a shame, Dom thought, that he hadn't gotten hold of her years ago, before she became too set in her ways to know how to let her hair down.

Still, she was here, which made Jordan and Mike happy. And she hadn't sniffed once.

Again, his gaze shifted to Jordan. Their nights, even now, were filled with passion, their days filled with laughter. Sometimes they fought, mostly about his cynical attitude or her insecurity, but the fights were quick and the making-up time a lot of fun.

Two nights ago, they'd been lying in bed when she'd asked him about the scar on his lip, said she'd been meaning to find out about that scar since the day she'd met him.

When he told her he had cut his lip on a can of tuna when he was a kid, she'd seemed disappointed. Hey, he'd told her, not all scars had violent histories. She'd agreed that it was so and that maybe that was an okay thing, after all. Then she'd kissed his scar and he'd kissed her belly, and they'd wound up pleasing each other. Safely, of course—after all, she was carrying his kid.

Yeah, Jordan was healthy as a horse, and he was about to become a biological father, a fact that made his chest swell, made him think all those corny my-boy-Bill kind of thoughts. Still, as fatherhood went, he didn't know how he could love a kid any more than he loved little Mike.

Once in a while he thought of Theresa and felt sad. She had wanted a child so badly, had sacrificed her life trying to be a mother. But life didn't always work out the way you wanted it to, and people didn't always behave in their own best interests.

And maybe, who could tell? Maybe Theresa was looking down on them right now from heaven and smiling her approval.

Hey, it was possible, wasn't it? Who the hell knew?

* * * * *

SILHOUETTE
SENSATION®

AVAILABLE FROM 21ST JANUARY 2000

BRIDGER'S LAST STAND Linda Winstead Jones

Heartbreaker

When two strangers met that cold and lonely night something special whispered in the air... But with their affair ruined before it began, that was so nearly the end of it—except that Frannie could identify a murderer and needed Bridger's protection. Suddenly, only Bridger's arms could make everything better...

THE LADY'S MAN Linda Turner

Elizabeth Davis believed in relying on herself. The last thing she needed was a self-appointed rescuer—even if he was a gorgeous government agent... Close contact with Elizabeth had Zeke forgetting what was so good about the single life!

KEEPING ANNIE SAFE Beverly Barton

The Protectors

Dane Carmichael was the only man who could keep Annie Harden safe. From the moment he laid eyes on stubborn, beautiful Annie, he knew she would be his... But Annie had never encountered a man so strong, so dominating, so absolutely infuriating as Dane. And never had she needed—*or wanted*—a man more!

THE MERCENARY AND THE NEW MUM
Merline Lovelace

Follow That Baby

Sabrina Jensen was prepared to do anything to protect her precious child, but the intruder standing over the baby's crib was the man she'd once loved beyond reason, the father of her daughter. *But Jack Wentworth was supposed to be dead!* What was going on?

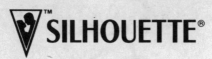

Look out in April 2000 for

A Fortune's Children Wedding

and the first book of a 5 part series

The Fortune's Children Brides

2 FREE

books and a surprise gift!

We would like to take this opportunity to thank you for reading this Silhouette® book by offering you the chance to take TWO more specially selected titles from the Sensation™ series absolutely FREE! We're also making this offer to introduce you to the benefits of the Reader Service™—

- ★ FREE home delivery
- ★ FREE gifts and competitions
- ★ FREE monthly Newsletter
- ★ Exclusive Reader Service discounts
- ★ Books available before they're in the shops

Accepting these FREE books and gift places you under no obligation to buy, you may cancel at any time, even after receiving your free shipment. Simply complete your details below and return the entire page to the address below. *You don't even need a stamp!*

YES! Please send me 2 free Sensation books and a surprise gift. I understand that unless you hear from me, I will receive 4 superb new titles every month for just £2.70 each, postage and packing free. I am under no obligation to purchase any books and may cancel my subscription at any time. The free books and gift will be mine to keep in any case.

S0EA

Ms/Mrs/Miss/Mr ....Initials...............................
                                                              BLOCK CAPITALS PLEASE

Surname ....

Address ....

....

....Postcode..............................

Send this whole page to:
UK: FREEPOST CN81, Croydon, CR9 3WZ
EIRE: PO Box 4546, Kilcock, County Kildare (stamp required)